Nicole

PRAISE FOR TH

'highly engaging and comp

'told with skilful flashbacks and a warm
understanding of hopes, dreams and kindness'
– *Woman's Day*

'tender, original, compassionate …
highly recommended' – *Herald-Sun*

'storytelling at its most adept' – *Canberra Times*

'a subtly mesmerising narrative that will charm
and captivate the reader' – *Toowoomba Chronicle*

'wonderfully written, creating a complexity
and sense of place that makes the journey
towards redemption an enjoyable one'
– *Bookseller and Publisher*

'poignant, emotive and insightful. Highly
recommended' – *Write Note Reviews*

'Wonderfully written … insightful' – *Book'd Out*

Also by Tess Evans

Book of Lost Threads
The Memory Tree

mercy street

TESS EVANS

FOURTH ESTATE
An Imprint of HarperCollins*Publishers*

Fourth Estate
An imprint of HarperCollins*Publishers*
First published in Australia in 2016
by HarperCollins*Publishers* Australia Pty Limited
ABN 36 009 913 517
harpercollins.com.au

HarperCollins*Publishers*
Level 13, 201 Elizabeth Street, Sydney NSW 2000, Australia
Unit D1, 63 Apollo Drive, Rosedale, Auckland 0632, New Zealand
A 53, Sector 57, Noida, UP, India
1 London Bridge Street, London, SE1 9GF, United Kingdom
2 Bloor Street East, 20th floor, Toronto, Ontario M4W 1A8, Canada
195 Broadway, New York NY 10007, USA

National Library of Australia Cataloguing-in-Publication data:

Evans, Tess, author.
  Mercy Street / Tess Evans.
  ISBN: 978 1 4607 5104 6 (paperback)
  ISBN: 978 1 4607 0567 4 (ebook)
  Abandoned children – Fiction.
  Child rearing – Fiction.
  – Families – Fiction.
A823.4

Cover design by Darren Holt, HarperCollins Design Studio
Cover images: girl silhouette based on photo by BLOOM image/Getty Images;
house and fence by Darren Holt; all other images by shutterstock.com
Typeset in Bembo Std by Kirby Jones
Printed and bound in Australia by Griffin Press
The papers used by HarperCollins in the manufacture of this book are a
natural, recyclable product made from wood grown in sustainable plantation
forests. The fibre source and manufacturing processes meet recognised
international environmental standards, and carry certification.

To Terry,
who has always believed in me

... mercy ... is twice blessed.
It blesseth him that gives and him that takes.

William Shakespeare, *The Merchant of Venice*, Act IV; scene I

I

'Another day ...' George speaks the words aloud before remembering that there will be no answering voice from the other side of the bed. 'I know – another dollar.' A silly joke, its origins long forgotten, but over time it had somehow become an intimate morning ritual. When they were younger, this was a signal for him to turn to her sleep-warm body, and often as not, they made love ... Today he winces as he flexes his arthritic knees and makes his way to the bathroom. The tiles chill his bare feet.

Still in his pyjamas, he heads for the kitchen, turns on the kettle and tips some cornflakes and milk into a bowl. His eyes narrow as he sniffs at the carton. *Nose like a bloodhound*, Pen used to say. He sniffs again. *Could be a bit off*. Putting on his glasses, he peers at the use-by date. Two days ago. With a fatalistic shrug, he pours the remainder of the milk into his tea and watches with a grim sort of satisfaction as suspicious white specks float to the surface. *I knew it*. Now not only are his cornflakes inedible, but his tea is undrinkable. He removes his glasses, looks around at the table, the chairs, the cupboards, as though he might find the answer (or, even more importantly, the question) inscribed on their surface. He passes a hand over his eyes, and his grip on the milk carton is suddenly precarious. *Saved!* George breathes out his relief. A near miss, though. He puts the milk back in the fridge before remembering that it's sour and needs to be thrown out. *Why has everything become so hard?*

George will have to go to the shops on an empty stomach. He could have had toast, but who wants toast without a nice cup of tea? As he opens the front door, his jaw trembles and he blinks behind his glasses. The milk was always fresh when Pen was alive. Walking down the path, he turns away from his garden and the spectacle of new-season roses. Their showy display assaults his senses.

He heads towards Station Street, past the giant wooden dog that guards Fairfield station. He hated it at first, but it's grown on him and now he says a silent *G'day* as though to a casual acquaintance. The coffee shop on the corner is not yet busy. Later in the morning, it will be full of young mothers with toddlers in strollers and babies in prams, and the occasional businesswoman or bloke with one of those mini-computers. There'll be groups of older women, too, their careful grooming no match for the youthful vitality that surrounds them.

It's a bit early for the usual crowd and there are only three customers, two women gulping down their pre-commute coffees and a young man in a *Save the Whales* T-shirt, reading a newspaper. Pen and her friends had coffee here every Friday after she retired, but he'd always been a bit intimidated by the easy camaraderie and the overwhelming *femaleness* of the patrons. Today, however, hunger drives him in for tea and toast.

Miserable and self-conscious, fidgeting at his table for one, he begins to regret this uncharacteristically rash decision. It's the first time since he and Pen married that he has eaten alone in public. Probably the first time ever, now he comes to think about it. Not that he and Pen ate out much. They'd go to the local club with friends a couple of times a month and to a fancy restaurant on holidays or special occasions. Pen always looked the part at a restaurant. Dressing right. Knowing what to order. Dealing with the waiters. Socially, he was safe with Pen. She'll be gone three years next May, and even after all that time, he wakes expecting to hear her silly, murmured response – *I know, another dollar.*

The early-morning sun slants across the Formica table, and tiny gold specks twinkle and wink in its pale yellow light. But George rarely notices such things. He splays his square, tradesman's hands, and checks for the telltale tremor that a few more years will surely bring. As he exhales, he becomes aware that he's been holding his breath and relaxes when he sees that his hands are steady as a rock. He has no idea why he does this; just that it's almost compulsive.

He wills breakfast to arrive.

The place is filling up and he experiences what it is to feel lonely in a crowd. It's only eight-thirty and there's a whole lot of day left to fill. When Pen was still with him, life had shape and purpose. Right now they'd be reading bits of the newspaper to each other.

The young waitress sets down his breakfast. 'Enjoy.'

'Thanks, love.' She reminds him a bit of Pen. Something about the way she moves.

He looks at his watch again. Eight-forty-five. George bites into his toast, and not for the first time, wonders if the whole thing is worth it.

When the whale-lover moves off, he leans over and snaffles the newspaper, grateful for something to look at, something to legitimise his place among strangers.

Much later, when he thinks back over this day, he realises that everything – all the good and all the bad things that happened – depended upon a carton of sour milk, the milk that sent him out hungry, took him to the café where he read the abandoned newspaper for just long enough, sent him to the supermarket where he decided to shop earlier than usual and loaded his bags just heavily enough for him to take the shortcut to his house. Most days, he avoids the lane. His bloodhound nose is offended by the smell of rubbish bins and cat piss.

*

At first he senses rather than sees them. Then he hears them – muffled footsteps that draw ever closer until he feels a short, soft exhalation on the back of his neck. The end of the lane recedes to a hazy distance. Paling fences, sagging, festooned with vines and covered with graffiti, crowd in on either side. Without turning, he speeds up as best he can, before his two plastic shopping bags break, their meagre contents tumbling out onto the cobblestones. Four cans of baked beans (Manager's Special – four for two dollars), an apple, a banana, a pear, three potatoes and a bottle of soda water roll away out of reach. The milk carton trickles its contents onto the cobbles next to him. He is outraged to see two expensive-looking trainers stomping on his coffee scroll.

'Hey. That's my morning tea.'

'Wanna make something of it?'

Forget the coffee scroll. The boy has a knife and he's shoving it at George's belly. What George feels now is fear – a fear long ago embedded in the marrow of his bones. They (he, his mother and Shirl) had felt like this on many nights as they'd listened for the scrabble of the key, the heavy tread in the passageway. George's dad had shouldered and flayed his way through their lives, sparing neither his children nor their mother.

So frozen, unable to either call out or resist, George stands with his back to the wall and feels the shaming trickle, warm and pungent, as it spreads down his trouser legs.

If only he could move his hand to his pocket. Give them his wallet. There's little enough in it – a couple of twenties (he never carries much cash), his driver's licence, his credit card and his seniors card. Not much to lose. But the knife holds him in thrall, tightens his airways, as the familiar wheeze begins to rise, hacking and shredding each breath.

The boy is young, but his eyes are empty and his voice flat. 'Get it.' This is addressed to an even younger boy, thirteen or fourteen at the most, who slips the wallet from George's pocket in one expert swoop.

'Got it.'

The knife moves up to George's throat, its pressure delicate and concentrated. 'You can forget about the cops. They come after us – we come after you.' Keeping the knife poised, he moves his face closer to George, who smells, of all things, toothpaste. *What sort of hooligan cleans his teeth and then goes out to mug pensioners?* His attacker indicates the wallet, now in his assistant's hand. The minty-fresh mouth becomes a wet, snarling cavern. 'We know where you live.'

George's knees sag with relief. They aren't going to kill him. After three years of hoping for death, he is surprised to feel the flood of gratitude from knowing that he's spared. He even wants to thank them for their latent compassion or common sense or whatever it is that sees the knife fold and disappear into the older boy's jacket. But his voice is lost in the wheeze, and as he slides down the wall, he feels a volley of vicious kicks to his ribs.

'Hey, you dickheads! He's an old man – leave him alone!' It's a girl's voice, screaming at them with shrill authority from the other end of the lane. At the sound of her voice, one of the boys plants a final, awkward kick before they both flee, calling the girl a name that shocks George. When pushed, he can swear with the best of them, but never in the presence of a woman.

'Ya got a puffer?'

George makes a feeble gesture at his breast pocket.

Again he finds himself rifled by the hands of a stranger, but these are the practical hands of a young woman who puts the puffer to his lips. 'Breathe. That's right. Slow.' She looks at him with satisfaction as the wheezing eases, then frowns as she peers down the lane. 'Those shits got away with your wallet.'

His breathing under control, George's attention is taken in equal measure by the crackling pain in his side and the fact that his rescuer is female. She is kneeling beside him, so it's hard to tell her height. Short, he guesses, and certainly overweight. Her hair, long at the back, sticks up on top in those spikes you see nowadays. And it's red. Not the satiny copper that had attracted him to Pen all those years ago. No. This is an unnatural, solid scarlet – an 'in your face' sort of colour that goes with the multiple nose piercings. He has seen girls like this before, and they seem somehow to manage a perverse sort of elegance. But this one has a frayed look. And hers is not the pretty plumpness that some young women carry off so well. Tight clothing accentuates slovenly curves that spill over the waist of her jeans and settle in unbecoming rolls of flesh, where her T-shirt struggles to conceal them.

All this George absorbs in an instant before a small attempt to sit up straighter causes him to cry out in pain. 'Shit! – Sorry, love.'

The girl smiles faintly. It's quite a nice smile. 'Heard worse. Can you stand up if you lean on me?' She moves position to his uninjured side and drapes his arm over her shoulder. 'One, two ...'

It's no good. Those mongrels must have broken his ribs. Though the lane isn't a popular thoroughfare, someone must have noticed them and called for help. Within minutes, a small crowd has gathered.

A frizzy, grey sort of woman puts down her shopping bag, eyeing George's rescuer with suspicion. 'I'll ring an ambulance,' she informs the milling spectators who have been waiting for someone to take charge. 'One of you call the police.'

The girl looks alarmed. 'No use calling the cops. They'll never get them now.'

George hasn't forgotten the threat. 'Didn't see them,' he says. *God, even talking hurts.* 'Couldn't describe them in a million years.' He is a man happy in his own company, but has lived long enough to know that people who get excited by events soon lose interest if any real action is required. Sure enough, the murmuring is in support of an ambulance only. *No police. They'll want witness statements.* Soon, all but the girl, the woman with the phone and a middle-aged man in overalls melt away.

George is suddenly aware of the state of his pants. He tries to cover the wet patch with his hands and is grateful when the bloke in overalls offers his newspaper. 'Could happen to anyone,' the man says, before heading back up the lane to watch out for the ambulance.

The girl clambers to her feet, brushing dirt from her already grimy jeans. 'Looks like you'll be okay, then.'

George regards her with a mixture of gratitude and embarrassment. In the old days, he'd have had those young tearaways on toast. Despite his humiliation at being saved by a female, a word of thanks is the least he owes her. 'Ta, love,' he says.

''S'all right. Gotta go and pick me kid up from Bree's.'

Kid? She was only a kid herself. 'Yeah. Well. Thanks.' He hesitates. 'M'name's George. I live round the corner in Mercy Street – number seven. Blue fence. If you … if I can … Well. You know where I live.'

She grins. *Makes the world of difference*, he thinks.

'Next time kick 'em in the nuts.'

*

The ambulance negotiates the narrow lane and George relaxes under the competent hands of the paramedics. 'What's your name?' the young man asks. 'Mine's Sean.'

George rouses himself at the question. Ambos always ask that. He'd had to call the ambulance for Pen several times, and one of the first things they did was ask her name.

'Penny,' she'd say.

'Is that Penelope?'

'Just Penny.'

Nice to meet you, Just-Penny.

That was his lame attempt at a joke the night they met at his cousin's twenty-first. She was almost half a head taller than he was, and while the other girls wore pink or yellow or aqua blue, she wore something soft in a greyish green – the colour of a gumleaf, he thought at the time.

Just-Penny folded herself into a chair with a fluid movement that he later realised was characteristic. That way of arranging her body. So natural. So – *composed*. After a polite smile at the joke she must have heard a hundred times, she explained that when she was born, her head was covered with bright-orange down. 'Dad said I looked like a brand-new penny. So they called me Penny, and if anyone asked why not Penelope, they'd say, "We're not Penelope sort of people".'

They weren't Penelope sort of people. They were good, old-fashioned working-class people, happy to have their Penny courted by a newly minted boiler-maker; secretly relieved that she had escaped marriage to a man damaged by the war. It was a sore point with George, who had been too young to join up. Long after the war had ended, he always felt less of a man when in the company of ex-servicemen. But he got on well with Ma and Da – better than with his own parents, that's for sure. He'd have tea there every Saturday night before taking Pen to the pictures or a dance at the town hall. She made her own clothes and was always twirling around in something new. *How does this look?* The simple fact was that to him she looked wonderful, and the new dresses were no more than a backdrop for her bright-copper hair. Long, with a natural wave, it bounced and swung and shone as though in delight at its own beauty. There had been prettier girls at the party, but Penny's slim, supple body and new-penny hair – they were more than enough for George.

They were much too much for his sister, Shirl. A few weeks after they'd met, when they were on their way out to a party, George turned the car. 'Time you met my sister. She's just around the corner.'

Penny smoothed her hair. 'Good,' she said. 'I've been dying to meet her.'

A flustered Shirl answered the door, heavily pregnant under a voluminous smock. She carried a toddler on one hip and a spoon in her free hand.

'Sis. How are you? This is Penny.'

The dishevelled Shirl ran her eyes over Penny's willowy figure, her glossy grooming, her fashionable party dress. 'Are you coming in?' Shirl attempted to pull out one of her hair curlers but was defeated by the spoon. 'It's all a bit of a mess at the moment.'

Despite the coolness of the invitation, George and Penny went in and the three of them endured fifteen minutes of self-conscious civility until George looked at his watch.

'Gotta fly.'

'Lovely to meet you,' Penny said.

'You, too,' Shirl replied. 'Nice dress,' she said before closing the door as quickly as she reasonably could.

Penny groaned. 'We should've told her we were coming.'

'Why would we do that?'

'So she could tidy herself up a bit.' Penny smoothed down her already smooth dress. 'I hope I never get like that when I have children.'

George never quite understood this. Even when his sister rang to berate him.

'There I was, looking all lumpy and frumpy with rollers in my hair no less, and in you come with that glamourpuss. It's not fair, George. It's just not fair.'

Women. George shook his head in disbelief. Still does, in fact.

But that was a long while ago. Before Penny's genuine kindness won Shirl over.

*

At the hospital, the ambos wait with him until he is shown to a cubicle. The nurse makes him comfortable then takes down his details.

'Name?'

'George Johnson.'

'Date of birth?'

'First of March, 1929.'

'So. That'd make you seventy …'

'Six.'

'Six. Right. Next of kin?'

'Penny … No. My sister – Shirley Adams.'

A young doctor (*when did doctors get to be so young?*) checks his vital signs and feels his ribs. 'Does this hurt?'

Bloody oath, it hurts. He swallows hard. 'Just a bit.'

An X-ray reveals that his ribs are not broken. 'Just badly bruised,' the young doctor says cheerfully. 'Lucky kids wear trainers nowadays.' But they didn't feel like trainers to George. *Steel-capped trainers*, he thinks with grim humour. He'd worn steel-capped boots all his working life and if you were kicked with steel-capped boots, you knew all about it.

They put him on oxygen to control the asthma and decided to keep him in for a few hours' observation.

Relieved to be taken in hand, he complies with good grace, but when Shirl comes to pick him up, he baulks at the suggestion that she take him back to her house.

'So you think he's fit to go home?' Shirl's tone suggests that she has a well-founded belief to the contrary. Snug in his cubicle, George hears her through the curtain and imagines the poor young registrar struggling to maintain his professional authority. He grins despite himself, imagining Shirl wielding her daunting bosom like some Amazon shield. He's not sure when it happened, but over the years his sister had become a warrior, her hair an iron-grey helmet, her blue eyes stern behind uncompromising glasses.

'I hope you're decent.' Without waiting for a reply, Shirl sweeps aside the curtain. *'Apparently'* – she emphasises the word for the benefit of the young doctor – 'you're well enough to leave. You'll come back to my place, of course.'

'I'm good, Shirl. Just take me home.'

His sister looks at him with that unique-to-Shirl exasperation. 'You told me yourself on the phone not twenty minutes ago. They said they know where you live.'

George glares right back. Women always make such a big deal out of everything. He might be getting on, but he isn't going to let a couple of snotty-nosed kids drive him from his own home. In a brief review of the incident, he has decided that it was the element of surprise that gave them the advantage. *Next time ...* he sees himself landing a punch on the big one and hauling the younger one by the collar; gloating as the lad stares in dismay at his crony spread-eagled on the footpath.

'Stop fussing, woman. If you're not going to take me home, I'll get a taxi.'

She isn't a bad old stick, his sister. On the way home (George is surprised to see that it's nearly dark), she calls by her place and grabs some soup and a casserole from the freezer. She settles him in bed, and making sure his painkillers and puffer are within reach, leaves him with a bowl of soup, a cheese sandwich and a pot of tea.

'Nothing much in the fridge, as usual.' Just as he's beginning to feel grateful for her ministrations, she has to add, 'Except for the grog.'

'For Christ's sake, Shirl. For once in your life, give it a break.'

She goes off in a huff then, and after finishing his soup, he begins to regret his irritability. Not that she doesn't deserve it. Always going on about the drink is Shirl, preaching about that God-bothering, wowser of a husband. *When Bill took the pledge, I knew for sure he was the man for me.* George bites into his sandwich. He has to admit that he can't blame the woman for wanting a teetotaller husband after all their mum went through.

The morning's incident has reawakened his childhood fears. Memories long-buried begin to surface. He was six, maybe seven years old, sitting at the dinner table with his mum and Shirl. His mum was talking to Shirl about ... what was it? A school play. That's right. Shirl was excited because she was going to be the drover's wife in the school play.

He was aware that his mother was only half listening. She was also listening for the scraping of the key. *Was he really so aware then, or is it only with hindsight that he knows this? Does it matter?* He remembers well enough how they all froze as his dad lurched into the kitchen and his mum leapt to her feet. In the silence before the storm, young George heard himself swallow, milk gurgling down his throat like water down the plughole.

'Started without me, have you? Never you worry about a man who's been working his guts out. That's right. Working my guts out so you can sit around on your fat bum all day reading your poxy magazines.'

'I've kept it warm for you. The children were tired ...'

'Like I'm not tired? A man who's been working all day? Fuck your poxy stew.' He flung the plate at the wall where the stew oozed, a greasy brown, down the faded wallpaper.

'The children ...'

'You kids. Get lost or I'll kick your bums till your noses bleed.'

Shirl took her brother's hand and they melted away, in desperate fear of drawing further attention to themselves. Young George put his hands over his ears but he can hear it to this day – the dull thuds, the muffled pleas.

Just that once, he found the courage to run back to the kitchen. His mother was cowering in the corner and his father, unsteady with the grog, was attempting to kick her.

'Stop!'

The man turned. 'Get out, you little prick, or I'll kill your mother. I swear I will.'

George fled, and later, when his mum dragged herself to bed, he was given a thrashing with his father's leather belt.

'That – will – teach – you.' His father thrashed and swore and thrashed some more until, exhausted, he fell in a drunken stupor onto the couch.

For a while after that his father called him *Mummy's brave ickle soldier.* It was the way he said it. With Frank Johnson, mockery was a finely honed art.

George, his reverie intensified by codeine, takes a moment to remember where he is, and is relieved to see the familiar green curtains and patchwork quilt. He pushes the quilt back. He's sweating, and his mouth is dry. He remembers his sister's crack about the grog. Shirl might go on, but he, George, isn't a drunk. True, he always liked a beer or two after work, and since he's retired, he keeps up the custom – two beers before dinner and one with his meal – and some nights (most nights) another one or two while he reads or watches a bit of telly. Although, come to think of it, he can't remember drinking after dinner when Pen was alive.

He looks over at the pillow beside his own. *Goodnight, Pen.* Every night for nearly fifty years, Pen's head lay on that pillow. He loved the way, in the early days, her hair spread across the white slip like marmalade, glowing with the colour of oranges and sunshine. Over time, she had it cut in what she called a smart, modern style. Over more time, the colour had faded and dulled, but the image he sees every night now is of burnished copper and marmalade.

2

Redgum has a key. They both live alone and it seems only sensible that a mate should have a key, just in case. *Just in case*, they joke, avoiding eye contact. *One of us will cark it one day and the other one can come in and pinch his stuff before the cops arrive.* They joke, but it's frightening, the thought of dying alone. In one way, George knows, we all die alone – even when we're surrounded by family and friends. Pen was alone in that moment when death called her name. Though he clung to her hand with both of his, his warm, desperate flesh was not enough to bridge the measureless gulf that opens between the living and the dying.

No. It isn't so much dying alone as not being found for days, weeks, months. You read about old blokes – old women, too, for that matter. They live by themselves and die by themselves and no one notices until a neighbour or a meter reader reports the smell. So he and Redgum keep a lookout for each other – if the newspaper is still in the letterbox by lunchtime, that would be a sign that there's something wrong.

When Pen was alive, George didn't need Redgum's help and he'd felt a superior kind of compassion when his mate was diagnosed with a dicky heart. *He's a couple of years younger, too. You never can tell.*

'A man could, you know – go all of a sudden.' Though Redgum spoke with his usual calm, his soft brown eyes were troubled. 'If you could sort of check on me if you don't see me around.'

'You have to feel sorry for Redgum.' George had squeezed his wife's shoulders as they watched him lumber back down the path. 'We're luckier than we think.'

Pen, wrapped deep in the folds of her cardigan, shivered and leaned into his warmth. She had a way of looking right into his thoughts, even before he thought them. 'Promise if I go first, you'll ask Redgum or Shirl to keep an eye out for you. It's different for people who have children.'

George found himself rattled by the intensity of her tone. 'Rubbish. You'll outlive me by years.' He didn't respond to the remark about children. He never did. They had tried and failed. It happens.

*

Redgum hasn't waited for lunchtime. 'Shirl rang,' he yells from the passageway. 'Said to check up on you. One of her grandkids is off school.'

'Up here.' George can see that there are some benefits in not having children. Even after they grow up, you're never shot of them. Those girls of hers run poor Shirl ragged. But they were nice when they were kids and he's still fond of them. Not that he sees them much, nowadays. Hard to believe, but they have families of their own, both of them. When they were small, Pen was always offering to babysit. She loved to read them stories and he had to admit it made a nice picture – Pen with the kids in their pyjamas, all rosy and fresh, snuggled up to her as she read their bedtime story. He had tried once, but it didn't work for him. He felt awkward and they wriggled and poked at each other as he read. It was their favourite story, too – *The Three Billy Goats Gruff* – but somehow he couldn't bring himself to stomp and roar like Pen did when she read it. He sounded flat and boring even to himself. As soon as he'd finished, they jumped off his knee. 'Thank you, Uncle George. Can Aunty Pen read to us now?' He was a bit hurt, but the sight of Pen reading to them in the lamplight – that almost made up for it.

*

Redgum is his best mate – probably his only mate, but George is not about to tell him the whole truth. 'Jumped by a couple of blokes in Seddon's Lane. Big bastards. Could've been bikies.' *Not really a lie. They most likely will be one day.*

Redgum shakes his head. 'Drugs,' he declares. 'It'll be drugs for sure. I mean there used to be rules about not kicking a man when he's down, but nowadays … You see it all the time. They'll do anything for drugs.' He flexes his fist. 'You and me would've made a mess of them not so long ago.'

Good old Redgum. They'd been in one or two pub fights in their time, nothing vicious, just a bit of pushing and shoving. Only ever started a blue once, but when things got going, they were unbeatable. Redgum is still a big bloke, but in his day … Working as a ganger for the railways, he used to heft around those red-gum sleepers as though they were kindling.

It was a fight that brought them together. George was enjoying a quiet drink when a couple of new blokes came into the bar, talking big about what they'd like to do to the redhead bird from the bank. George wasn't tall, but he was strong and nuggety and completely fearless.

'That's my wife you're talking about.' He punched one of them in the gut and this big bloke joined in. The strangers were no match for George's fury and the big bloke's powerful punches. They made a right mess of their opponents, who took off together when the cops came to sort things out. In those days that meant looking the other way unless there was a weapon involved. And these bastards had insulted his wife.

The cops understood. 'Fair enough,' they said. 'Just get out of here.' They did, and George shook Redgum's hand, discovered that they were neighbours and the rest, as they say, is history.

*

'Bugger of a thing to happen.' Redgum is uneasy around sick people. All that clucking and tutting and questions and sympathy – that's what women are for. He opens and shuts his big hands hanging useless by his side. 'As long as you're okay ...'

'Good as gold.'

'I'll push off, then.'

'No worries.'

*

Redgum had brought in the newspaper and George reads the crime articles with more than passing interest. His assailants have grown in his mind. They might have been young but they were big and mean-looking. Then there was the knife. He thought it was probably a switchblade – it seemed to open and close with a flick. A man would have to be crazy to mess with a knife-wielding junkie. You have to wonder what the parents are thinking – letting their kids roam about the streets with knives and God knows what. If he'd had sons they'd have been tough, that goes without saying, but when push came to shove, they'd have been good kids. A bit of rough and tumble – *boys will be boys* – up to all sorts of mischief, no doubt, but nothing mean or vicious. And respectful of their elders – he and Pen would have made sure of that.

He sometimes sees his boys – they even have names – Eddie and Jeff. (Jeff with a 'J'. They weren't Geoff with a 'G' kind of people.) When he was younger, he used to imagine them climbing trees, playing with their dog, Digger. (*What else would you call a dog?*) A few more years and they'd be playing footy and cricket for their school teams. Later, they might have batted for Australia, played full-forward for the Blues. Who knows? It's George's dream and he can make them exactly as he pleases. So they remain forever ten and twelve. He's always been a bit vaguer about their younger sister, Annie. He gave her copper curls like Pen and eyes like his mother's, but after that, his imagination ran out.

He wonders, as his vision of Eddie, Jeff and Annie blurs and fades, why he never spoke to Pen about these children who lived in his head. Did she, too, have a raft of phantom babies that grew into sticky, sturdy toddlers? And later to schoolchildren with scabby knees and eager faces that shone with each new and wonderful thing they learned?

Despite his own experience of beatings and derision, George has faith in schooling. One teacher. That's all it takes to fire you up. Miss Walsh was strict, but she was the one who took the trouble to find out that he had no books at home. Every second Friday, she'd take her class of nine-year-olds to the local library, where they were allowed to borrow two books. They could keep them for a fortnight, but George always finished his within a few days. Then Miss Walsh would take him back to the library alone. In her own lunchtime. That was the sort of teacher who made up for all the rest.

Teacher's pet! Suck! After a few visits, George told Miss Walsh that he was sick of books and didn't want to go to the library anymore. He can relive that moment, years later. As a boy, he thought it was him she was cross with, but over time he came to realise that her anger wasn't directed at him at all. 'Oh, George,' she'd said. 'Such a waste.'

After he married Pen, he felt safe enough to join the library again. In those days a library had weight to it. All those books, all that knowledge lined up in orderly ranks so high that they had sliding wooden ladders to help you reach the top shelves. There were tall, dusty windows and heavy timber fittings. When he first walked back into a library as a man, the silence, the fusty smell, the general solemnity transported him to another world where people like him, outsiders really, had access to thousands of books. He now goes to a light, modern building, where children sit listening to stories and the librarians all seem to be pretty young girls. He reads detective fiction, war stories, adventure stuff like Len Deighton and Wilbur Smith and, of course, the memoirs of his sporting heroes. These are manly enough to pass muster. In a shifty sort of way, he reads books on astronomy, geology and even history (as long as it involves a war – but then what history doesn't?). He wishes he had the nerve to borrow the rest of the Biggles series he missed out on when he told Miss Walsh that he was sick of books.

No point in dwelling on the past. All the same, he regrets not talking to Pen about Eddie and Jeff. And Annie, too, of course. It might have eased the pain of their childlessness just a little. Or it might not. He'll never know now.

After folding the newspaper, he drifts off to sleep, then wakes to hear Shirl clattering around in the kitchen. His stomach begins to rumble. He wouldn't mind some more of that vegie soup.

*

Never one to lie about in bed, George is back on his feet three days after the bikie incident, as he's come to call it. His ribs remain very painful, and when Shirl and Redgum are there, he shuffles about with a faint air of martyrdom. He doesn't want to become dependent. You never know what might happen if you give in to that sort of thing. The trouble is, he quite likes the attention. He hasn't felt so cared for since Pen died and remembers well enough the initial fuss and bother that surrounded him then.

She had lots of friends, did Pen. He was happy just with her. And Redgum. (Every bloke needs a mate.) But Pen had numerous friends and relatives, who, in that first couple of weeks, visited his hollowed-out house, bringing comfort in the form of soup, casseroles and cake. What is it with fruitcakes? He could die, fully content, without ever seeing another fruitcake. There's still one in the freezer. Been there nearly three years. It doesn't seem right to throw it out.

In the weeks that followed the funeral, visitors sort of drained away, leaving random scraps of food and pity in their wake. Soon there was only Shirl and Redgum and he told himself that was the way he liked it.

Shirl's Bill made an effort, but they'd never had much to say to each other and he suspects Bill was as relieved as he was when the visits stopped. (Mind you – not without some carry-on from Shirl.)

So it's natural for a man to be wary of becoming dependent. Support can go down the gurgler at any given moment – even, perhaps, when it's your sister and your best friend. Certainly when it's your wife's friends.

When Pen was alive, people seemed to drop in all the time. He knew they were there for her, and he'd just say 'G'day' or 'How's Peter (or Harry or Serg or whoever)' before going on with what he was doing, but he has to admit that it was good to live in a house that was … that had … He searched a long time for the right words. Then he found them. When Pen was there, 7 Mercy Street pulsed with life. It had a heart.

*

After she retired, Pen started a patchwork group. Six women (seven counting Pen) spent Tuesday afternoons in the lounge room cutting, sewing and talking. And laughing. George was amazed at the number of things they found to laugh about. Patches littered the carpet as kneeling women measured and cut and stitched the bright scraps of fabric. They were like bees, he thought. 'Busy buzzing bees.' He took to calling them the Bee Bee Bees and the women laughed good-naturedly and threatened to make him patchwork trousers.

When the AIDS epidemic sent cold waves of fear through the community, the quilters, led by Pen, took on a new task. The quilts, once for their children and grandchildren, were sent instead to the AIDS quilt project.

One day, he and Pen were having breakfast and she read, with growing horror, an article on the social effects of that terrible, wasting disease. 'It says here that people with AIDS are being shunned like they have leprosy.'

'Mmm.' An absurdly healthy male, George wasn't much interested in medical matters, couldn't imagine what it might be like to be sick, and tended to refer to the unwell as whingers and moaners. He moved on to a more appealing topic. 'They reckon this Stephen Silvagni's going to be a star one day, just like his dad.'

'They need volunteers at Fairfield hospital. It's practically next door. I think I might check it out.'

'What? What are you checking out?'

'Volunteering to work with the AIDS patients.'

George lowered his newspaper and stared at his wife. 'AIDS patients? Drug addicts and poofters? Over my dead body.'

Penny stared right back. 'If it has to come to that ...' She smiled then to soften her response. 'Now I've got all this time to spare, I want to do something. When all is said and done, they're just people. Maybe I could read to someone, or just talk.'

George's voice rose to an unnatural pitch. 'You can catch AIDS. Why else would they put them in an infectious-diseases hospital?' His stomach began to heave and growl, indicating the level of his anxiety.

Penny stood up and came around to his side of the table, then put her arms around his neck, her chin on his head. 'I'll get all the information first,' she reassured him. 'If there's any danger, I won't go. Promise.' She ruffled his hair. 'Come on, woolly-head. Your tea's getting cold. I'll make us a fresh pot.'

Pen got her way. Every Tuesday morning she would visit her 'boys', as she called them. Every Tuesday at lunchtime, she'd want to talk about them. 'Peter's parents finally came to visit him,' she said once. 'But they won't talk to Mike. Their son is dying and they won't talk to the other person who loves him best in the world. If I had a child ...'

George understood then, and stopped calling them junkies and queers. Still, he was happier to encourage the quilting. In his book, it was a lot safer.

*

He is surprised to hear the doorbell. Shirl and Redgum both have keys. Who else would be visiting at (he checks his watch) nearly three o'clock in the afternoon? So instead of answering the door, he dithers about in his slippers and dressing-gown and starts to wonder. Instead of wondering who is at the door, he wonders at a line of poetry from his Fourth Grade Reader – *He stood in his shoes and wondered*. Or maybe it was *wandered*. But would you *stand* and wander? No. It must have been *wondered*. He jumps when the doorbell rings a second time. He'll have to be careful. These wandering (*wondering?*) thoughts might be an early sign of Alzheimer's. He does a quick hand check for tremors.

Opening the door, he squints into the afternoon sun. 'Yes?'

'You don't remember me, do you?'

It's the girl. At least she looks like the girl. 'In the lane,' he says. 'We met in the lane.' Good grief. He made it sound as though they'd been formally introduced. He stares from the doorway, holding the dressing-gown tight to his chest.

'Can we come in?'

She has a child with her, a waif with stringy yellow hair and wary eyes that narrow in a very unpleasant way when they meet his. He flinches at that judgemental stare before remembering his manners. 'Of course. Come in.' He gestures at the dressing-gown. ''Scuse the clobber. Bed-rest. Doc's orders.'

'Can't stay,' the young woman says. 'Got a couple of things to do.'

That's a relief, thinks George, but, feeling beholden, he mutters something conciliatory. The visitors are standing just inside the door. George goes to speak but finds he has nothing to say. He scratches his chin. Perhaps he should thank her again.

'Don't want to stay with that man.' The child (*What would she be – three? four?* George is no expert) clings to her mother's hand and slides up against her skirt like some little animal seeking refuge.

'You got to. Aunty Bree can't look after you.'

What did she say? He must have misheard what she said. 'You're not expecting to leave that kid here?' The sweep of his arm takes in the whole house, from front door to back.

Her reply is short. Affectedly patient. Even, it seems, from her point of view, logical. 'I told you. Bree can't do it.'

Bree? 'What's that got to do with me?'

'Poison toe. She's got to go to the doctor's, so there's nowhere to leave the kid.'

George smarts at the exasperated tone, the patronising way she rolls her eyes. It puts him on the defensive. *Watch your tone, young lady. Don't think you can treat me like I don't know what day it is.* He doesn't say this aloud, but makes do with glowering over her head at the lamppost beyond the front gate. It requires some effort, deciphering the young woman's shorthand. He's almost certain he doesn't know a Bree. But why would she think he did? And why should this Bree's poisoned toe lead them to his house with such a ridiculous request?

'Why here? Why me?' Of course he doesn't want to be responsible for this disagreeable child (or any child for that matter). But that's not the only thing. It is so unsuitable. Not to mention dangerous. What could be so important that she would risk leaving her child with a stranger? Clutching his bruised ribs, he draws a painful breath and begins to sputter. 'You want to leave the kid here? With me? You don't know me from a bar of soap. I could be a child molester for all you know.'

'You're not, are you? Wouldn't've saved your life if I thought you were.'

'Of course I'm not. But you don't know that. And anyway ...' (He's doubly mortified by her claim to be his rescuer.) 'They put the knife away before you came.'

She shrugs. 'Say what you like, Granddad, from what I saw, they were kicking you. *And* you were having an asthma attack.'

George deflates under his dressing-gown. 'True enough, girlie.'

'So you'll mind the kid, then?' This time she tries a smile. 'Her name's Aurora-Jane.'

Aurora-Jane? What sort of name is that? Honestly, the names people give their kids these days. What's wrong with just Jane? Or Patricia. Or Annie? For some reason he is able to picture his Annie much more clearly. Perhaps because she's the opposite of this unlovely child with the sallow skin and guarded eyes.

'I can't. It's not right. Look at her. She's terrified.' *And so am I. What do I know about kids?*

George looks at Aurora-Jane and she looks back at him. The dislike is both candid and mutual.

As one, they turn their eyes to the young woman. *We don't want this,* their eyes say. *Don't make us. You have to stop it before it's too late.*

She doesn't stop though, does she? No matter that George has made his feelings quite plain.

'Interview at the Job Centre. Lose me benefits if I don't go. Look. I got no choice. It's too hard with a kid whining round me ankles. Besides ...' She measures the effect with her eyes. 'You told me where you live.'

George almost feels sorry for the child. Perhaps he does owe the mother something. 'How long?'

'Half an hour. An hour at the most,' she says, her voice (*in deference to his age?*) getting louder as she disappears down the path.

'Just this once,' George yells after her. 'Don't get any ideas.'

*

George is perplexed. 'Now what can we do with you?'

The kid is crying, beating on the door where her mother has just disappeared. 'Maaarm. Mummy.' She works up to a high-pitched shriek. 'Maaarmeee!'

What on earth will the neighbours think? What would Pen do? What should he do?

'Shh. Shh. Stop it. Aurora-Jane! Mummy'll be back soon.'

The crying continues, punctuated by demands for her mother and the odd venomous *Hate you* directed at George.

'Stop this minute. Do you hear me?' George's heart is racing uncomfortably as he struggles for control. Perhaps he should ring Shirl. She could be here in ten minutes. Fifteen at the most. Then a flash of inspiration. 'Hey.' The wailing subsides. 'How would you like a biscuit?'

The kid looks at him from under her arm, which is still beating on the door. 'Maaarmee!' she counters.

But negotiations have begun. *Holding out for a better offer, are you?* George plays his last card. 'What about an ice-cream?' His one self-indulgence is to buy a packet of Choc Wedges at the supermarket each week. There must be one or two left.

His faith in this tactic is confirmed when he waves one in her direction and the tears dry up as quickly as they'd come. He's quite chuffed. Fancy him managing to quieten an upset kid. 'Now,' he says, 'you just sit here at the table.' He goes to help her up but she puts down the ice-cream and clambers up by herself. Despite his dislike, he recognises independence when he sees it. A determined little bugger; he has to give her that. But she might have said 'thank you'.

*

Aurora-Jane, having finished her ice-cream, climbs down from her chair, trots into the lounge and sits, large as life, on Pen's nice velvet couch, looking expectantly at the television. Children shouldn't watch too much TV (even George is aware of that), but he doesn't want her crying again, so they watch *The Price Is Right*. George chooses to sit on the straight-backed chair. Getting up and down on the couch is still pretty painful. Besides, he doesn't feel comfortable with the thought of sitting beside her. Watching TV together on the couch suggests an intimacy beyond their brief and hopefully short acquaintance. With Annie it would have been different. They would have sat cuddled up together as fathers and daughters do. Or better yet, they'd be outside on the swing. It would be a mild evening, very much like this one. The swing would have been a birthday present. Or (George is quite carried away by this thought) brought by Santa in his magic sack. Redgum would have come round to help him put it up on Christmas Eve after Annie was in bed.

'I hate this show.' Aurora-Jane's whine cuts into his reverie.

'Too bad,' he says.

'I hate you.'

'I don't like you much, either.'

They glare at each other for a bit – then George goes back to watching TV. He has to admit she's right. It is a stupid show – he never watches it unless he's desperate to hear another voice. On the other hand, it doesn't do to let a kid rule the roost. 'Say please.' That's what Pen would say if she were here. 'Say please and I'll find another channel.'

This remarkable show of firmness results in renewed bellowing. He looks at the clock. Twenty past five. *Half an hour,* she'd said. *An hour at the most.* And the wailing goes on and on. 'Maarmeee! Maarmeee! Maarmeee!'

He clicks through the channels and finds a cartoon. Kids like cartoons. Especially if there's a bit of biffo. *Wham!* Captain Cool dispatches two bad guys with one punch. Aurora-Jane pauses. Takes stock. When she flicks a glance in his direction, he swears there's a glint of triumph in her eyes. There's certainly no trace of tears.

Moments later Shirl arrives with his tea – a nice chicken pie and vegetables. When she comes into the room, the look on her face is priceless. 'George, I … Who is that child? And what on earth is she doing with her shoes on Pen's good velvet couch?'

You get a good deal of satisfaction out of seeing someone like Shirl nonplussed. 'Her name's Aurora-Jane.' *Why make things easy?*

'Shoo, girl! Shoo!' Shirl puts down the plate and flaps her hands at the child as though she were shooing a chook. 'Get off that couch this minute! George – she's all sticky. Do something.'

George tries to be reasonable – not always the best approach with Shirl. 'She's just finished an ice-cream,' he explains. 'Bound to get sticky.'

Meanwhile, Aurora-Jane burrows her way into the cushions and sets up another bout of wailing. 'Maarmeee. Maarmeee. Maarmeee!'

'Now look at what you've done. She was fine till you came in flapping and shooing.'

'I hope Pen had that couch stain-guarded, that's all I can say.'

Of course despite this claim, she can say a lot more – and does. While George goes into maybe-she'll-shut-up-soon mode. He had perfected this as a boy. The staring as though he were listening. The occasional nod. The total refusal of the words that spatter the surface of his consciousness and slide away like rain off a plastic raincoat.

'Her mum'll be back soon.'

'Who on earth is she?'

'Aurora-Jane. I told you that.' Hearing her name, the child looks up, and catching Shirl's expression, decides to return to the relative safety of the cushions.

'Not the child's name, you old fool. Who's her mother? Where do you know her from?'

To George's relief she doesn't pursue him about the mother's name. Just as well because he's sure he doesn't know it. (Although you never can tell. He may have forgotten.) 'She was the lass who helped me after the bikie incident.' Shirl's expression changes at the margins and George pursues his advantage. 'Got my puffer for me and everything. I'm just helping her out for an hour or two.'

He sees this has placated his sister, who is moved to study what she can see of Aurora-Jane with more interest. 'Well. Yes. Hmm.' Turning on her heel, Shirl marches off to the bathroom. 'Washcloth,' she announces and proceeds to wipe the child's hands and face. Not without a fight. George has to admire them both. This is a battle of equals.

At the sound of the doorbell Shirl is in the passageway before George can haul himself to his feet. *We're in for it now.* He sinks back into his chair to watch events unfold.

Shirl all but frogmarches the young woman in. 'You had no right to leave your child with a stranger. Tell her, George. She has no right at all.'

Aurora-Jane's wailing resumes and her mother grabs her by the arm. 'Shut up, Rory. I'm here now. If you're good we'll get fish 'n' chips for tea.'

George realises he's been holding his breath. No one could mistake Shirl's disapproving stare, but most of the time you can rely on her to say the right thing. Nevertheless, he hears shards of ice crackling in his sister's voice as she shepherds the pair to the door. 'We owe you our thanks, I believe. For helping my brother after the bikie attack.'

George winces. His white (?) lie will come to light and he'll look completely ridiculous. He shoots a hopeless glance at the girl.

'No worries,' she says and winks at him behind Shirl's back.

Encouraged by George's grateful expression, the young woman plunges on with a reckless disregard of Shirl's increasingly horrified stare. 'Don't get me wrong, I got nothin' against rippin' people off, but kickin' a bloke who's old enough to be your granddad – that's just crap.'

Shirl returns from the door and gives him one of her looks. *We both know you've done something stupid/thoughtless/rash*, a look like this says. There are subtle differences in her repertoire of looks, and as a youngster he lacked the skill to interpret them. Over the years he has learned to read them like the morning paper and responds to this one with the traditional slight shrug. He glances at his watch and wishes, not for the first time, that it was a stopwatch. The next step is to see how long Shirl can refrain from comment.

Ten seconds. Shouldn't be long. She inflates an indignant bosom. *Time!*

'Did you hear what she said?' She exaggerates the girl's broad accent. (*Just like yours used to be*, thinks George.) '"I got nothin' against rippin' people off." That's what she said. Bold as brass! In broad daylight, too.'

While his sister pauses for breath, George ponders the implication that such a statement might be acceptable at night. (Or at twilight. Or even, at a pinch, on a cloudy day.)

'I can't believe you gave her your address.' Shirl's growing outrage is evident in the hectic red spots that spread high across her cheekbones, the rapid blinking behind her glasses. 'And the first thing she does is dump the child on you. With an injured man. A stranger, no less. Honestly, George, I'm speechless.'

With remarkable self-control George bypasses the obvious rejoinder. 'She helped me, Shirl. I'd have been a goner for sure. There's a debt. Me to her. That's the way I see it.'

'Don't the Chinese say that if you save someone's life, it's you who owes them?'

She never gives in, the old Shirl. George's expression is mild, even affectionate. 'But we're not Chinese, are we?'

*

Angie scowls at the door, which the dragon lady has shut, practically in her face. Dragging a protesting Rory in her wake, she seethes over her day – Bree and all that bullshit about a poisoned toe, the kid carrying on about being left with George. That bitch at the Job Centre wanting to know why she hadn't applied for any jobs in the last month. *Duh! Like there's any point.* Then along with all the other crap, in comes that up-herself Shirl woman.

The old bloke seems all right, she concedes, tucking away this assessment for future reference. Survival is her one, finely honed skill. And *you never know,* she thinks as she shepherds her daughter into the fish 'n' chip shop.

*

Shirl gives her hapless brother terse instructions about how to heat the pie, and heads off in the direction of her own well-ordered home. She grips the steering wheel as though it might fly off out the window. Would you believe it! Just as George seemed reconciled to his life as a widower, he goes off and gets himself mugged. Not satisfied with that, he seems to feel some sort of obligation to his rescuer. Shirl has always prided herself on her sense of fair play, and it's clear that he owes the girl something. But he could have given her money. Much less bothersome than babysitting. He was never very good with Marianne and Claire when they were little and they're his own flesh and blood. So how could he expect to look after the child of a stranger? A child who, if she were honest, is no more than a grubby little brat.

3

The Sticky Wicket isn't what it used to be. Now it isn't even The Sticky Wicket. It's The White Clipper Bar and Bistro and there isn't a sticky glass stain or a flake of sawdust in sight. A few old-timers huddle in the darkest corner, providing authenticity, while the thirty-somethings sit at dinky chrome tables and sip wine or that foreign beer.

Redgum, already on his second drink, is leaning against the bar when George limps in, an unusual fifteen minutes late.

It's been ten days since George was roughed up, but he looks buggered, crossing his arms around his ribs as he eases himself onto the bar stool before taking a deep draught of the beer Redgum has ordered. 'That hits the spot.'

'Any more visits from Wonder Woman?' Redgum wipes some froth from his upper lip and surveys the fancy-schmancy artworks more in sorrow than in anger.

'Yeah. She came yesterday and asked if I could look after the kid while she goes to a job interview.'

'What'd you say?'

'Nothing much I could say, except I would.'

'Shirl's not gonna be too happy.' Redgum and Shirl had discussed the situation and he had to agree that his mate was too soft. You could take advantage of a bloke like George.

As though controlled by a single string, the two men tip back their heads and drain their glasses.

'Same again,' says George to the barman hovering by the tap.

Without a beer, Redgum isn't sure what to do with his hands so he wipes them on his pants. 'When?'

'When what?'

'When's she bringing the kid?'

'This arvo. Two o'clock. Interview's at three.'

'Yeah. Well, make sure … you know …'

'No worries.' They talk desultorily of this and that before George swigs the last of his beer and puts down the glass. 'Best be going. It'll take a while to get back home. I still can't drive.'

Redgum acknowledges this with a fractional movement of his glass. He knows better than to ask if he can help.

*

'What sort of job did you say it was?' George, doubtful, frowns at his young rescuer enveloped in a jumble-sale of mismatched clothing.

'Office,' she says. 'Some plumbing-supply place.'

George had been a boiler-maker all his life, but Penny had worked in an office and she always went off looking smart. High heels, makeup, one of those nice skirts that showed off her good legs and neat little bum. It isn't for him to say, but even in these casual times, surely you have to look a bit neater working in an office. He wishes Pen or even Shirl were here. They'd put the girl right.

'You can type, then?' he asks.

She grins. 'They call it keyboarding now – computers and stuff. They made me do a course.'

'Good luck.' He hopes he sounds more confident than he feels.

The girl totters along the path on those big wooden-heeled shoes, pulling at her skirt, which rides up over her thighs. George looks down at the unappealing child in the stained pink T-shirt. She fixes him with a ferocious glare but doesn't wail like last time. That's a blessing, at least.

'What's your mum's name, then?' he asks as she climbs up onto the couch. (He'd prepared for this, covering the cushions with an old blanket.)

The child gawps at him, an *Are you for real?* expression on her face. 'Mum,' she says. 'Her name's Mum. You got any more ice-cream?'

George unwraps a Choc Wedge. He's sure the young woman hasn't told him her name, but it seems too late to ask and he'd hoped her daughter could tell him. 'My name's George,' he says, handing her the ice-cream. 'And yours is Aurora-Jane. That's what other people call us. What do other people call your mum?'

The child takes a large bite, sending a shower of chocolate flakes over the blanket. 'Pete used to call her Babe.'

'What do other people …' George suddenly remembers. 'What does Aunty Bree call her?'

'Angie – Girlfriend, sometimes.'

Angie – Angela? Angelina? Angel? She doesn't look like an Angel, that's for sure.

They stare at the television until the mother returns, responding to George's inquiry about the interview with a brief expletive. She bends over Rory, fussing with the zip on her jacket. 'They said they'd contact me but I could tell as soon as I walked in that they didn't want me.'

George is surprised to detect the panic underlying her bravado.

'Maybe next time,' he says.

'Bullshit. But thanks for minding the kid.'

'Any time,' George hears himself saying.

*

George is right in his intimation of Angie's real feelings. Despite past experience, she had thought that this time her luck may have changed. How many jobs can you go for without getting at least one? She is superstitious in the way of the luckless, and believes that because of her good deed with George, she is now entitled. But the woman who did the interview had looked at her like she was a dead cat. Angie had glared back. Gave as good as she got. The old bloke was nice about it, though. Bullshitted her and that, but he was trying to be nice. And he gave Rory an ice-cream. She grabs her daughter's hand and pulls her away from the fish shop. 'Baked beans tonight.' She nearly says 'on toast' but remembers in time that there's no bread.

*

It bothers him, the fact that the girl (Angie – he has trouble thinking of her as Angie) has no idea about how to get a job. Going off in that weird get-up with the spiky hair. And he's almost certain that you wouldn't find black lipstick in your average office.

He puts this to Shirl when she 'pops in' (Shirl's vernacular for 'visit uninvited') on the way to her 'Save the Children' charity shop roster.

'Don't tell me she dumped that child on you again. You're a fool, George Johnson. Always were. Always will be.'

George waits. It won't be long. His sister likes nothing better than a project – especially when that project involves the personal improvement of someone who is (it always seems so obvious to Shirl) incapable of self-improvement. She clears her throat.

'If she comes again, maybe I could give her a few pointers. Even find something suitable for her to wear at the shop.' She pauses and all but wags her finger. 'But you mustn't let her take advantage. That sort always know which side their bread is buttered on. The sooner she has a proper job, the better.'

George sees Shirl (still talking) to the door. He notes her nicely fitting grey trousers and pale-pink shirt. (Not something he'd normally notice, but the contrast to Angie couldn't be more marked.) He understands that Shirl, despite the extra weight she's gained over the years, knows how to look smart. (*A fine figure of a woman*, Redgum always says.) To George's relief, the responsibility he's been carting around all week is now tucked away in one of the many compartments of his sister's formidable handbag.

But when all is said and done, it's unlikely that Angie will return, George thinks as he closes the front door. Although he had said 'any time'. But the young woman must know that 'any time' is just an expression. The whole thing is unsettling and he doesn't like being unsettled. At his age, he values routine. It's only natural. And things like babysitting are certainly not on his daily to-do list. Of course he isn't averse to minor deviations. He just needs advance warning. All she has to do is ring and ask. She's sure to have one of those mobile phones. Perhaps he should give her his number. He can hardly expect her to ring when she doesn't know his number.

Who does he think he's kidding? Suddenly forlorn, he looks at his mostly silent phone and sits down to a solitary lunch.

*

Shirl heads straight for the charity shop and flicks through the racks. She's annoyed to find that she's rostered on with that Isobel woman, who for some reason thinks she runs the whole show. Undeterred, Shirl makes virtue of necessity, and explains to Isobel that she's looking for an outfit for a 'young single mother' who needs it for a job interview.

'What size is she?' Isobel asks.

'Hmm, she's quite plump. Not tall. Fourteen? Sixteen? Do you know Fran who works here on Mondays? A bit like her, I'd say.'

They become quite chummy, do Isobel and Shirl, as they examine the possibilities, and Shirl has to admit that Isobel, being younger, has some very useful suggestions, selecting smart but loose-fitting clothes, suitable for a job interview.

'Not that I expect her to be grateful,' Shirl confides as they fold and bag the chosen garments. 'They never are.'

'I'm afraid you're right, Shirl. Still, "There but for the grace of God …"'

'True enough.' Shirl begins to sort a new bag of donations without further comment. She doesn't want to go into all that.

So she takes the clothes home and bides her time. She has contended with two teenage daughters of her own (though blessedly neither of them is at all like that slovenly young woman), but even the best teenage daughters in the world don't welcome interference in their lives. Especially when it comes to clothes. Better to wait until there's some urgency.

*

Another Christmas arrives, his third without Penny. Waking alone on Christmas morning, George remembers his first Christmas in their new house. They had decorated the tree the week before, but Pen liked to leave wrapping the presents until Christmas Eve. Her eyes sparkled as she looked up from her struggle with the odd-shaped bowl she had chosen for Shirl. 'Who knows, next year we could be playing Father Christmas right about now.'

'Fair go. Even if we started a baby tonight, it'd be a bit young for all that.'

Pen ignored him. 'A teddy. There'd have to be a teddy, although someone's sure to give us one when it's born. Never mind. A child can never have too many teddies.' She tied a triumphant bow and the recalcitrant parcel was secured. 'There. I hope Shirl likes it.' She sat back on her heels. 'That's the last one.'

'About time.' He helped her up from the floor. 'If we're going to play Father Christmas next year, we'd better get a move on.'

She giggled. 'And there was me worrying about what to get you for Christmas. I should've just tied myself up in red-and-green paper.'

There's a painful lump in his throat. Even later, when there was no child to anticipate, Pen always had a tree.

So, for the third year, there is none of the bustle, the present wrapping, the traditional 'get-togethers' with friends – none of this happens. For the last two Christmases he has refused all invitations except lunch at Shirl's. This year there are no other invitations. He always knew their friends were just being kind. He always knew that it was Penny they wanted. So he goes to Shirl's and eats his turkey and plum pudding, opens his present (a new shirt) and distributes his own to Shirl and his nieces' children. Thank goodness the kids are old enough to appreciate a gift of money. The thought of shopping was more than he could bear. He leaves early and spends the long afternoon and evening watching a M*A*S*H marathon.

*

For several weeks now, a packet of Choc Wedges has remained unopened in the freezer, a sight that depresses George for some reason he can't explain. Then, a few days after Christmas, the doorbell signals the young woman's next appearance. He gets to the door before the visitor has time for a second ring. 'G'day,' he says. 'Um, Angie.'

She's holding the child's hand. Neither of them looks any cleaner or tidier than before, and there are dark smudges around the young woman's eyes where that mascara stuff leaves her looking like a tragic panda. Pen had worn mascara, so he knows what those smudges mean – Angie has been crying.

George can't quite get his head around this. She seems so tough. In control, in her own anarchic way. Perhaps she has a cold. *Runny eyes and nose. Probably just as damaging to mascara as tears*, he decides. Waiting for her to speak, he notices a supermarket trolley behind her on his front path, loaded with – *stuff*.

'Got chucked out of our room, didn't we?' She indicates the trolley. 'Our bags weren't big enough.' Next to the trolley are a battered purple suitcase and a bulging backpack.

George doesn't know what to say. He looks from mother to child to trolley and back to the mother. 'What happened?'

'Needed that job at the plumbers. Owed too much rent so they chucked us out. Waited until after Christmas. Said they were like, doing me a favour.'

Fair enough — she wants money. No real harm, he thinks, creating a channel to the tender voice of Penny's ghost and a mental bulwark against the prospect of a very real Shirl. Things like this need a balanced perspective. He never spends all of his pension, and there's still a tidy nest egg from his and Pen's superannuation. A bloke'd have to be some sort of bastard to let them sleep rough. 'How much do you need for the rent?'

She looks at him sideways, not quite meeting his eye. 'Not much point. They won't let me back.' With some effort she dredges up a smile with just enough pathos. 'Thought me 'n' Rory might doss here for a coupla nights. Just till we find something else. Bree thinks she knows a bloke ...' She peers around him into the hallway. 'You got a big house here.'

Three bedrooms. Hardly a palace. George feels cornered. *They can't stay here.*

Aurora-Jane — Rory — begins to sniffle. 'You said he'd give us a Choc Wedge.' She wipes her nose on her sleeve. 'I want a Choc Wedge.'

'Please,' George says. 'Little girls should say please if they want something.' *Bloody hell. I'm starting to sound like Shirl.*

Angie's response is brisk. 'In you go. And say please.' Rory slips past him and runs down to the kitchen shouting, 'Please, please, please, please.' Distracted, George steps back, and before he can protest, his hallway is invaded by a resolute young woman armed with luggage. 'We're used to sharing.' She makes it sound as though the concession is all hers. 'Where can I put our stuff?' She looks back at him over her shoulder. 'You can help us with the trolley after I stow these.'

Long ago, each bedroom in George's house was allocated a purpose. There is their room, of course. His and Pen's. Then there's what Pen used to call 'the guest room', although no guest has stayed there since she died. It has two nice single beds with patchwork quilts, a white dressing table and a two-door wardrobe. There's a mat beside the bed, and a reading lamp and crystal vase on the dressing table. The third room, next to theirs (his) was going to be the nursery. It had never been furnished and over the years became a storeroom of sorts. George hardly ever goes in there. Only when he can't find something. Even then, he tries all other possibilities before stepping over the threshold and rummaging through the boxes and shelves and the old chest of drawers that slouches by the window. He hates that room. Full to overflowing it may be, but he senses the emptiness at its heart.

Ushering Angie down the passage, he opens the door to the guest room. 'Here,' he says. 'But only for a couple of days, mind.'

'Awesome.'

Despite himself, George preens a bit at the admiration in her voice. 'I'll get Rory that Choc Wedge,' he says. 'While you get organised.'

'Thanks, George.' She grins. 'Betcha that sister of yours'll be surprised.'

Shirl! He's managing his injuries much better now and she's stopped coming every day. *That being the case* … He does a rapid mental calculation. She came yesterday, and on current indications, he has three, maybe four days. And Angie had said that Bree would have something organised in a couple of days. It all depends then on what 'a couple of days' might turn out to be.

Meanwhile, there's only a bit of mince in the fridge. Not enough for an extra two servings. 'I'm just heading down to the supermarket,' he tells her. 'Do you want me to return the trolley?'

'You gotta be kidding.' She calls out after his retreating figure. 'I'm outta smokes.'

It takes George three-quarters of an hour to do his shopping and it never once occurs to him that he might return to a house stripped of his few valuable possessions.

In the event, he's not quite as lucky as that. On his way to the kitchen, he looks into the lounge to see Rory glued to the television and her mother sprawled on the couch with a cup of tea. 'Kettle's boiled,' she tells him, as though it's her house and he the interloper. 'I used the last of the milk.'

George grunts and packs away his shopping. He'll do chops and veg for their dinner. And he bought a tub of ice-cream. Choc Wedges aren't cheap and Rory seems to devour them at an alarming rate.

He puts his head around the door. 'I'm getting dinner ready,' he announces.

'Cool.'

Cool? No offer of help. He fancies his ribs are extra painful after carrying the shopping, and aggrieved, bangs a few pots and slams the cupboard doors. But the twinges in his ribs remind him that he's repaying a debt. When Angie intervened in his mugging, he knew she had seen the knife. What would have happened to the kid if she'd been wounded, or even killed? It doesn't bear thinking about. He'll have to explain to her (*tactfully, of course*), that she should have left him to his fate. You can't do things like that when there's a kid relying on you.

He isn't sure how much his guests will eat, and adds another carrot and an extra handful of peas to the saucepan, just in case. He'd eaten enough meals at Shirl's in the old days to know that kids don't much like vegetables, so he bought a treat – frozen chips that you just put in the oven. *No chips until you eat your veggies*, he imagines himself saying. Pen and Shirl, had they been there, would probably have given him a lecture on healthy eating and the evils of bribery, but surely a kid like Annie deserves a treat once in a while.

He passes a bewildered hand over his eyes. *Rory.* He means Rory.

Mealtime is a shambles. His guests both tuck into the chips and while Angie gnaws on a chop, Rory pushes hers aside. 'Want fish fingers,' she says.

'Haven't got any.' Both mother and daughter shuffle their vegetables to the side of their plates.

'Eat your veggies,' he says to Rory. 'They're good for you.'

'Mum isn't eating hers.'

It's a reasonable observation, and Pen would have known to spoon them up with encouraging noises. He'd seen her do it with Shirl's kids. *Yum. Lovely orange carrots!* He looks at Angie, but she continues to worry at her chop bone. 'Yum,' he says with a singular lack of conviction. 'Nice green peas.'

Rory stares at him. 'Hate peas.'

At least she drank her milk. George scrapes the plates while Angie takes Rory to have a bath. By the sound of things, the kid likes the bath even less than she likes peas. He's drying the dishes when mother and daughter emerge from the bathroom. Now that it's clean, he notices that Rory's pinched little face is freckled. Penny had a light sprinkling of freckles on the bridge of her nose and across her cheeks and shoulders. She was always trying to powder over them, but he loved every single one. There's something about freckles, he always thought. Something tawny and wild. Pen said they made her look like a schoolgirl, but George knew better. With her lithe body and golden freckles, she had a grace that could only be described as feline.

This pitiful mite looks more like a skinny feral cat, with her green eyes and sharp, pointy teeth. She's wearing the same pink T-shirt and grubby white tights she had worn all day (when had he started noticing such things?).

'Pyjama time,' he demands rather than asks. He's tired now, and dispirited. He just wants them to go to bed and leave him in peace.

Angie manages to look both embarrassed and sullen. 'Only had one pair. Grown out of them, hasn't she?' Her hands span the child's shoulders as though demonstrating the amazing growth spurt that had brought this to pass.

It's George's turn to be embarrassed. 'Yeah. Well – I'll get some sheets.'

'We got sleeping bags.'

'Not when you're guests in this house,' George says, with a curious dignity. 'Pen would never forgive me.'

Pen loved visitors. Especially when they stayed overnight. Her elderly Aunty Kath from Bendigo, for instance. She used to stay with them when she came to Melbourne for her regular medical appointments. The evening before Kath was due, Pen buzzed around like a firefly, preparing the guest room. After a full day's work, too. *All that energy*, George thinks ruefully. But he loves to remember her that way. She dusted and polished and then took out the crisp white sheets, burying her face in their folds. 'Mmm. Aunty Kath loves lavender. Smell, George.'

He had reeled back in mock horror. 'Take it away. Too girly for me.'

'Is it too girly to cut some roses?'

'Only for you.' George went and found some choice blooms which she arranged in the crystal vase. 'Is the room well aired enough, do you think?'

Before he could answer she was off to make Aunty Kath's favourite lemon pie.

George burrows in the linen cupboard. The smell of lavender is accompanied by a surge of nostalgia. 'I'm doing my best, Pen.'

'Can you give us a hand?' Angie returns to the kitchen as he's wiping down the bench. 'Gotta put the mattress on the floor. She's not used to a bed ...'

Something inside George responds to the shame in her voice. He pats her on the arm. 'No worries, love. Kids will be kids.'

*

It's after eight-thirty before Rory settles, her soft, animal snore drifting out into the passageway. George stops at the door and listens. *Funny little kid.*

'She's asleep,' he announces.

'About time. I'm dying for a smoke. Didja remember to get them?'

George has remembered them but did wrestle with his conscience. He hasn't smoked since Pen was diagnosed. Talk about life being unfair. Pen had never smoked. Not even as a dare, or to give it a try as a kid. She couldn't see the point, she said. Better things to do with her money. Then she got the cancer and he, George, got off scot-free. Except for losing Pen, of course. Except for watching, in those last weeks as, eyes bright with fear, she sucked with a terrible greed on the tube from her respirator.

When the bored young woman behind the counter handed him the cigarettes, George looked at the box. In his smoking days they used to be so fancy. There was something slimy-looking and phlegm-green and disgusting on the back of the packet. *Passive smoking kills*, the caption said. Well, that's true enough. George had put the cigarettes in his pocket. He'd work out what to do later. Thank God he'd lost all appetite for nicotine.

Now Angie is appealing to him with a look he knows only too well – the look of a smoker dying for a fag. *Dying! Good one, George.*

He has to try. 'Pen – my wife – died from lung cancer,' he says. 'It was ...' He shudders. 'It wasn't nice.'

'You sound like me nanna,' she snaps. 'Waited till the kid went to bed, didn't I?'

George sighs. There's some virtue in that, he supposes. He takes the packet from the drawer. 'Here. But don't smoke inside. Me asthma's been much better since I stopped.'

Angie grabs at the cigarettes and scrabbles in her handbag for a lighter. 'Ta. I'll go out the back and then I'll have a shower.'

No offer of money for the cigarettes. No *I'll have a shower if it's okay with you*. George might be a bit rough around the edges, but his mother had taught him manners. He switches on the telly and flicks through the channels, settling on a documentary about sharks delivered in the breathless tones of a David Attenborough wannabe. He had been going to finish his book, but he wants to assert his authority, even if it's only in the choice of television programs. 'The Great White, though potentially lethal, is a thing of beauty ...' George's hand reaches for a beer and finds it closing on nothing. He'd forgotten all about it. No wonder he feels edgy. He hasn't had a beer all night.

*

Angie, meanwhile, sits on a garden chair drawing greedily on her cigarette. Eyes narrowed, she observes the drifting smoke, and savours the satisfaction of a job well done. In the fading light she scans her surroundings. She's in a small paved courtyard, enclosed by a trellis on two sides. The shabby wooden table is shedding paint and two of the chairs have faded and slightly tatty cushions. There are pots of various sizes, some with healthy-looking plants, others somewhere between dying and dead. She stubs her cigarette in one of the pots and stands up to peer around the trellis. A path leads to a rotary clothesline and further on what looks like a shed is covered with some sort of creeper. There's a patch of lawn in the middle and bushes around the edge. It all looks so ordinary that she almost cries with relief. They'll be okay here, her and Rory. Even though sooner or later they'll have to move on. They always do. But right now, they're on to a good thing and she congratulates herself on finding such a nice place. Especially without any help. She pauses outside the lighted window. 'Told you I can stand on my own two feet,' she tells the absent Bree.

*

By the time she returns from her shower, George is on to his second can. Should he offer her one? It's an unwritten law of hospitality that you offer your guest a beer, but with her newly scrubbed face, she looks so young. He dithers. 'Last can,' he lies, holding it up to demonstrate its rarity. 'Sorry.'

'Don't like beer. What about a Bacardi and coke?'

'Only got beer (*thank goodness*). Anyway, how old are you?'

'Twenty-five.'

George is not so easily fooled. 'Who do you think you're kidding?'

'Twenty,' she says. Adding with some bravado, 'Nearly twenty.'

'And Rory?'

'Nearly five.'

'Jesus!'

'Mum and Dad threw me out. Went to me gran's for a while but she got sick. And she carried on over every little thing. Been in a few different places since then.' Her eyes skitter across his face, and sensing a dawning empathy, she continues. 'Some of them were okay, but the last one – a mattress like, two centimetres thick. Hardly any hot water … Crackheads next door …' Twisting the tassel on one of Pen's cushions, she glances up at him from under still-matted eyelashes. 'Don't look like that. We're doing all right, Rory and me.' She turns to the television. 'Do you always watch such crap TV?'

4

Yellow ones with the pink butterflies – or the blue ones with mermaids? This is all new to George – he passes Kidz Biz on his way to the pub every day, but has never been inside. Well, why would he? There are always mothers and children in the shop, so he figures it's his best bet for finding kids' pyjamas. Now he's found them, but there are so many decisions. Size four or five? Rory is nearly five, but she seems small to him. Doubtful, he holds up the size five. They look pretty small, but they would, wouldn't they?

A tiny woman with a large pram smiles at him. 'Pressie for your granddaughter?'

'No. Yeah. I'm not sure what size to get.'

Assisted by the young woman, he chooses the smaller size in the yellow. Halfway to the checkout, he goes back and adds the blue mermaid set and a pair of fluffy dog slippers. It only makes sense to add the slippers – you can't let a kid put on smelly socks after a bath. He peers into the bag the moment he gets out of the shop, and all the way back to Mercy Street, savours the glee bubbling in his throat.

Rory and her mother are out when he gets home, and the sparkling droplets of glee begin to drain away as he remembers the reality of the child. She is whiny, snotty-nosed and grubby. Greedy, too. And rude. *Hate mermaids* – that's what she'll say and he'll be left looking like a real galah.

So instead of giving the gift directly to Rory, he gives it to Angie as she prepares her daughter's bath. 'Happened to see these in the shop,' he mumbles. 'Thought they might come in handy.'

Angie opens the plastic bag and looks at him all funny. 'You're not a bad bloke, George,' she says, before hurrying off to the bathroom.

George clanks around with the dishes and listens to Rory's protests. Who can fathom the ways of kids? Tonight, it seems, she doesn't want to get out of the bath. By the time he sits down with his book, there's a blessed, if suspicious, silence. Then Angie's voice. 'Go on. Show George.'

Rory, wearing the mermaid pyjamas (a perfect fit) shuffles along in the doggie slippers, right up to George's chair. She's trying not to smile and for a moment he sees beyond the watchfulness in her green eyes. *She likes them.* 'You look very smart,' he says.

Her stare is so intense it drills right into his head. 'G'night, George,' she says, stony-faced.

*

He expects Angie to mention the pyjamas again. He wants her to. They've been a great success as far as he can see, but after her cigarette, she just slumps on the couch, staring at the television. The program is *So You Want to be a Model*. A series of very thin young women glower and sulk into the screen to a breathless commentary by an even thinner older woman in black. The tone of the commentary reminds George of the nature programs he likes to watch. The same note of wonder and intimacy. As the sullen-looking models preen and prance, a delinquent thought causes him to snigger. *Next we'll have the mating ritual.*

'What's so funny?'

George is embarrassed, almost as if he had spoken aloud. 'Nothing. You want a cup of tea?' An affirmative grunt sends him to the kitchen, fuming. Can you believe it? There she is, lounging about on his couch like Lady Muck or someone – expecting him to wait on her hand and foot.

He never minded making tea for Penny. She cooked all the meals and it was fair enough that she could put her feet up at the end of the day. He takes down her special china cup – the one with the blue cornflowers, and cradles it in his hand. Sees himself, clear as a bell, pouring the tea, putting a biscuit or a slice of cake on her plate. She always smiled up at him when he came back with the tea. 'Just the thing,' she'd say, after the first sip. It was regular as clockwork. George brushes his hand across his eyes and returns the cup to its place. Right up until the last few days, Pen sat or lay on that couch smiling and saying, *Just the thing*. Even when it was no longer 'just the thing' and she was able to take only a few tiny sips.

He opens the fridge and takes out a can. He feels like a cup of tea, but he takes out a beer. Drinking tea on the couch. That was a George and Penny thing.

By the time he brings the drinks in, several girls are crying and hugging each other. 'Felicity's into the next round,' Angie informs him. 'Hope she doesn't win. She's a real cow.'

George needs to talk. 'Penny, that's my wife, she taught me to cook, you know. When she knew she was – sick.'

'Laura should of won. I reckon they rigged it.'

'Just simple things – chops, parma …'

'She probably slept with the producer or someone.'

'… a bit of pasta, a roast …'

'What?'

'Nothing.' No point in sharing his memories with this lump of a girl. With some spite, he mentally compares her with the weeping beauties on the television. *No hope for you, love.* Penny would have compared more than favourably, but she was too practical to waste time on such things. When they were young, he managed to overcome his shyness a few times to tell her how pretty he thought she was. She always looked pleased and a bit embarrassed. He wishes now that he had told her more often. When her hair had fallen out, and her cheeks were puffy and sallow; when the dark caverns of her eyes glittered with pain; then, when she needed to hear how beautiful she was, her beauty had been devoured with such savagery that he was unable to utter the words.

It was inevitable, George supposed, that Shirl would come before Bree's contact managed to find them lodgings. The next day, she 'pops in', as she has a habit of doing, at just the wrong time. Rory is scooping up the last of her cereal (much of which has found its way down the front of her new pyjamas), while George, toast in hand, reads his newspaper.

Shirl is in and down the hall before he realises she's there. 'I just thought I'd pop in – George! You have that child again.'

He can hardly deny it. 'So?'

'That young woman dropped her off this early? Before she's even had breakfast?'

George mumbles into his newspaper.

'Mum's still in bed,' Rory volunteers, dipping her finger in the sugar bowl.

'Don't do that, child. Your fingers could have germs on them.'

Rory examines her fingers for said germs but George's eyes are glued to the print that crawls ant-like across the page.

Then the implication of Mum being still in bed hits Shirl. 'She stayed the *night*? That ... *person* stayed the night?' Shirl thumps herself down on the nearest chair as though, in this new world order, her legs can no longer be trusted to do their job.

George gets up and pours her a tea. 'It's just for a day or two. Bree has this friend who knows ...'

Shirl makes a little moaning noise. 'A young woman. Living here. With you. What will the neighbours think?'

George realises that he doesn't care a toss for what the neighbours might think. 'Steady on, Shirl. They had nowhere to go. What was I going to do? Throw them out on the street?'

'George gave me these pyjamas,' Rory says, picking off the cornflakes and placing them on her tongue. 'And doggie slippers.' She lifts her leg as high as it will go, to show off the furry, brown footwear. 'There's one for the other foot, too.'

Shirl's smile is strained. 'Very nice, dear.' She turns to her brother. 'Honestly, George, you have to be the most gullible person I've ever met.' She lowers her voice. 'Just look at her. A sly little miss if ever I saw one. And as for her mother …'

George isn't having any of this. 'You're the churchgoer, Shirl. What about all that Bible stuff, "Do unto others …" and so on. Where would our lives have been if we hadn't known how to forgive?' *Where would his have been if Penny hadn't known how to forgive?* The thought comes unbidden and he pauses before continuing. 'It's all give and take,' he says. 'In the end, that's what life is.'

'In this case, you seem to be doing all the giving,' his sister responds tartly. 'Now please tell me you haven't been sleeping with that girl.'

George hasn't had a good laugh in a long time. Now, the suggestion that he might be sleeping with Angie (or any young woman for that matter) sends him into a series of genuine guffaws, snorting tea through his nose in a violent explosion of mirth. 'Give us a break!'

Shirl begins to giggle. 'You'll be the death of me,' she says, wiping her eyes. 'But they'll have to find somewhere else sooner or later. You know that.' She's struck by a sudden thought. 'If you're lonely, you could get a dog.' Seeing George's jaw tighten, Shirl shifts her gaze and changes the subject. 'Washcloth – don't worry. I'll get it.'

George remembers very well the last time his sister had offered the solace of a dog. That was just after Pen had left him. Even after all this time (fifty years ago in May), the pain is deep and sharp and real. Bruised ribs will heal well before this old wound. His fingers curl into fists at the thought.

'The washcloth lady's here,' Rory announces as her mother makes a brief appearance in the doorway before wandering out for a smoke.

George is still chuckling when Shirl comes back from the bathroom. *Washcloth lady. Doesn't that describe her to a T?*

Being forewarned, Angie waits until Shirl leaves before coming back into the kitchen. In the meantime, Shirl had finished her tea, wiped Rory's face and hands (none too gently, George thinks) and left with an ominous parting shot. 'Get rid of them. That young woman is a loser.' (George's eyebrows had shot up at that. Shirl had obviously picked up some of the argot from her daughter's generation.)

'In Mum's day, they called them battlers,' he retorts and is vindicated when she closes the gate behind her without further comment.

Shirl isn't happy. She hates being put in the wrong and George's rebuke (for that's what it was) continues to sting. She has no idea why she used the word 'loser'. She has often enough reprimanded her daughters for using that very expression. The truth is, she finds herself increasingly disturbed by the girl's casual incursion into her brother's household. She, his older sister, has always been his protector, and now her influence is slipping away as George becomes further entangled in the lives of Angie and that scruffy child of hers.

Needing some outlet for her frustration, she toots at the car in front. The driver responds with a two-finger salute, then roars off as the lights turn amber, leaving her to wait for another set of lights. Once through the intersection, she pulls over. Her heart is beating unnaturally fast and she feels like she might pass out, right there in the car. She recognises that it's not a heart attack. Shirl is inclined to frustration, annoyance, irritation, even indignation. But this is anger, something she rarely feels – an anger born of the responsibility, and yes, the love she has for her brother. She breathes her way through to comparative calm. She'll just have to be extra vigilant and speak her mind to both George and this Angie person whenever the need arises.

*

After breakfast, Angie dresses Rory and tells George they're off to Bree's. It seems that Ming thought that Daz might know a chick whose cousin's mother has a spare room.

'I'm doing a load of washing,' George says before they go. 'Do you want to put anything in?'

Angie disappears into the guest room and returns with a small bundle. 'We'll need these for tomorrow.'

George hangs out the tatty bra and two pairs of knickers – one small and greyish and a larger red pair in a bikini style with ragged lace edging. He's uncomfortable handling these intimate garments and makes sure they are on the middle wire of the rotary clothesline. Not that he cares what the neighbours think of him, but Angie's poverty isn't a thing to put on display for the whole world to see. The small white tights have runs and there's an intractable stain on the T-shirt. He remembers the cornflakes on the pyjamas and wonders if he should have washed those as well. Then he wonders that he wondered. It seems that the more carelessness his guests display, the more fastidious he becomes. He washes the breakfast dishes and goes to put them away. What is he doing? Since Pen's death, he's never put the dishes away – he just washes them and lets them drain on the sink for next time. Of course, it's different when there's more than one set. So he stacks them on the shelf, sweeps the floor and looks at the clock. Angie and Rory have been a long time at Bree's. What time should he expect them back?

*

Once at Bree's, Angie discovers that the chick Daz knew had a fight with her cousin so the room at the end of the complicated chain is no longer an option. This doesn't surprise her. She's more than happy, in fact, although she doesn't admit this to Bree. Better to keep all options open.

Angie slouches in a chair while Bree produces some picture books from the kitchen drawer.

'How about you have a look at these while Mummy and I have a talk?'

Rory accepts them with a limp hand. 'Seen these before.'

'There's a new one about a giant.'

'Say thank you to Aunty Bree.'

'Thank you, Aunty Bree.' The child looks thoughtful. 'I don't mind giants.'

'You're lucky to have an aunty.' Angie means it, too. Bree isn't her sister but she's the closest they have to family.

The two women settle down to coffee and a fag. 'What's he like, this George bloke?'

'All right, I guess. Ancient.'

'You sleeping with him?'

Angie snorts into her coffee. 'You gotta be gagging.'

'Just ripping him off, then?'

Angie chooses to be offended. 'Yeah, like I'd rip off an old man.' She uses her finger to corral some spilled sugar. It takes some time to shape it all into a miniature volcano. 'Well, I might be. But not in a mean way. He needs company. I need a place to stay. Simple.'

'Fair enough.'

Angie looks at her friend with something like gratitude. Bree has a live and let live attitude that suits Angie's slippery moral landscape. She's good with Rory, too.

As mother and daughter walk back to the tram, Angie tries but fails to imagine George hitting on her. He's just not that sort of bloke. She's seen the wedding photo on top of the telly, and though she's not sure what he saw in his wife, they're looking at each other all lovey-dovey. It's a real downer, thinking of it. All those years looking at each other like that then *wham* – one of them is dead.

Maybe they stopped, she thinks. Stopped looking at each other like that. Most people do. That's one thing she knows for sure. Even so, it's nicer to think that maybe they looked at each other like that right up until the end. It's nice to think that some people might.

*

'No luck,' Angie says. 'It was more like a cupboard.' She seems quite cheerful about this and gestures towards George's spare room. 'At least here we got two beds.'

At least? There's gratitude for you. 'No one's forcing you to stay,' George replies in a fair imitation of Shirl.

He sees her stiffen. Calculate. 'Don't get me wrong. It's a great room. Me 'n' Rory love it, don't we?' She nudges her daughter, who frowns before climbing onto the couch with the TV remote. '*Rugrats* is on. You said I could watch *Rugrats*.'

Angie, aware of her slip, chooses to be placatory. 'How about I make us some tea while the kid watches telly,' she says.

They go out to the kitchen and Angie makes a great show of pouring the tea. (Pen always used a pot and George tries to keep up these fragile markers of their lives together.) He's inclined to nurse his resentment but thaws when she brings his tea over, passing him the sugar as nice as pie.

'Need to talk about a coupla things,' she says in an off-hand 'just thought I'd mention it by the way' sort of tone.

'Fire away.' George bites into his biscuit.

She ticks off item one on her finger. 'First. Can you mind Rory on Wednesday? I got another job interview. Dunno why I bother, but they make you go or you lose your Newstart allowance.'

Why should he make things easy? 'Wednesday,' he says, drawing out the word as though he has a diary cluttered with Wednesday engagements. 'I'm fairly sure … Let's see … Tuesday's no good. Yes. Wednesday should be okay.'

'Great.' She approaches the next item warily, an eye on George's reaction. 'The other thing. The holidays are nearly over. Rory starts school in two weeks.'

'School?' *Surely she's too young for school.*

'It's just that every so often I'm going to need someone to pick her up. You know, if I get a job and Bree's got other things on.' She leans back in her chair. 'Thought we could say you were her grandpa or something and I could give permission for you to get her after school.'

Half listening, George is processing the information that Rory is old enough to go to school. Angie taps her foot and fiddles with her hair. 'Why not?' he says, after a full minute has passed. Then, 'Poppy. I'd rather be her Poppy.'

'Whatever.'

Grandpa, his dad's dad, was a surly drunk; but he'd loved his Poppy – trusted him. Poppy's calm and security were as much a part of him as the soft flannel shirts he wore summer or winter. George can still feel the worn fabric on his cheek. The large hand cupping his head.

When things were really bad, his mum would take him and Shirl around to Nanna and Poppy's for a few days. The two children had decided that they wanted to live with Nanna and Poppy and had asked him more than once. 'Can't take you away from your mother,' he'd say. 'You're all she's got.' Poppy's eyes were a faded blue and always kind of troubled when he saw them off at the gate.

Those bright, rare spots that punctuated his childhood – so vivid yet so long ago. His life with Pen – not so long ago in the scheme of things – has to his bewilderment, lost some of its clarity. Worse, when he tries to recall the last three years, he can see people and movement, but they're sifted and blurred like a television with a badly adjusted aerial. Now, apparently, it's a new school year and George no longer feels grounded in time.

What was she asking? He must look like a dithering old fool.

Angie is summing up in her own abbreviated way. 'Poppy, Grandpa – whatever.'

Mission accomplished, she stands up. 'Need a ciggie.'

And to George's chagrin, he's left to rinse the tea things.

When Shirl hears about Angie's next job interview, she arrives with an assortment of clothes, blustering but gratified. 'Well, I'm here. It's nice to be needed once in a while, I suppose. The sooner she gets a job, the better,' she continues before George can draw breath. 'Then she won't be here sponging off you. This bag' – she indicates a large green rubbish bag – 'has some things Peta has grown out of. They might do for the child. These' – she indicates several wire hangers, the garments shrouded in plastic – 'are for madam to wear to her interview.'

Angie was out, attending a mock interview with her case manager. 'Waste of time,' she'd asserted before she left.

They take the clothes in to Rory, who is clean for once – George has seen to that. (It's so much better when his sister rings first instead of popping in.) As Shirl opens the door, Rory hops down from the couch and disappears for a moment, returning with a washcloth.

Nonplussed, Shirl looks at her brother while Rory stands, head tipped back, waiting.

'She calls you the washcloth lady.'

'Little monkey. If I thought you were being cheeky …' But Rory's expression is so solemn that Shirl has to laugh.

That's the second time in a week George has seen his sister laugh and he joins in as much from surprise as amusement. Three years older, she has always been bossy, but they'd had good times as kids. One benefit of their fractured home was that no one seemed to miss them when they went off for hours at a time. Young George had no real mates of his own and Shirl and her friends alternately tolerated and petted him, but for years he was always allowed to tag along. He resented it when she reached her teens and no longer wanted his company. And when she married, he felt abandoned. In some ways she had taken on the role their mother couldn't seem to manage.

Rory suffers the red cardigan, the denim pinafore and the pink-striped top with the zip. Now she's had enough and stands her ground, arms rigid, as Shirl tries to coax her into the dark-blue dress. 'I'm thirsty,' she decides. George goes to the fridge and takes out the milk. Shirl and Rory follow. 'Not milk. I hate milk.'

'How about some lemonade?' George bought some especially for her. All kids like lemonade.

'Milk, water or nothing.' Shirl throws a warning look at her brother and a steely glare at the recalcitrant child, who saves face by declaring that she isn't thirsty anymore before escaping to her room.

Shirl has to give up on the dress. 'I think we can say that most of these will fit.' She holds up a red parka with white snowflakes and a fur-trimmed hood. 'Peta used to look gorgeous in this. They grow up so quickly.' Her voice is tinged with regret. Shirl's granddaughter, Peta, is now an independent nine-year-old. 'Lucky Marianne didn't toss it all out.'

George is grateful. 'Thanks.' He gestures at the bag of clothing. 'Fact is, they don't seem to have much at all. Couldn't let the kid go off to school in rags.'

'Doesn't the school have a uniform?'

'Never thought of that. Do they wear uniforms nowadays?'

Brother and sister look at each other. They both well know that schoolyard hierarchy is implacable, and clean, well-dressed children can be merciless.

'Find out,' Shirl says. 'If she's the only one in civvies ...'

'Maybe you could come with us to buy one.' George isn't at all happy at the prospect of a shopping trip. 'Or even take her yourself.'

'I suppose I can make the time.' Shirl sounds put-upon but can't hide her satisfied smirk.

So Shirl waits for Angie to come home then marches her off to the bedroom. George can hear their raised voices.

'Do you want a job or not?'

'Not if I have to look like a dork.'

'Better than looking like a scarecrow.'

'Scarecrow! You old cow!'

George is alarmed to hear scuffling noises, but continues to stare at his newspaper. Recalling his own childhood, he is saddened to see Rory taking it all in with blank equanimity. He endures the kerfuffle a while longer, then Rory jumps up and shouts at the bedroom door. 'Hurry up, Mum. I got new clothes, too.'

George is surprised then when Angie, meek as you like, comes out in a pair of black pants and a black top trimmed with red and orange. Her wayward hair is confined in a short ponytail and her makeup is, well, less obvious. She primps a bit, then scowls. 'So?'

Rory takes her hand. 'You look lovely and beautiful, Mummy.'

George smiles. 'Very nice, love – a real office girl.'

Shirl, tousled but triumphant, passes her own judgement. 'You'll do.'

*

George, on Shirl's advice, drives Angie to her interview.

'Don't wait for me,' she says, getting out of the car. 'I'll drop in on Bree afterwards.'

'She still trying to find you a place?' George wonders why all Angie's house-hunting eggs seemed to be stowed in Bree's basket.

'Could have something. She says Amp might know someone.'

George tries to imagine Bree. He sees a magnetic young woman around whom swirls a whole cast of characters with improbable names and dubious possibilities. She is a wheeler-dealer, an organiser of the less able, keeping all her contacts in a fine balance of usefulness to her and to each other. Except that, in Angie's case, the usefulness has been questionable, to say the least.

*

So thanks to George, Angie arrives five minutes early for her interview. She hovers at the entrance and checks her letter – Trenerry Imports Pty Ltd. Calling on her meagre store of confidence, she steps inside.

The office is light and modern-looking, decorated in shades of grey and white. On the wall over the desk there's one of those baffling pictures that are all splotches and streaks. Nice colours, though.

The woman at reception smiles. 'Call me Dina,' she says.

Caught off-guard, Angie almost smiles back. Once the interview starts, however, she answers in monosyllables and can't look her interviewer in the eye. 'Show some enthusiasm,' her case manager had advised, but who can be enthusiastic about sitting at a computer all day?

After stumbling over the questions about experience, Angie is given a data-input test.

'Finished already?' Dina looks surprised. 'I hope your accuracy matches your speed.'

'Dunno.' Angie leaves, none the wiser about how she went.

As the bus winds its way through lookalike streets, she yanks the elastic from her ponytail. All that fuss about what to wear. A lot of good it did her.

She calls in on Bree for coffee and a whinge and leaves still feeling hard done by. Bree is in one of her moods and doesn't even see her to the door. On top of that, she has to wait twenty minutes for the next bus.

Walking down Mercy Street, Angie is struck by the unfamiliar notion that she's coming home. The thought is far from comforting. In fact, it terrifies her. To Angie, 'home' is a place that beguiles you, that whispers promises and endearments, before discarding you like so much rubbish. By the time she's closed the front door behind her, she is so despondent that she barely looks up when Rory, despite the summer heat, comes dancing out in her new parka.

'The washcloth lady gave it to me,' she chirps.

'Yeah, nice, love.' It's the best response Angie can muster.

She is similarly abrupt when George asks about the interview. 'Said they'd ring. I'm not, like, holding me breath.'

*

A few days later, they do ring.

'Got the job,' she tells George in that off-hand way she has. But he can see that she's struggling to hide her delight. 'They said I did real good on the computer test. Start Monday.'

George wonders at the quality of the other applicants but is more than happy for her. For himself, too. A job means she can find other accommodation more easily and his life will return to normal.

He says as much to Redgum when they meet at the pub that afternoon. 'She doesn't contribute a cent,' he complains. 'And I do all the cooking and cleaning. I mean, bugger it – I'm too old for all this.'

Redgum looks at him over his beer. 'It'll be quiet when they go.'

On Friday, the staff are back at school and the three of them set off to introduce George to the principal. A careful woman, Ms Fontana. The school community is small, and as far as possible, she likes to meet all those who will have regular contact with her pupils.

'You do remember what to call him?'

Rory gives her mother a withering look.

They've been coaching her to call him Poppy. 'But his name's George,' she pointed out. 'I call him George.' She thrust out her chin in that stubborn way she has. Staring pointedly at the television.

Angie shrugged. Her method of disciplining the kid leaves a lot to be desired. Ask her to do something. Yell when she refuses. When she continues to refuse, give up.

'I have an idea,' George said. 'What about Poppy George?'

Rory, less inclined to buckle than her mother, assessed the proposal and decided it involved minimum concession. 'Okay,' she said. 'But only at school.'

'Fair enough.' George tried not to look smug. Maybe he had a way with kids after all. He just hasn't had the practice.

George finds Ms Fontana daunting. It isn't that she's unpleasant, but her military posture, her confident manner and appraising eye send George straight back to his own school days. Here he is in the principal's office, and she'll know he's lying. He shuffles and coughs and stares out the window where a bloke with a dog ambles across the oval. The grass is littered with those little yellow daisies; Shirl and her friends used to make them into long chains to loop around their necks and hair.

'So, Ms Wilson ...' The principal's voice cuts through his reverie and he jumps like a guilty child. (*Wool-gathering,* his teachers used to call it. *More interested in what's going on outside than what I'm saying. Isn't that so? No Sir/Miss.*) But in his experience, teachers have a sixth sense when it comes to lies.

Angie, introducing him as her granddad, has no such fear. George listens half in dread, half in admiration as she goes on to say that Poppy George has permission to collect Rory after school.

Ms Fontana sits back in her chair. Her voice is crisp. 'We have to be very clear that Rory may not be ready for school. As I told you in the interview, she'll be one of the youngest in her year and without the benefit of preschool—'

Alarmed, Angie becomes unusually articulate. 'Me case manager, Karen Something – she wrote you a letter – told me she spoke to you on the phone and everything. Rory's a special case, she said, because we got no real home.'

George bridles at this, but says nothing. Who is he to question the assessment of a case worker?

Ms Fontana looks at the young mother as though she's a naughty and not very bright child. 'I understand that. But you have to do your bit. Make sure that her attendance is regular and that she has a good breakfast before school. And a good night's sleep.' She turns to Rory. 'Not too much television.'

Ostensibly, she addresses Angie and Rory, but George feels the message is for him.

Ms Fontana continues in her cool, impersonal tone. 'Her assessment was borderline. Home support is essential if she's not to fall further behind.'

Further behind? George is outraged. Young Rory might not be the most lovable kid, but she's smart as a whip. *Perhaps your teachers aren't up to scratch*, he wants to say. *I'll bet they're not all like Miss Walsh. Not by a long shot.* Instead, he hears himself saying, 'I'll make sure she comes.' He sounds so mealy-mouthed. He hates being that way but recognises that sometimes it's necessary.

*

George's life moves to a new rhythm. He gets up at six-thirty, has breakfast and wakes Angie at seven. More often than not, this requires a good deal of exasperated cajoling. Doesn't she care about being late? After the first morning, she stays in bed as long as possible, cutting her margins finer and finer. So George supervises Rory's breakfast, makes her lunch and ensures she is dressed properly. (This is rarely a problem. Rory's quite proud to be wearing a real school uniform.) He got into trouble about the lunch, though. After his first effort, Rory brought home a note to say that lunches needed to be healthy. Apparently white bread, Twisties and a chocolate frog are not acceptable fare for a growing child. They even had the cheek to send home a list of suggestions. He, George, has eaten white bread all his life and anyone can see he's as fit as a fiddle. Nevertheless, he quietly replaces white bread with wholemeal and adds apples to his shopping list.

In this new regime there's a bit more cleaning and laundry, but that's okay – he likes to be busy. He still meets Redgum at the pub but earlier, so he can be back in time to collect Rory from school. Although he's impatient to see her, he notices with concern that she's never part of that bubbling, brimming entity that flows down the steps like lava – an entity that on closer inspection comprises myriad groups and pairs. On the contrary, Rory walks quietly, alone, looking around for him with an anxiety he finds both touching and troubling.

George's favourite time is the few hours before Angie comes home. He gives Rory lemonade and a biscuit (chocolate Teddies are firm favourites for both of them). They have their snack at the kitchen table, not saying anything much, but sort of ... cosy.

George sees how the other children meeting their mothers all talk *nineteen to the dozen*, as Shirl would say. He does try. 'What happened at school today?'

'Nothing much.'

She trots along beside him, meeting every overture with a monosyllable at best. George remembers his own childhood. Uncles, aunts, even Poppy would ask about school. What sort of reply did they expect? He'd been an obliging child and several times tried to answer. *Four times tables. Spelling. Mr Green read us a story about Simpson and his donkey.* But he had soon realised the inquirers weren't all that interested. It was just what you said to kids when you didn't know what else to say. So after a few attempts with Rory he chooses silence in preference to empty questions. He's not exactly garrulous himself.

She still watches television, but that gives him a chance to get the tea on. When Angie comes home, he asks how work went. 'All right.' She's as bad as Rory. But he persists with Angie. An adult (and she is an adult, despite her many immaturities) should be able to take part in a civilised exchange. Besides, he's genuinely curious. She's so lazy around the house. Has no idea of time. Is she late back from lunch every day? Does she work at a reasonable pace? He finds it difficult to imagine that during working hours she's capable of overcoming her customary inertia.

*

'For you.' Angie plonks a plastic bag on the table in front of George. 'It's a coffee mug,' she explains, as though an explanation is required. 'I got it at the two-dollar shop.'

'For me?'

'Yeah. To say thanks and stuff.'

George takes off his glasses, wipes the lenses, puts them on again and reads the caption. '"I am the Walrus". That's … interesting.'

'I dunno what it means either, but it was in the bargain bin.'

George is not sure whether to laugh or cry. Angie isn't used to giving gifts. That much is obvious. Nor does she want him to see it as a sign of weakness. Fair enough. He's never been very good at receiving gifts. Pen always had to nudge him into enthusiasm every time Shirl arrived with his birthday present.

He notices that Angie is making for the door. 'Hey. Thanks, love. It's just what I needed.'

'Yeah, well …'

Should he have hugged her? In his limited experience, that seems to be what people do. He's never been much of a one for hugging. Nor has Redgum. *It's a woman thing*, he decides. To make up for the lack of hugging, he'll have his tea in the mug from now on, even though he prefers a cup.

*

Angie has fled to the bathroom. Bree was right. No harm in sucking up occasionally. George seemed pleased. And she was pleased, too. Unaccountably, if truth be told. But Angie found herself to be pleased, nonetheless.

5

Angie works until four on Fridays and for the first three weeks comes straight home. But on the fourth Friday, she rings. 'A few of us from work are goin' for a drink,' she says. 'Might be a bit late.'

George doesn't mind. Young people should have friends, and apart from the shadowy Bree, Angie seems to be a bit of a loner. Like George himself, when he comes to think of it. But he understands the importance of socialising with workmates. You all have to get along together hour after hour, day after day, and Friday-night drinks or an occasional counter-lunch help to smooth things along. So he doesn't mind looking after Rory. It isn't as if he has anywhere else to go.

'I could be late. You might have to put her to bed. Bye.' And she's gone before George can demur.

When he agreed, he expected her home about six, seven at the latest; at least in time for a late dinner. But when it comes time to eat, there is no sign of her. George and the child eat together and he's too tired to argue over the vegetables. As soon as the meal is over, she wanders off to watch television. George looks at his watch. Angie has always been here at bedtime. What about the kid's bath? The idea of giving her a bath makes him deeply uncomfortable. It isn't as though he's her father, or even her real Poppy. George has a natural sense of propriety. It just doesn't seem right.

So when the time comes, he washes her face and hands and scabby knees with a soapy washcloth. 'We can skip the bath tonight,' he says. 'Now, into your pyjamas.' He'll be glad to have her settled and is looking forward to a beer. 'G'night, then, sweetheart.'

'Where's Mummy? Mummy always puts me to bed. I want Mummy.' Rory stands at the bedroom door, fists clenched, face red and mutinous.

'Mummy's running a bit late,' George tells her. 'She wants you asleep when she gets home.' He tries to pick her up, but she flings herself onto the floor and curls up in a ball. 'No! No! No!' She's screaming like she's being murdered and George throws a worried glance through the window at the house next door. No lights, thank goodness.

It's awkward picking up the little bundle, and her wriggling hurts his ribs, but in the midst of it all George is moved by her lightness, her sharp-boned fragility. He puts her into the bed and pulls up the covers.

'Mummy's gone away,' she sobs. 'I don't like going to bed by myself.'

George is alarmed to hear the beginnings of a wheeze. Angie had mentioned that Rory was asthmatic, but it seemed to be under control. 'Your puffer,' he says. 'Where is it?'

But Rory has already brought it out from under her pillow. Her breathing improves almost immediately but those are real tears running down her cheeks. 'I want Mummy. Where is she?'

George looks around for a doll or a teddy – something to keep her company. Surely she has one toy. There's nothing. 'I'll be back in a minute,' he says. There are some chocolate frogs left in the packet and any lingering qualms regarding bribery are far outweighed by necessity. Just as he opens the fridge, the phone rings. *No. He doesn't need a new roof. Not even if it's a special deal for pensioners.*

By the time he returns to the bedroom, Rory is asleep. He tiptoes over to straighten the covers. Her face has begun to relax, although her forehead is puckered and her cheeks streaked with recent tears. She's breathing evenly and cradles a strangely familiar shape on the pillow close to her cheek. A bit worse for wear but recognisable – it's one of her fluffy dog slippers.

*

'It's not good enough.' George is determined to be firm about last night. 'Rory was very upset. It brought on an asthma attack. I had trouble getting her to sleep.'

Angie is sulky and probably hung-over – she didn't get up until after eleven. Black-rimmed eyes challenge him over her teacup. 'At least I came home. Coulda stayed at Bree's.'

'Bree's? Wasn't this a work thing?'

'Hooked up with Bree later.' She puts her arm around Rory. 'George is mad at Mummy. Look! His face is all growly.' They both snigger. 'You're not mad at Mummy, are you?'

George wrestles with his jacket. 'Make your own lunch. I'm off to the pub.'

*

Angie grabs two pieces of bread, adds butter and Vegemite and slaps the slices together. She cuts the sandwich into rough halves. 'Here.'

Rory shoves the plate back at her mother. 'George makes triangles.'

'Well I don't.' Angie is getting tired of being told how George does things. They've managed without him well enough until now.

*

George finds Redgum at the pub, watching the telly above the bar. 'Might put a bet on later,' he says. 'Got a tip in the second from Phil.'

Smarting from the scene in his kitchen, George isn't ready to discuss horse racing. 'It was like they ganged up on me,' he says. 'After all I've done for them.'

Redgum is busy with the form guide, but there must be something in George's tone because he looks up from his calculations. 'Watch it, mate. You're startin' to sound like Shirl.'

George grunts. Surely a bit of gratitude isn't too much to expect? The way they'd looked at him – a gang of two. All at once he was Short-Arse George, the small, skinny kid the other boys picked on. He is aware of that same scooped-out hollow in his gut. For once he thinks of his father with a wry gratitude. The only gift his old man had ever given him was to teach him how to defend himself. How to fight dirty, if necessary.

Frank Johnson had found his son crying in the lane behind their house with a swollen lip and bloody nose. 'What's happened to you?' No sympathy in that voice, thick with alcohol and contempt.

'Mark Hamble and his gang. They pick on me.'

'Pick on you? Pick on you? Christ Almighty, I might as well have had two girls.' He put up his fists and George winced. 'I'm not gonna hit you, Mary. Just teachin' you how to fight. Come on. Watch me.' He took a balanced stance, then danced, light and graceful as an autumn leaf, feinting with his left hand. 'The jab and the hook. Work on those and you'll be sweet. Let's go. Fists in guard position. Like this. That's right. Okay. We're aiming for the nose.' They persisted for a week, every night in the back lane. Like his father, George was small and light on his feet. Quick with his fists, too. Even after so many years he's never forgotten the look in his father's eyes when he displayed some aptitude for boxing. His jaw had relaxed for an instant and it was as close to paternal pride as George was ever likely to see.

'That'll fix them,' his father said. 'If they're too big, fight dirty. Kick their kneecaps. Grab 'em by the balls. Bang their heads into the wall if there is one.' He demonstrated his last point by slamming George's head into the fence, which fortunately had some give. Then he turned away. 'No more nancy-boy snivelling. Give as good as you get. End of lesson.' George's father left then, throwing a strange look back over his shoulder. 'Better not try any of this on your old man.'

Young George stood in the lane, with love and hate in his heart. One day, when he was big enough, he might just do that. But he hung on to that look of pride in his father's eyes as though it were a lifebuoy.

Redgum continues to ramble on about this horse, so George fishes for his wallet. 'Put a tenner on for me,' he says. 'I gotta get going.'

*

George arrives home to find a motorbike parked at the kerb and Rory sitting on the front step. What's the matter with her? She never plays like other kids. Like Annie would, for instance. Just sits around doing nothing or watching television.

'What you up to?' he asks, easing himself down beside her.

'Nothing.'

That's true enough. 'Where's your mum?'

'Inside with Amp.'

'That Amp's motorbike?'

Rory nods. 'I don't want to go inside,' she mutters.

'That's okay. Sometimes it's best to be outdoors. Let's sit on the seat; it's a bit hard for Poppy down here.' They sit for a while, side by side, on the small garden seat and George shuffles and harrumphs with the uncomfortable feeling that he needs to say something. Along the front fence Pen's rose bushes are jostling each other in summer's final, extravagant display. They'll be due for a prune soon. *You can never cut them back too hard.* That's what Pen used to say. Then she'd worry that he'd pruned too deep. *It drove me crazy,* he thinks with affection.

George scans the sky, feathered with high, cirrus clouds. He looks at the veins, knotted and grey, on the back of his hands. (Steady as a rock.) He looks at the house and its closed blue door. 'What if I tell you a story?'

She fixes those strange, green eyes on his. 'You only have stories at school.'

'Not true. You can have stories anywhere.' He racks his brain, trying to remember a children's story – one Pen had read to their nieces. (*It's a worry how his mind goes blank sometimes.*) Rory begins to look sceptical so he's forced to start, not at all sure where he's going.

'Once upon a time, there was a young … mermaid called Annie who lived in the sea with her mother and father and six brothers and three sisters.' *Should he have said that? The kid has no father or brothers or sisters.* He glances at her but she's watching him, waiting for the story to continue. 'They lived in a castle made of sand and seashells and shiny pearls and Annie was very happy except for one thing …'

The solemn little face looks up at him as he scrambles for inspiration. 'Except ... except ... that she wanted to fly!'

'Why?'

'Well, she was sitting on a rock one day and she saw a seagull and she wanted to fly just like him.' George reckons he's getting the hang of this now.

'It was a boy seagull.'

'That's right. So when everyone else was busy, she swam to the surface − that's the top of the sea − and she found some feathers on the rocks. And ... and ...'

'There you are.' Angie sways in the doorway, looking even more dishevelled than she had earlier. 'Oh. Hi, George. You wanna beer?'

She sounds conciliatory so George creaks to his feet. 'Come on, Rory.' As they walk down the passage, George feels a timid hand slip into his. The palm is surprisingly rough. He'd always imagined Annie's hand to be soft.

'Will you finish the story later?'

'Course I will, love.'

'This is Amp,' Angie says. 'Amp, this is George.'

The introduction is courteous enough but the leather-clad brute, sprawling at George's table, does no more than raise a finger from his beer. 'Yo,' he says. The beard, the tatts, the chain-draped leather − it's all there. As if one of his imaginary bikies has materialised in his own kitchen.

George feels his stomach lurch and Rory's grip tightens − the bikie story has suddenly become a menacing possibility. What is this − this *Amp* − doing in his house? Drinking George's beer, too, by the looks of it. An arrogant bastard – the way he's sitting, for instance, slumped but alert, pelvis thrust forward to the edge of the seat. Amp has positioned himself sideways, arms and legs spread as though a mere kitchen chair is too small to contain his bulk. He's a big bugger, that's for sure – and George is sensible (and scared) enough to see that there's no way to get rid of Amp unless he wants to go.

Where had he heard the name 'Amp' before? Something to do with Bree – didn't he have a cousin or someone who knew someone else? He takes the gamble, hoping his voice sounds normal. 'You found Angie a place, then?'

Amp's voice is lighter than he might have expected and quite well modulated. 'Nothing yet,' he says. 'How about a beer?'

George nods and Amp hands him a bottle of Jürgen's Pale Ale – one of those boutique beers that poofs drink. At least he hasn't raided the fridge. George takes a swig. 'Not bad,' he has to admit. 'Never had one of these before.' Now the threat is diminished, he appraises Amp more closely, his eyes making swift sorties to the other man's face, retreating when in danger of catching his eye. So this was Amp – bulky, but with arresting dark-blue eyes that were both shrewd and remote; a straight, almost delicate nose; and, half hidden by the beard, a mouth (George recoils from the thought), a mouth that can only be described as sensual. He would have been good-looking as a young man, but his features have coarsened and the folds and lines on his face and neck suggest that he's well on the wrong side of forty. *It can't be what it looks like. Angie's only nineteen.*

'I'll leave the rest of the grog in the fridge,' Amp says amiably enough. 'Time to go.' He wraps one leather-clad arm around Angie's head and kisses her long and hard. It's an act of possession, a marking of territory, and is as much for George as for Angie. Rory slinks closer to George, who responds with an arm around her shoulders. Barely acknowledging their presence, Amp saunters off down the passageway, Angie trotting after him. 'See you, babe.'

'Yeah. Stay cool.'

*

'What? What?' Angie is on the offensive.

'For a start,' George says, anger splintering through his natural diffidence, 'this is my home. I don't expect to come back and find strangers sitting in my kitchen.'

Angie rolls her eyes. 'A stranger? He's *Amp*.' She stresses the name as if this will legitimise his credentials.

Rory burrows even closer and this makes George more articulate than he might otherwise have been. 'It's not only me. What about … ?' He inclines his head towards the small figure at his side. 'I found her out on the front step. She didn't want to come inside without me.' *She's scared of him*, he wants to say, but as the child is within earshot, he chooses to be more diplomatic and mouths, 'I don't think she likes him.'

'She didn't like you either, at first.'

True enough. But does everything have to be a battle? 'Well I certainly don't like him,' George says. 'He must be – what? Twenty, thirty years older than you? It's not right.'

Angie executes a long-suffering sigh. 'When did they make *you* me dad?'

'I mightn't be your dad,' he says. 'But you're Rory's mum.'

Rory abandons George and runs over to her mother. 'Don't go, Mummy.'

'Course I won't go. We're happy here with George, aren't we?'

Wrapping her arms around one denim-clad leg, Rory grins up at her mother. George has to turn away. This demonstration of the child's trust, restored so easily, invokes a kind of dread.

'George was telling me a story,' Rory says. 'Can you finish the story now, George?'

'I've got to start dinner soon. Let's wait until bedtime.' By then, he hopes, he'll know how it ends.

*

'So,' George continues, 'the little mermaid put the feathers in her purse and swam back down to the castle under the sea.'

'To her mum?'

'To her mum. They had a delicious seaweed pizza for tea and after they did the dishes together ...' (*It's his fairytale and the dishes are still a sore point.*) '... Annie went to the palace next door. It was a creepy palace because a witch lived there.'

'I don't like witches. Was she scared?'

'Uh – this was a good witch, just a bit old and ugly like me so she wasn't scared a bit.'

'You're not ugly. Your face is just a bit funny.' Rory giggles and squirms down further in her bed.

George grins. 'That's what they all say. Anyway, the witch took the feathers and made her a pair of beautiful wings, all white and soft as ... froth on ...' (He can't say *on a beer*, can he? Not in a children's story.) '... As soft as a cloud.'

'How do you know how soft a cloud is? You can't touch them. They're too high.'

Should've stuck with the beer. He improvises. 'Because a scientist told me. They know all sorts of stuff.'

'What's his name – the scientist?'

'Redgum.' He's becoming impatient. 'Now let's get on with the story. But the witch warned Annie. "Be careful. These wings will only fly once."'

'I'd like some wings.' Rory's eyelids are heavy.

George bends down, hesitates, then pulls back and ruffles her hair. The gesture is tentative and clumsily executed. 'You think about that and we'll save the rest for tomorrow night. Okay?'

That was the easy bit. The hard bit is to lay down the law with Angie. But fair's fair – he has every right to say who can and can't come into his home. He heads for the lounge room and turns off the television.

'Hey. I'm watching that.'

Shoving the remote into his shirt pocket, he swallows. 'Not until we have a proper talk.'

Arms folded, foot tapping her impatience, Angie is the very model of long-suffering. 'Spit it out, then.'

Keep calm, George tells himself. *Be logical — she's an adult, after all.* He clears his throat and she smiles faintly. 'It's like this, Angie. You saved me from serious injury and I'm grateful for that. Always will be. You came here for help, and because I owe you, I'm helping as best I can.' Angie frowns and he blinks behind his old-fashioned glasses, feeling as pathetic as he sounds. 'The truth is, I'm not getting any younger and I can only take so much. Amp is your business, but I don't want him in the house.' She starts to speak but he raises his hand. 'No. I want to finish. If I find him here again, you'll ...' *How can he say it? The ultimatum — you'll have to go. Knowing she'll take Annie — Rory — with her.* Apart from the odd bet on Redgum's tips, George isn't a gambler. But he gambles now, mindful all the while that he risks losing the child. (*Why does he see this as a risk?* he wonders. *It's not like she's his real granddaughter.*) No. He can't say he finds her lovable, but he feels sorry for her, and in a funny sort of way, admires her. The kid's had a lot to put up with, one way and another. But she's not broken.

Now he's aware of Angie, looking at him with fear. The fear of homelessness — it's a powerful weapon.

'You can stay,' George continues. 'I'm inviting you to stay, but you must promise never to bring Amp here again. And that goes for any other men.' He hands back the remote. 'You have a daughter,' he says more gently. 'Men like Amp — they're not good for little girls like Rory. I'm going to make some tea. Think about what I said.'

When he comes back with the tea, the television is still switched off.

'Did you mean it?' she asks. 'About staying here?' Teeth tearing at her already ravaged nails.

'I do mean it. But I need that promise. You mustn't bring strange men here again.'

She gives him a wry smile. 'Most men I know are strange, but I promise.'

Cleared the air. That's what he's done. And now, as they sip their tea, he feels comfortable enough to ask the question. 'Rory's dad. Do you ever see him?'

'Nah. Hardly knew him.' She responds to George's raised eyebrows. 'You're shocked? It's all changed since your day. I was fourteen then and I was fat, with pimples and crap clothes.' She gestures, arms wide, to indicate the extent of her unattractiveness. 'I was the ugliest girl in my class and when a boy wanted to do it with me, I wasn't going to miss the chance.'

She bites hard into her biscuit, sending crumbs all over the couch. 'Turned out it was all for a bet,' she murmurs, hurt and humiliation evident in her flushed cheeks and unnaturally bright eyes. She gnaws at her lip and picks at the biscuit crumbs. 'We only did it a few times and then I found out he laughed about it with his mates later. When I knew for sure I was knocked up, me stepdad wouldn't have anything to do with me. Said he didn't want another brat to feed. Mum had four other kids and she was scared of him but scareder of being left by herself. She was an ad– She wasn't well and couldn't work.' Angie shrugs but can't look him in the eye. 'She gave me twenty bucks and said I'd have to go – wouldn't admit it had anything to do with me stepdad. Just said she was sorry but they had to keep me sisters safe from a slut like me. What a joke! Me big sister, Shiloh, was having it off with half the school, but Mum thought the sun shone out of her bum.'

George's lips twitch.

'By the time they knew, it was too late for an abortion, so in the end I went to me gran's.'

'She looked after you, your gran?'

Angie's tone softens. 'She was brilliant, but she wanted me to give up the baby for adoption. I was goin' to do it an' all – I didn't want a baby. Not for a million bucks. But when I saw her, so tiny and all squishy …' Her voice is shaking and George senses resentment behind her admission. It's as though she doesn't want to expose her weakness in the face of her baby's need. 'I guess I like, ended up with her after all.' She shrugs. 'Well, you know …'

George doesn't know. He can only imagine. 'So you kept her.'

'Yeah. Gran tried to help out, but Rory cried all the time. In the end, it was better to go. Gran's got this heart thing and she wasn't getting any sleep, so we snuck off when she went to Outpatients.'

'And you were what? – fifteen?'

'Goin' on sixteen by the time I left.'

George hasn't thought before of what it would be like to be sixteen and homeless, with a baby to care for. How on earth had she managed? He regards her with new respect.

Whatever the sad and sordid details of Rory's conception, this young woman (*girl*), has been resourceful enough and brave enough to persevere and raise the child as best she could. She isn't what you would call a good mother in the general way of things, but she's good enough and deserves a break.

'Here's the plan,' George finds himself saying. 'Stay here with me until you get on your feet and you can afford to rent a nice place. Have you got a bank account? Yes? If I see you're putting away a bit each week, you can stay here for nothing – but you buy your own smokes. And remember your promise about not bringing blokes here. Fair enough?'

'Fair enough. And George …' A twinkle supplants the usual wariness in her eyes. 'I'm almost glad those bikies didn't kill you in the lane.'

'Cheeky young bugger.' He stands up and stretches his back. 'Bedtime, I'd say. It's late and we both need our beauty sleep.'

Surprisingly docile, she says goodnight and goes off to bed, leaving George feeling like a real dad. There had been a connection – an exchange of jokes had created a connection. He sleeps well that night. *The sleep of the just*, their minister used to say. Drifting off, he addresses the red jowly face that had so terrified him the few times he attended Sunday School. *You might find me in heaven after all, Reverend Thomas.*

We'll see, the face replies. *This is only day one.*

*

For her part, Angie sleeps the sleep of the young. It's not just that she's hung-over, but her immediate problems have melted away. She has no doubt that she can keep to George's conditions. The world seems to be a good place when you're sleeping between clean sheets in a situation that has magically stabilised. At last, here is the good luck she'd earned. *He'll come around when he knows Amp better,* is her last, hopeful thought before falling asleep.

*

George finishes his story the next night. 'So Annie took the wonderful white wings and swam up to her rock. First she planned to fly over the land to see all the things that she had heard about in stories – mountains and cities and cows and elephants. Then she was going to swoop and dive and somersault in the clouds before coming back home to her rock.'

'And her mum.'

'And her mum. But when she reached her rock, what did she see? A little girl crying as though her heart would break.'

'What was her name?'

'Her name was – Rory, and she was sad because when she was at the beach a big wave had taken her out to sea and now she was stuck on the rock all alone.' Rory's eyes are fixed on his face and she looks so worried that he decides to cut the story short. 'So Annie gave her wings to the little girl.'

'To Rory.'

'To Rory. Annie was sad that she'd never get to see an elephant or a cow or a city or a mountain, but she was sadder for Rory and told the wings to take her home to her mum. So Rory waved goodbye and flew off into the clouds, while Annie went back to her palace under the sea.'

'And they all lived happily ever after?'

'That's right, sweetheart.'

George pauses at the door, struck by a new anxiety. If only he could be sure that Rory would live happily ever after. He heads for the fridge. *No point in worrying. She'll be gone in a few months.*

*

George has no illusions about Angie. Accepting that she'll continue to come home late whenever she pleases, he seeks the help of his sister. Not with any great enthusiasm. Ask Shirl for advice about how long to boil potatoes and she'll have you cooking a five-course banquet.

'It's like this, Shirl.' He chooses the phone – a form of communication over which he has a modicum of control. 'Angie has to … work late sometimes, and I have to put Rory to bed.' He allows time for the 'tsking' before continuing. (He's seen the word in books, but his sister is the only person he knows who actually 'tsks'.) 'I don't feel – you know – *right*, giving the kid a bath. Is she old enough to leave alone?'

Shirl is not sure. She tries to think back to her own children and finally decides to err on the side of caution.

'She's a bit young, yet, I think. Why don't I come over and teach her how to have a shower? You can't drown in a shower.'

So Shirl arrives at seven o'clock and whisks Rory away to the bathroom. 'You're a schoolgirl now,' she says. 'Schoolgirls don't have baths. They have showers.'

'That's the way.' Shirl adjusts the height and temperature of the shower and suffers a drenching as Rory clings to both her hands. 'Come on, schoolgirl. Use the soap.'

George, lurking in the kitchen, hears a good deal of squealing, which to his relief, turns into smothered giggles.

For all the fuss, Rory emerges pink and dry in her yellow butterfly pyjamas. Shirl, wet but triumphant, tells George that all is well. 'I'll help out for another day or two, but she'll manage by herself in no time. When she does, I promised I'd bring her some animal soap.'

'Not above a bribe, then?' Despite his gratitude, George can't resist the opportunity.

'Not a bribe, George. A reward.'

6

The Asian bloke from next door stops George on the way to the pub. The Nguyens are an elderly couple who keep to themselves. George has never had much to do with them, but Pen used to say hello to the woman over the fence and they'd exchanged a few home-grown vegetables from time to time. They seem decent enough – even came to the funeral, solemn and awkward in black, unable to converse properly with the other mourners. Afterwards, they'd brought in some of their Chinky food and he'd said thanks, of course, but didn't eat it. You can't be too careful with foreign food.

Now Mr Nguyen is tugging at George's sleeve as he walks past. 'You have granddaughter stay your house?'

What's it to you? 'Yeah,' he says, moving off. He can hardly deny it, but he wasn't going to blab all his business to some foreign bloke

'Like swing?'

George stops. *What's he saying? Something to do with singing. Couldn't possibly be right.* 'What?' George stares back at him. Squints into the sun.

'Swing.' The man sways his body back and forth and gestures towards his backyard. 'Swing. For granddaughter.'

'Swing? You want to give Rory your swing?'

'Yes. Yes. You come and take. Need friend help us maybe?'

The Nguyens have three children and any number of grandchildren, but even the grandchildren are all too big now to play on the swing. George is touched and shakes his neighbour's hand. Like his own, it's calloused – a worker's hand – or maybe it's all that gardening. 'Ta, mate. Good of you. Tomorrow?' His own hand describes a loop that is supposed to represent tomorrow.

Fortunately the gesture isn't necessary. 'Tomorrow. Yes. Very happy for little girl … mate.'

George finds himself smiling as he walks the block to the pub. 'You never can tell with people,' he observes to Redgum, who's agreed to help with the swing.

'Take people as you find them. That's what I always say.'

'Live and let live.'

'Too right.'

The two philosophers stare into their ale. If only everyone thought as they did. The world would be a better place, that's for sure.

*

Hands on hips, the three men stare at the swing. They'd managed to pull out the hoops anchoring it to the ground; now they have to work out how to get it next door.

'Over the fence?' Redgum suggests. 'That side gate's a bit narrow.'

''S'all right for a big bugger like you,' George points out. 'The fence must be six-foot high.'

Nevertheless, George and Mr Nguyen go around to the other side, and Redgum, despite his dicky heart, heaves the swing to the top of the fence and over.

'Hey. Fair go, lady. No need to hit me.'

George looks over the fence to see the tiny woman swiping at his big friend, who is kneeling in the middle of her veggie patch.

'I'm sorry, missus.' Redgum is trying to dodge her blows while scrabbling about in a futile attempt to repair the damage.

He looks so crestfallen that George begins to laugh and Mrs Nguyen stops her attack and joins in with a harsh, high-pitched cackle.

Even her laugh sounds foreign, George thinks.

'Go. Go,' she says, exasperated. 'Help at swing.'

The swing erected, they test it for stability and with folded arms survey their work. Mrs Nguyen comes over with green tea, and although Redgum and George would have preferred a beer, they drink the tea cheerfully enough, with much nodding to express a general goodwill.

'Time to pick Rory up,' George says, looking at his watch. 'Why don't you stay here until she comes home?'

He sees the Nguyens straining for comprehension. 'Stay and see Rory,' he says, his hand approximating her height. 'Little girl.'

'Yes. Yes. We stay.'

The school is only two blocks away and George always walks. Those women in their four-wheel drives are capable of intimidating the strongest man as George discovered the day he tried to park Penny's old Corolla. It was a particularly nasty encounter. He had no idea that women could be so aggressive. So after that he walks, and enjoys the feeling of Rory by his side as they make their way back home. They still don't talk much, but George hopes that will come in time.

Today though, he's fair bursting with his news. 'Got a surprise for you.'

'Tell me. Tell me.'

'Wouldn't be a surprise, then, would it?'

She's such a serious kid. 'No,' she says with a judicious pursing of her lips. 'So we'd better hurry.'

When they arrive home, George pauses at the back door. 'Cover your eyes. No peeking.' He leads Rory the few steps around the trellis. 'Now.'

Rory takes her hands from her eyes. 'A swing. A real swing. In our own backyard.' She looks up at George, her face alight. 'Can I have a go right now?'

Redgum and the Nguyens smile at each other as she clambers onto the seat and George begins to push.

'Higher. Higher.' Rory is squealing with delight and only consents to stop when George pretends to be more tired than he is.

'Now say thank you to Mr and Mrs Noo-win.'

For one awful moment, George fears that the kid might turn all sullen. It wouldn't be the first time. But no. He's proud to see how nicely she thanks them.

'And say thank you to Uncle Redgum for helping.'

She looks at the big man with awe. 'You're the cloud man.'

Redgum is puzzled. 'Cloud man?'

'Long story. I told her you're a scientist.'

'Got to go, little lady,' Redgum says, ruffling her hair. 'Got some sciencin' to do.'

*

Redgum has been won over, but George is yet to tackle Shirl. She'll have to know of his offer to Angie sooner or later. Nevertheless, he is grateful for the breathing space that occurs when Marianne's eldest comes down with bronchitis, keeping Shirl occupied with extra child-minding. But knowing his sister, George is not surprised to see her at the door on her grandchild's first day back at school.

'Cuppa?'

Shirl looks at her watch as she steps inside. She always seems to have somewhere to go, but on this occasion, she's carrying a banana cake. George's heart sinks. Banana cake means an extra-long visit.

Shirl makes the tea. George always regresses when a woman is around to do women's work. (Except Angie, of course. Her cooking skills range from the burning of toast to the heating of baked beans, so he has to make an exception there.)

'They're still here?' Shirl's gaze takes in the undies airing on the clothes horse, the furry slippers on the floor and the quantity of breakfast dishes waiting to be washed.

Best get it over with. 'I've asked them to stay. Just till they get back on their feet.'

As he expects, Shirl lets fly. 'I can't imagine that they were ever on their feet. Or ever will be. You'll be stuck with them, George. They'll bleed you of every penny and move on without so much as a thank you. Don't look at me in that manner. That's exactly what they'll do. Marianne works with people like that every day. It's her job. And for every success there are a hundred failures.' Shirl bangs down her cup, rattling it in the saucer. 'Take them to the Salvos and let them deal with it. They need professionals.'

'Finished?' George, usually so obliging, pushes out his jaw, and for the first time in his life, really stands up to her. 'Whatever you say, it's my house and my money. Don't worry. There'll be plenty left for your kids when I die.'

Seeing the shock on his sister's face, he regrets the harshness and (he has to admit) the total injustice of his outburst. 'Shirl. Please. That was a terrible thing to say.'

Shirl stands up, knocking over her chair, and blinded by tears, fumbles for her handbag. 'That's the cruellest thing anyone has ever said to me.'

Stricken, he leads her, weeping, to the couch, and sits beside her, a cushion's width away. If only he could take it back. He can't look at her and stares instead at the blank screen of the television.

His voice comes out as a low mutter, and eventually Shirl leans in slightly in order to hear. 'You've always stuck by me, Shirl. You and the girls are the only family I've got. Marianne and young Claire – they're special. No one could ever take their place. That's what I wanted to say, but it came out all wrong.'

She's calmer and the tears have all but abated so he continues, gathering diffuse thoughts that have been long hovering on the brink of his consciousness, shaping them into words.

'At first I was just paying back a favour. But when I heard Angie's story – I know it's against all logic, but I thought, this is something I can do. Give them a chance.' Desperate, he dares to reference a subject they have never broached. Not once in all these years. 'You know, Shirl, if Bill hadn't done the right thing by you, I reckon Dad would've kicked you out – just like Angie's stepdad did.'

She flinches but acknowledges the truth of what he says with a brief nod.

'You were lucky enough or smart enough to pick a good bloke.' *He is a good bloke, teetotaller or not*, George thinks, surprised. 'I understand that you don't like Angie, but you can't take it out on the kid. I know it sounds barmy, but I think it's fate. I'm *meant* to help Annie.'

'Annie? I thought her name was Angie.'

Confused, George has to pause before answering. 'Rory. I'm meant to help Rory.' He puts his arm around his sister, an uncharacteristic gesture that surprises them both. 'You do good stuff all the time, Shirl. Pen did, too. Is it so bad for me to want to do this one thing?'

Dry-eyed at last, Shirl puts her hand over his. 'Not so bad, I guess. I just don't want to see you exploi– hurt.'

George looks at his sister with affection. Shirl can be bossy, even overbearing, but she has lots of good qualities and he has never told her how much he admires her. He'd said a hurtful thing today and he needs to make amends. 'You 'n' me,' he says, 'we had a totally crap family life. But you've been a terrific mother – me and Pen always said that. I've often wondered, though' – he's genuinely puzzled – 'how did you know what to do?'

Shirl takes a long while to respond. She smiles. 'I suppose I had a baby brother to practise on – and my kids had a good dad. Now you have Rory. But you have to remember she's not yours. I'm serious, George. Love her enough, but not too much.'

George is surprised. Who said anything about love? *Women*, he decides. *They just can't help themselves.* 'No worries there. Now let's go back and tuck into some of that banana cake.'

They finish their tea and Shirl prepares to go. 'I'll help where I can.' She turns back at the door, diffident. 'Thanks for saying I was a good mum. All we can do is our best.'

*

The day after setting up the swing, George meets Rory after school as usual. 'Poppy George,' she says. 'I got a gold star today.'

'A gold star!' This is more than she has ever told him about school and he's aware that his response is inadequate. 'Um – amazing.'

'Don't you want to know what I got it for?'

'Of course I do.' *Pen would have asked that straight away.*

'It was for Show and Tell, about my new swing. And I got a surprise for you.'

'I don't get many surprises.'

'Me neither. But here …' She dives into her bag. 'I drew a picture of you pushing me on the swing and this is the shed and that's a bird. And that's the star. It's in the sky but it's daytime!' She giggles as George admires the picture and chuckles along with her. 'And it's for you.'

George looks down at the animated face, listens to the artless chatter and realises that they have become comfortable together. At this moment, they look like all the other parents and children. He's unpractised in this adult–child communication, but he'll do better as time goes by.

He grins down at her and the grin is returned. 'We'll put it on the wall,' he says. 'Right next to the calendar.'

'It's been like a flood,' he tells Redgum later in the week. 'She's become a real chatterbox.' But the talk is all about classroom activities. There's no mention of friends.

Annie the mermaid becomes part of their nightly ritual and George is chuffed to find he's never short of ideas. On the way, Annie becomes a hybrid of Mother Teresa and Supergirl as George seeks to instil in Rory some of the values he holds dear.

After a while, the child becomes bored with all this goodness and self-sacrifice. There's something else, too. 'Isn't Annie ever naughty?' she asks one night.

'No.' George sets her mind to rest. 'Never ever.'

'Then I don't want any more Annie stories.' Rory turns on her side and refuses to look at him.

'Come on, love. What's the matter?' He has begun to read her moods and understands the extent of her distress. What can possibly be wrong with Annie stories? She used to enjoy them.

'You only like good girls,' Rory responds, her back still turned. Muttering. 'Not bad girls like me.'

'Don't be such a silly.' George has become as distressed as she is. 'My very favourite girls are a lot good and just a bit naughty. Not bad. Naughty. So they're just like you.' He pauses. 'And you're my very favourite girl of all.' This, with a silent apology to his Annie who, without question, would have been his very, very favourite.

Mollified, she turns back to him. 'Ms Hamilton thinks I'm bad.'

'Your teacher? Why would that be?'

''Cos I am. I hate school.'

*

George stays up late to report this conversation to Angie. She clatters in after midnight and isn't inclined to talk, but George is adamant. 'It's important,' he says.

Angie listens to him with barely concealed impatience. He sees her fingers twitching for a fag. 'You're always fussing, George. Nobody likes school.' She stretches and yawns. 'Gotta get up early in the morning.'

But George isn't about to let her get away with this. Usually in bed by ten, he is tired himself and she owes him (and Rory) a hearing. 'I think you ought to have a word with the teacher.'

Angie is horrified. 'Most kids get into trouble at school. It's just the way things are. And it's not as though Rory's the worst kid on the planet. That stuck-up principal was enough for me. I'd rather pull out me eyelashes than front up to another teacher. Anyway,' she adds, as George looks at her in disbelief, 'gotta go to work, don't I? If you think it's so important, you do it.'

'Someone has to,' George says to her disappearing back. He finds it difficult to contain his fury. Some people don't deserve to have children. Life can be so unfair.

7

If any couple deserved children, George and Pen did. Especially Pen.

They had tried from the moment they were married. 'A honeymoon baby,' they joked. 'That'll have them all counting.'

In post-war Australia, everyone was having babies. How difficult could it be? George and Pen enjoyed a vigorous sex life so the odds should have been well in their favour. One, two, three years passed, the sly comments ceased and they became aware that they didn't quite fit in anymore. Pen's peers were pushing prams or discussing teething, or rubbing satisfied hands over burgeoning bellies. And all the while, Pen's figure remained as slender and flat as a girl's. Friends and family were not sure how to react. Was this a deliberate avoidance of parenthood and thus a reproach to their own parental status? Did poor Pen have, you know, a woman's problem? Or (snigger) was nothing much happening between the sheets? Pen went to baby showers, admired nurseries and knitted bootees, bonnets and lacy woollen jackets. They were godparents to Shirl's Marianne and one of Pen's sister's children. It seemed that they attended christenings every other week. It was raining babies, but none landed in the neat blue-and-white weatherboard house in Mercy Street.

'Doctor Donoghue is sending me to a specialist,' Pen said. 'There might be some blockage in my tubes.'

'Fair enough, love.' George enjoyed Pen's body but was embarrassed by detail. He wasn't sure what tubes she was talking about and if he were honest, he'd admit he didn't want to know. Women's bodies were beautiful and desirable but ultimately a mystery. That was how it was and how it ought to be. It never occurred to him to offer to go to the gynaecologist with her.

She had to have tests. Wait for results. And it was three months before all the results were in.

'Good news,' Pen told George, who was waiting outside the doctor's surgery. 'Doctor Parsons says there's no blockage, and no other medical reason as far as he can see.'

George took her arm as they walked back to the tram. 'So what do we do next?'

She grinned. 'Could be worse. He said we should relax, maybe take a holiday. That sometimes it just happens out of the blue.'

So they decided on a holiday. Having two jobs and no children meant more disposable income, and their friends were envious when they decided to go to Mermaid Beach on the Gold Coast. They had never been interstate before.

Never been on a plane. In a taxi on the way to the airport, they held hands and smiled in anticipation.

Anxious to impress, George confided in the taxi driver. 'Off to the Gold Coast,' he said. 'Two weeks at Blue Waters Motel.'

A grunt. That was all George got in response. 'Surly bugger,' he muttered as the driver flung their cases from the boot. But his elation was such that he wasn't going to dwell on the snub. He grabbed their luggage. 'Come on, Just-Penny. Let's begin our holiday.'

It was March, and the sun's rays were warm and benign. In those days the Gold Coast was just that – a wide stretch of white-gold sand where the breakers rolled in with a rhythm that threaded through your days. No bloody high-rises then – just modest holiday shacks dotted along the esplanade, with tropical-looking gardens and windows shaded from the sun. George sometimes wished that they'd stayed in one of those houses. But he'd wanted to make it special, so he'd booked them into the best motel he could afford.

They enjoyed their days on the beach. Fair-skinned Pen covered up when she wasn't in the water, but George tanned easily and lay in the full sun, as relaxed as a flounder on a slab. They walked along the water's edge and ventured (not too far) into the white-capped waves. The roll of the surf, the blue of the sky, the improbably large and impossibly bright tropical plants all served to intoxicate them, and they roamed together through sun-soaked days in a kind of oblivion. But as time went by, George (and, he suspected, Penny) came to dread the nights.

Four or five days into their holiday, they remembered they were on a mission. After time on the beach, they usually showered and changed and went for a walk along the sand or around the Point, where they talked or they didn't. It was all good. Now they were suddenly grateful for the falling dark that shrouded their faces.

'No real twilight up here,' Pen said. 'Blink and you miss it.'

'Yeah … not like home.'

'It's like the sun is swallowed up in one big gulp.'

'Yeah … Well …'

Pen struggled on. 'We've been lucky with the weather.'

'Too right.'

Poor Pen. She tried, but soon all conversation dried up.

'Better have a bite to eat, then,' he said, and with this small reprieve, they went back to their motel, where they ate in its half-empty restaurant, spending a good deal of time discussing the food.

'The water's nice and cold.'

'Lamb's a bit tough.'

'I wonder what this green thing is?'

The waiter was hovering, and realising that they were the last customers left, they had no option but to go back to their room.

Up to this point, their lovemaking had been — it probably sounded sissy, but the only word that would do was *joyful*. Sometimes playful, sometimes tender, but always passionate and with that element of joy. Now it became clinical, tinged with desperation. Pen's body, once

117

supple and responsive, became tense and ungenerous. Fearing the effects of his reciprocal tension, George didn't dare to linger over foreplay and was relieved when the act was completed. Afterwards, instead of snuggling into his shoulder as she used to, Pen lay on her back, legs elevated and closed her eyes as though she, too, was relieved to have done with it.

Two days after they arrived home, Pen's period started. Neither of them commented, but George inhaled his wife's pervading sadness with every breath.

That's why what he did was unforgivable.

Pen had come back from an appointment with the gynaecologist weary and subdued. Nothing unusual in that. Perhaps he should have spoken before he had his beers, he thought later. Although he wasn't drunk. He did his best to be meticulous in his appraisal of the incident and in the end found he couldn't blame the beer. It had been his own fault, pure and simple.

He was in the kitchen making tea, when Pen appeared out of nowhere. 'We need to talk,' she said. He turned to face her and when he saw her expression – tentative, a bit fearful – he swallowed his jokey response and stood, teapot half raised like a plea.

She handed him an envelope with a name and phone number scribbled on the front. 'This is from Doctor Parsons. He said there's no reason why I can't have a baby.' She stressed the *I* – he remembered that later, but it hardly registered at the time. 'He said you should have some tests. There might be something wrong with your … sperm …'

That's when he hit her. A backhander to the side of her head that sent her spinning against the door. Clinging to the handle, barely managing to stay upright, she regarded him with a look that seared him to the marrow.

'Pen.' He took a step forward and she flinched. 'Pen.' But she'd gone, closing the door with care. George would have preferred her to slam it. Yell at him. He became aware of their bedroom door closing with the faintest of clicks. He had never felt so alone.

He tried to focus, but the kitchen began to shift shape, dipping and weaving, refusing the fact of its everyday solidity. The oven, the green-painted cupboards, the teapot with its knitted cosy floated before his eyes. The cupboard handles – hadn't they chosen those flash handles only weeks ago at the local hardware? He centred his thoughts on the handles, and leaving the kettle on the bench, managed to sit down with his beer. He shouldn't have hit her. That goes without saying. The way she flinched – he felt like a brute. His mother. She had flinched, too. More times than he could count. He wasn't like his dad, though – was he? But whatever way you looked at it, this situation was extreme. His manhood was in question. You had to admit that any bloke would have the same reaction. It was one thing for that quack to suggest a problem with his wedding tackle, but for Pen to even give it a second thought ... Size wasn't an issue – he was sure of that. And he'd never once failed her. Not once. And here she was telling him there was something wrong with his sperm. His *sperm*, for Christ's sake. Using a word like that made her sound like a whore.

Another beer, a couple of shots of whisky. All the while, stoking his indignation. The envelope lay at his feet, and with savage satisfaction, he kicked it under the table as he drained his glass. Unlike his father, George was a brooding, maudlin drunk. *Who knows with women?* he mourned. He had worshipped the ground she walked on and this is the thanks he gets. Tears of self-pity welled in his eyes and he brushed them away with a childish gesture. 'Not much point anymore,' he mumbled, wrestling with the can opener. 'A man can't do one bloody thing right.' He lurched into the lounge room and flopped onto the couch. It was cold, but the cold reinforced his grievance and pandered to his sense of injury. Time passed, the righteous anger wilted, and he began to snore, the still unopened can clutched to his chest.

He awoke to find Pen standing over him, dressed for work. Dragging himself into a semblance of consciousness, he squinted at the clock. Six-thirty. Why was she going to work at six-thirty? *Bloody hell!* Memory of the night before trickled into his sleep-fuddled brain. 'Pen?'

She picked up her suitcase and swung around with sharp finality. Moving, as always, with such precision, such graceful economy of movement that he, slow and leaden, was humbled into silence.

'I'll be staying at Susan's until we can sort out something more permanent.' High heels tapped their way down the passage; the front door opened and closed; and George, frozen in a half-sitting position on the couch, was left with his new reality.

Sliding back down, he pulled the blanket over his head, then stopped. Surely there hadn't been a blanket when he lay down. *Had Pen … ?* The effects of last night's binge prevented him from following that thought. A hammer pounded in his skull. His mouth was rancid, foul. With any luck he'd die right here on the couch.

Work! He sat up to meet the hammer that thwacked him between the eyes. Putting on the kettle, he lit a cigarette before going out to urinate in the backyard. Pen would never allow that, but she wasn't here anymore, was she? He watched the stream with grim satisfaction before going inside for his tea. He was already late and decided to take a sickie. He'd go back to bed, then clean up a bit and have things looking nice for when Pen came home.

He stood outside with his tea and cigarette, squinting against the sun that seemed exceptionally bright for the time of morning. A magpie trill rippled through the pain in his head. He was trying to rationalise, but knew in a visceral way that there wasn't any point in cleaning up for Pen. She was a strong woman, his wife. Her stern face swam up through the sun glare and he understood that she wasn't coming home. Filled with dread, he realised that he no longer knew how to live without her.

*

Before Pen left, if you had asked George was he a bad person, he would admit that he wasn't particularly good or bad – that he was good enough in his own way (which was as much, he believed, as the general run of people could claim). He would have professed to being an honourable man, but after Pen left, he'd behaved dishonourably. Despicably.

What to tell Shirl and Redgum, not to mention his workmates? That his wife had cast aspersions on his virility and as a consequence he'd hit her? That she left because she was afraid of him? Because he was too proud to undertake the tests?

'Pen's gone off with a bloke from her work,' he told Shirl, who had, even in those days, often *popped in, just for a minute.*

'I knew right from the beginning. She was a bit too much of a glamourpuss for my liking. Poor old George. After all you've done for her. A lovely house. Holidays. Clothes. What more could she want?'

'The thing is,' said George, 'I don't know what to tell the blokes at work. Don't want them thinking I can't hang on to me wife.'

'Tell them nothing,' she said. 'It's none of their business and how often do they see her anyway?'

Not at all, when George came to think about it. Work was work and home was home.

So he said nothing at work.

That left Redgum. George had a need to confess, or at least explain, and Redgum was not a man quick to judge. The Sticky Wicket was a real pub in those days, and not long after Pen left, the two men breasted the bar.

It had taken two weeks, but it was better to say it short and sharp. 'Pen's left me,' George said. 'My fault.'

Shamefaced and miserable, he twisted his glass in shaking hands and refused to look his mate in the eye.

Redgum took a long, slow draught, replacing his glass with care in its own sticky ring. He didn't look up. 'That's no good, mate. Reckon she'll come back?'

George didn't know. He couldn't forgive himself for hitting her, so how could he expect her to forgive him? Unlike Shirl, Redgum didn't ask why she left and George wasn't sure he could answer the question. Like competing weeds, shame and pride struggled for ascendancy, and like weeds each grew strong because that was its nature.

Redgum, eyes kind and mild, was waiting for a reply.

'Come back? No. Why should she?' George looked deeper into his beer. 'Fact is, I hit her.' Fearing Redgum's response, he didn't dare raise his eyes, and despite the pub noises, felt as though they were alone, just the two of them, the judge and the accused.

Redgum cleared his throat but said nothing and signalled for another round.

George, compelled to fill the silence, began to plead his case. 'She wanted me to go to the quack to see ... to see if ... We've been tryin' to have a kid ... She was talkin' about tests.' *Help me here, mate.* He ventured a look at Redgum and saw perplexity, concern, and at the periphery of his consciousness – censure. That's when George panicked. Even his best mate condemned him.

'You have to see my point of view. It was like she was sayin' I'm not man enough for her. Not man enough to father a kid.'

'Tests, you say?'

'Yeah.'

'Just tests?'

'Not just any test.'

Redgum downed his beer. 'It's up to you, mate. Gotta go.' He hesitated. 'She's a good woman, your missus.'

George bristled. 'Whose side are you on, anyway?'

'Your side, mate. Never a doubt.'

George watched Redgum all the way to the door, where a sudden shaft of sunlight pierced the bar gloom. A few minutes later, he too left.

*

Two months have passed since his ultimatum to Angie, and George's plan is humming along nicely. Having managed to save just over a hundred dollars, she's proud to show George her bank receipts. True, he wonders if she might have managed just a bit more, but he has no idea what she earns. She seems to go out a lot, but George is more than happy to have Rory to himself.

Nevertheless, events overtake him before he can arrange a visit to Rory's school. The following payday, Angie tells him, in that *wanna-make-something-of-it* way she has, that she's spent most of her savings. She leans against the doorway, watching as George peels the potatoes. Despite her casual posture, she seems poised for flight.

'Thirty dollars left,' she tells him. Daring him to complain.

Shirl had warned him. 'People like her have no idea how to handle money.' George's anger is tinged with panic. Angie has broken their agreement. There is no choice but to ask them to leave – but how can he bring himself to send a little kid out onto the street?

'For something important?' *Please make it for something important.*

'A bike for Rory. I got it at the Target sale. I'm leaving it at Bree's until her birthday.'

A bike for Rory's birthday. Foolish, but surely understandable. 'Her birthday. When's that?'

'The fifteenth of May.'

'Right, we've got a couple of weeks, then. Let's give her a party.'

'Never had one meself.'

'Me neither.'

They become conspirators. *A surprise*, they agree. *We'll make a list.*

Birthday cake, George writes. *Balloons.* He clicks his pen, hesitant. 'Lollies?' He fears lollies are frowned on nowadays.

But Angie appears to be unaware of the finer points of the modern child's diet. 'Yeah. Bags of lollies.'

What else? 'Shirl used to have party pies and sausage rolls for her kids. And bread with hundreds and thousands.' He adds these to the list. 'I'll ask Shirl if she has any other ideas.'

'Hmm,' Angie says. 'Shirl. I dunno about Shirl.'

To George's relief, she is reconciled, but only when he points out that neither he nor Angie knows how to make a cake.

They continue their planning, then, mid-list, he stops. There's something more important than food. 'She doesn't seem to have any friends,' he says. 'Who do we invite?'

Angie crumples. 'No friends. How can we have a party if she's got no friends?' She rubs and smudges black-streaked tears with the heel of her hand, looking at him with the face of a disappointed child. 'It's not fair. She's a good kid.'

She is a good kid. With awkward kindness, George pats her arm. 'I'll have a word to her teacher tomorrow. See if she knows some kids who might come. Then we'll invite Shirl. And maybe Redgum and Mr and Mrs Noo-win from next door.'

'And Bree.'

'And Bree.' With some excitement, George envisages his kitchen table with a nice cloth, a birthday cake and balloons. Party hats! He's forgotten party hats. And those whistle things. 'Don't you worry. She'll have her party all right.'

*

Ms Hamilton takes some time to respond to George's question. 'Aurora ...' (He corrects her.) 'Sorry. She never told me she's called Rory at home. Well, *Rory* seems to have difficulty making friends,' she says, smoothing her sleeve. 'She can be a wee bit ... aggressive.' Her hand moves to her necklace, telling each bead like a rosary. 'It might be the making of her though. I'd suggest maybe two children. There's Kirsty – a mature child – she has a disabled brother and had to grow up quickly.'

'The other?'

'Maryam. She's very shy. A lovely child, she and Aurora – sorry, *Rory* – should be good for each other.'

George writes the names down and thanks the teacher before going off to Station Street, where he spends a pleasant hour shopping for the party. He also buys a pink safety helmet with sparkly stars – glad that Angie hadn't thought to buy one. It's a nice present and George is impressed with his forethought when he remembers to buy a gift bag to put it in – Pen had always wrapped their presents, but George, aware of his limitations, is satisfied that a bag is easier than wrapping paper and sticky tape.

*

The bike and (by association) the helmet are a great success. The bike has training wheels and Rory wobbles up and down the back path, a huge grin on her face.

Angie is equally delighted. 'I'll take you to the park to practise some more,' she says, winking at George. 'As soon as we put on some birthday clothes. Have to look nice on your birthday.' It's to be a lunch party, and Angie's job is to keep Rory out of the way while George and Shirl prepare the food.

George waves them off and scurries back inside to phone his sister. 'All clear,' he says and minutes later Shirl arrives laden with boxes and bags. *You have to give it to the old Shirl*, he concedes. She could organise a Coronation feast if asked, and love every minute.

'I'll start the balloons,' he tells her as she ties on her apron. It's not long before the huffing and blowing make George so breathless that she suggests he take a break. Set to work on the fairy bread (who could possibly fail fairy bread?), George gloats as he dips the buttered bread in the bowl of sprinkles as he's been shown. By the time he's finished the bread and balloons, Shirl has prepared the oven, set the table with an assortment of goodies, and put the lolly bags aside for later. There are candles for the cake, and paper cups, plates, party hats and whistles at each setting.

'One more thing.' He had almost forgotten. (*Again.* A worry he sets aside for later.) 'Help me with this.' 'This' he unfurls with a flourish. 'Happy Birthday' the sign says, all spelled out with pink and silver glitter. He's glad he paid the extra couple of dollars for the nicest sign. It isn't every day he gives a party. If only Pen could see him now.

The Nguyens and Redgum arrive together at exactly eleven forty-five, followed a few minutes later by Kirsty and Maryam, whose mother, to George's surprise, is wearing a hijab. 'She'll be fine,' Shirl assures each of the mothers, as she ushers the children inside.

Once more George finds himself watching his sister with amused admiration. Thank goodness it isn't down to him – the welcoming, the reassuring. He fiddles with the lolly bags, straightens the chairs and looks at his watch. Rory should be back in a few minutes. His stomach churns and rumbles. What if it turns out badly? What if the children fight, or one of them falls off the swing, or hates the food? Do Muslims eat fairy bread? What if Rory becomes *aggressive* – as Ms Hamilton said she could be? What if she falls off her bike and ends up in hospital?

He's distracted by the sight of Redgum drinking a paper cup of lemonade. George catches Shirl's eye and indicates his friend with a jerk of his head. 'That's something I never expected to see.'

'More's the pity.' Shirl leavens her remark with a smile. 'Don't be nervous, now – it'll be fine.'

It is fine. The finest thing to happen in a very long time. 'Surprise!' they all shout as the birthday girl, like a sudden flame, comes rocketing down the passage. It isn't just the red pants and orange top Shirl has given her – under the flying hair, her face is alight in a way George has never seen before.

The other two children rush over with their presents and they all whisper and giggle as little girls are supposed to do. They take turns on the swing, the bike and Redgum's broad back as he gallops and snorts his way around the yard. *Giddyup*, they call. *Giddyup ol' horse.*

Shirl is checking the oven when Bree arrives. George answers the door to a woman older than he had imagined, dressed in black with complicated earrings and a panther tattooed on her left breast, most of which is visible, along with its unadorned mate, above the deep and unnerving vee of her T-shirt. 'Bree?' George steps aside and is rewarded with a distracted smile.

She's closer to forty than thirty, he surmises, taking in the small face, with fine, regular features that have become brittle with time and circumstance. Bree is the sort of woman, he thinks, who inevitably invites the opinion that she 'must have been quite pretty when she was young'. Now, her thick black hair scraped up in a ponytail, she flaunts a shabby sort of glitter that touches him. There's something gallant, even courageous, in her demeanour, and George, recognising a lack in himself, has always admired those qualities in others.

Directed to the backyard, Bree hands Rory her present, a set of flavoured lipsticks and false fingernails of various hues. They are clearly designed as toys, but Shirl purses her lips and Mrs Nguyen frowns. Unaware of elderly disapproval, the children fall upon these treasures, squealing with delight.

'There's enough nails for everyone,' Angie says as she and Bree apply the lipstick. The fingernails, Shirl tells them with obvious relief, are attached via a plastic sleeve and not glue. Redgum, and Mr Nguyen, who had been in charge of the swing, look crestfallen at the children's defection and hang about, hands in pockets, shuffling their feet in the pine-bark.

'Party time. Come and wash your hands.' Shirl's tone is so authoritative that Redgum scurries along to the bathroom with the children, who, divested of their nails, are soon tucking into the party food.

'Haven't had this since I was a kid.' Redgum is on his fourth slice of fairy bread.

'Made it meself,' George replies. 'Not hard if you got the knack. You don't sprinkle it on the bread, you just spread them on a plate and ...'

But Redgum has moved on to the party pies.

'Ooh!' The cake appears, shaped like a butterfly, with pink-and-white wings.

Rory glows. 'My Aunty Shirl made the cake,' she tells her friends. 'She can make any cake you like. For shops and rich people and everything.'

While waving aside this embellishment of her skills, Shirl preens at her unexpected promotion to Aunty. 'I'm glad you like it, dear,' she says, smoothing her skirt with an embarrassed smile. She leans over to George. 'Just fancy – Aunty Shirl! She's really quite a sweet child when you get to know her.' She claps her hands for attention. 'Time to light the candles now. You can do the honours, Redgum.'

'Happy birthday,' they sing. 'Happy birthday, dear Rory.'

George, singing along with tuneless gusto, feels his chest expand with goodwill. All the parties he never had. All those gifts ungiven. All those unsung 'Happy Birthdays'. His own sense of deprivation melts away in the all-engulfing blaze of Rory's joy. He looks across at Angie, who gives him a delighted thumbs-up.

Mrs Nguyen wraps pieces of cake in paper napkins for Rory to give to her guests, then helps Shirl with the dishes, while Mr Nguyen takes charge of the rubbish. George sees Redgum to the door, picking his way through wrapping paper and balloons.

'You did good, mate,' the big man says. 'She won't forget today.'

'Me neither.' They're both a bit misty. 'Have you got your cake and lolly bag?'

'Yep. And Shirl gave me some leftover sausage rolls.'

'See ya, then. And thanks.'

'No worries.'

When George returns, Angie and Bree are smoking in the backyard. They're certainly animated. He watches the emphatic gestures and thrusting shoulders, amused when Mr Nguyen, rubbish bag in hand, sidles past them, looking alarmed. When Bree has clearly had enough, she throws down her cigarette and grinds it under her heel. Swinging around, she spots George and tosses her head, lips tight. Leaving Angie sulking, she says her goodbyes and gives Rory a swift hug. 'Happy birthday, sweetie.' Then she vanishes, trailing storm-clouds neither she nor Angie see fit to explain.

By bedtime, the birthday girl is tired and cranky and Angie is subdued. 'Bath time,' she says. And for once, brooks no argument.

By the time George goes in to say goodnight, Rory is curled up in her sleep position, her doggie slipper joined by the shaggy purple elephant Maryam gave her.

'There you are, birthday girl.'

'Goodnight, George.'

'Goodnight, love. Did you like your party?'

'It was the best party ever in the whole world.'

'Can't say fairer than that.'

George switches off the overhead light. The fairy night-light, a present from the Nguyens, suffuses the area with a benign glow. Angie, on velvet feet, steps into the room, and he lingers to watch her kiss her daughter goodnight, to listen to her murmur as she strokes the little girl's head. They make a pretty picture, mother and child. For a fleeting moment, the woman in the shadows is Pen, the small figure in the bed, their Annie. George swallows hard. It's his fault that there's no Annie or Eddie or Jeff. He should have let Pen go. Left her to become the mother she was meant to be.

*

Penny! Having entrusted his shame to Redgum that night in the pub, George was mortified by his mate's reaction. True, Redgum wasn't married. But surely he could understand that Penny's request was not only unreasonable, but deeply hurtful?

So George felt twice-abandoned and, as he left the pub, the words 'a good woman, your missus' took on an annoying rhythm in his head, like the first song of the morning that embeds itself for the day. He even felt his steps adjust to the beat as he turned off into the park. *Good woman, your missus* – tum TUM tum tum te tum. He tried to distract himself with 'Waltzing Matilda', but somehow each note curled around the words he wanted to ignore.

Good woman, your missus.

Good woman, your missus.

So why has she left you,

You undeserving cur?

Where did that come from? George, head down against the wind, hands in pockets, strode beyond the beat, beyond the melody, beyond the meaning, until he reached his front door. Stepping inside, he felt the indifference of an empty house. No cooking smells. No music playing. And the underlying reek of dirty dishes. When he awoke the next morning, the *thrum-thrum* of the beat with its accusatory refrain continued to march through his head. He sat up. 'Okay. Give a man a break.'

George switched on the kettle and rolled up his sleeves before running hot water into the sink. Arms plunged into the fresh suds, he scrubbed at the caked-on food, dried and put away the dishes, then took out the broom.

Sweeping up the crumbs and fluff, he was forced to face the fact of the letter, still lying under the table. It was grimy, but the phone number was just legible. George picked it up as though it might explode. He held it away from his body, between two fingers, this scrap of paper that had come between him and his wife. It was the hardest thing he had ever done, but he went out to the hall, lifted the receiver and dialled the number.

'Doctor Fraser's office.'

'An appointment,' he said. 'I need an appointment.'

*

Despite the orthopaedic mattress and feather doona, George's bed had exuded a chill, an unyielding negation that blew in with the cold wind of Penny's death. Without her warm, sleepy presence, neither his mind nor his body could truly rest. The night after the party, however, he falls asleep as one might fall into a mass of sweet, powdery marshmallows. He experiences a liberating lightness – not flying, but he is no longer subject to gravity. And all around, the cloud-like sweetness, enfolding and protecting him. On Rory's birthday, he had ventured beyond his own pain and bent all his energies to making her happy. Rewarded with a good night's sleep, he wakes up refreshed and full of zest for the coming day.

He makes his way to the kitchen and is surprised to find an envelope on the table. His name is written across the front in large, childish handwriting that he recognises right away. Why would Angie leave him a note? A sense of foreboding prevents him from opening it and he puts it back down again. *I'll make a cuppa, then read it.*

His morning cup of tea is like a warm-up for the day's activities, and George shakes his head and even smiles at the complete unfoundedness of his fears. *Probably a thank you for the party.* Ignoring the improbability of this explanation, he takes out his reading glasses and tears open the letter.

Hi George Forgot to tell you I got the sack. Amp and me are of to do some fruit picking the pay is good and well come back for Rory in a coupple of months. You got my mobile if you have to ring. Awsome party. Tell Rory Ill see her soon. Thanx Angie ☺xxxx

It can't possibly say what I think it says. George reads and rereads the letter. It's clear enough. Angie has sailed off for

God knows how long and left Rory in his care. What on earth will he tell the kid? For some reason (one he can't fathom for the life of him), Rory loves her mother. He recalls the extravagant present, the party, the extra-tender goodnight. Angie knew she was going days, maybe weeks ago. Yesterday was a salve to her conscience. The argument with Bree – he'd bet his life's savings on the reason. Bree was trying to talk Angie into staying.

The clock strikes seven and George, elbows on the table, puts his head in his hands. Rory will be awake any minute. What on earth should he tell her?

'Mummy had to go to work early today,' he improvises as she gives him a sleepy smile. 'She might have to work late tonight, too,' he adds. 'They're very busy at her work.'

Rory accepts the news without comment. 'It's time to get dressed,' she says. 'I want to get to school early and play with my friends.'

*

Angie is drinking coffee in a roadhouse a hundred kilometres down the highway. Last night, as she packed her things, she almost weakened. It had nothing to do with Bree and all that garbage she went on with after the party. No. It was the party itself. She and George had never had a birthday party and it was like they were sharing something special. Something nice and normal. Almost like she was living in somebody else's luckier life.

Despite this, she'd left Mercy Street before dawn and crept around the corner to meet an impatient Amp revving up his bike. Climbing on behind him, she felt daring and romantic – like on a TV show. No regrets. In her own way, she'd said goodbye to Rory last night and as for George, well, he had the note. When someone as cool as Amp wants you to be with him, you have to jump at the chance. Angie has no illusions about her attractiveness and wonders what he sees in her. Must be the sex. She's good at that.

She loves Rory. Of course she does. But the kid has been around forever, or so it seems. *I just need a bit of time to have some fun*, a plaintive voice bleats in her head. *I'm owed.*

8

It's been a difficult morning, what with Angie's letter and all, but George notes with pleasure that Kirsty and Maryam are waiting for Rory at the school gate.

'Goodbye, sweetheart.'

Busy with her friends, Rory offers a brief wave, then disappears into the muddle of children, leaving her 'Poppy' in turmoil.

Sooner or later (probably sooner, if he faces it squarely), Rory will have to know that her mother has gone. 'A couple of months,' he mutters, feeling his stomach lurch at the thought. Angie's promises are slippery and her sense of time hazy at best. A couple of months could mean anything. Forever, even. Angie's a good enough kid, but she has no sense of responsibility, so it's quite possible that she would mean to come back, but weeks, months, even years might pass before she got around to it.

His agitation is such that he walks past his house and on to the park. His heart begins to thump in a way that seems ominous. What if he has a heart attack? He brightens at the prospect. Someone else will have to sort it all out – not such a bad thing. Lets him off the hook. He tries to conjure up central chest pain but salvation-by-coronary eludes him.

Sitting on a bench, he watches some Indian mynahs fighting over a half-eaten hamburger, and a man and woman in green overalls trimming the shrubbery. A bus rumbles by behind him and a plane flies almost directly overhead. People, birds, buses, planes – all with somewhere to go and something to do. Busy. Busy. And here he is, wishing for a heart attack to escape even thinking about what he must do. The mynahs fly away as a woman comes down the path with a dog straining at its leash. George checks his watch. Maybe he should call in on Redgum, despite the fact that after so many years of friendship he has been to his mate's house only twice. The pub is their natural habitat, but he can't wait for their normal meeting time. Redgum has a way of seeing through all his bluster and palaver, his ego and his fears. He doesn't say much, but the big man provides a compass that never fails to point in a direction that's straight and true.

Redgum's house, built sometime in the seventies, is an ugly cream-brick. The lawn is mown but patchy and the garden comprises a single gum tree. The hallway, when Redgum answers the door, is bare of pictures, the only furniture being a chair which seems to serve as a hall table. You would have guessed easily enough that this was the house of a man who has always lived alone.

'Is everything okay, mate?' Redgum is startled and stares at George as though he can't quite decide who he is and what he's doing there. Discomposed, he shuffles aside and the two of them stand in the hallway, unsure how to proceed.

'How about an early start?' George suggests. 'I could do with a drink.'

Relieved, Redgum grabs his wallet from the lonely chair. 'You look like you've seen a ghost,' he says, as he locks the door.

They walk to the pub talking desultorily of this and that. There's a protocol to these things – no questions and no confidences until after their first beer. George drags his feet. This is big. Not as big as when he told Redgum that Pen had left him. Not as big as when he shared the news of her cancer. But it's easily the next biggest. Major issue number three in decades of small confidences.

They drink their first beer in silence and wait for the second. George stares moodily into his glass, looking like he needs a nudge to get things going.

'Somethin' on your mind, mate?' Redgum asks.

George is grateful for the opening. 'It's bloody Angie. She's gone off fruit picking. Up and left without so much as a by-your-leave.' He snaps his fingers. 'Just like that.'

'But Rory's just settlin' in. She even started calling me "uncle" after I helped put up the swing.'

'You don't get it, mate. It was Angie who left. Rory's still with me.'

Redgum gives a long, low whistle. 'Wotcha gonna do?'

George doesn't know. That's why he's talking to Redgum. 'I suppose I should take her to social services, or the police, or even the Salvos.' He shakes his head. 'Then it'll be foster care for sure. They'll send her to complete strangers when I ...'

Redgum waits for him to complete the sentence but George remains tongue-tied. 'When you ... ?'

'When I'm practically family. She calls me "Poppy George".' (Only at school-times, but that's a technicality George chooses to ignore.)

'You're attached to the kid,' Redgum tells him.

'Am a bit.'

'Let me get this straight. Her mum left her with you. Not social services or the cops?'

'No. She left her with me, all right.'

'Well, then.'

They finish their beers and walk down the street together, kicking idly at the autumn leaves until their paths diverge.

'Thanks, mate.' As usual, Redgum has articulated, in that abridged way of his, what George has known all along. It will be his job to look after Rory until her mum comes back. She'll be a burden in some ways, but he remembers an old text, one of Reverend Thomas's favourites. *My yoke is sweet and my burden light.* He experiences a disconcerting hotchpotch of inadequacy, excitement and trepidation. And an overwhelming need to protect. He feels, in fact, all those things he may have felt as a young father had he been able to look into the soft, baby face of his never-born Annie.

He returns to his house with a lot of thinking left to do. True, the major decision has been made, but how will it work in the real world of snoopy teachers and social workers – his own sister for that matter? He makes a sandwich and a pot of tea and takes them out to the table in the small courtyard he had made for Pen. Frowning at the flower pots, he makes a mental note to water them. There are so many things that just happened when Pen was alive.

As he puts down his plate and mug, he notices the flaking paint. He'd promised to do that for her. She was going to choose a colour. He chips a bit of paint with his thumbnail. Towards the end, she lost interest in things like that, but he can remember when she was always out in the garden, snipping and weeding and watering. This is the place where he feels closest to his dead wife.

He looks up at the scudding clouds. 'Could be in for a bit of rain.' He speaks aloud, but there's no reply. She'd be pleased, though. *There's nothing like rain for a garden.* That's what she would have said. He can almost see her there, in that old checked shirt, hands on hips, admiring her camellias.

Am I doing the right thing? Will I be able to cope? He nearly says *without you* but stops himself. *What would you do, Pen?* Deep down, of course, he knows. Knows exactly what his Pen would do. 'Okay, love,' he says. 'Okay.'

That's 'the what'. Shaking himself back to the specific, George picks up his sandwich. The 'how' requires more tactical thinking. He has to get things straight in his head. *So what next, Just-Penny?*

Write it down.

Always the organised one, he thinks with affection. Leaving his half-eaten sandwich, he goes back inside for a

142

notebook and pen. First the heading – 'Rory'. He underlines the word and writes the figure one. After some thought, he lists the questions that have been worrying him the most.

1. When should I tell Rory?
2. Should I tell her the truth?
3. What about the snoopy do-gooders?
4. How to tell Shirl?

If her mother was only going to be gone a few days, he might get away with the busy-at-work thing. There's a treat he'd been planning but hasn't got around to – he's going to join Rory up at the local library. *Tell her after that*, he decides, drawing a frame around the first question and underscoring the key word with two heavy black lines. So that's 'the when', but 'the what' is a lot harder. He imagines them sitting on the couch with one of those nice picture books and a Choc Wedge. *Mummy had to go away for a while.* Not *away with Amp.* He won't mention Amp. *She's going to get some money so you can have a nice place to live when she comes back. While she's gone, I'll look after you and we'll have a great time going to the library and riding your bike in the park.* Once he gets started, the words come easily.

So far, so good. His next problem (a more difficult one, in practical terms) is social services and the school. *We won't tell anyone that Mummy had to go away for a bit. We'll tell them ...* What could he tell them? Not the truth, that's for sure. *Her mum's run off with a bikie.* He might as well send her to a foster home as let that cat out of the bag. Social services had taken him and Shirl a couple of times. What's more, they'd split them up. His foster parents were good people, but he'd missed his own home, his mother and sister, and even in some strange way, his father. He had been a boy who disliked change and fretted himself ragged until they decided it was safe enough to send him home.

No foster care for our little girl, he promises the figure by the camellias. The rain, which has been threatening all day, begins to patter on the iron roof. *Thanks, Pen.* He takes a last look at her garden. Although he still has no strategy, he goes inside confident in his determination to keep Rory safe with him.

*

'Why are we going this way?' Rory (she's sharp all right) sees they're taking an unexpected turn.

'When I was a schoolboy,' George tells her, 'one of my favourite places was the library. So I thought we might go and borrow some books.'

'Silly old George. The library's at school.'

'Ah, but there's one even bigger than the one at your school,' George says, 'with more books than you've ever seen.'

When they arrive, George fills in a membership form and the librarian directs them to the children's section. Rory and George look greedily at the shelves crammed with books of all sizes. Some are facing cover out, offering an enticing glimpse of what to expect inside. So many books. So many stories.

They choose seven. 'One for each night of the week,' George says. 'Then we can come back for more.' He hands her the books. 'Now I need to get a couple for me.' His eyes slide around the older children's section and there they are. New editions of Biggles. Without even looking at the titles, he slips two of them in among the picture books. In the adult section he finds an interesting-looking account of life on an Antarctic station and a Wilbur Smith he hasn't read.

He puts the pile of books on the check-out desk and the librarian raises her eyebrows. 'I'm not sure that Biggles is the right book for your granddaughter.' George ducks his head and she grins. 'Oh, I see. Enjoy.'

*

Spaghetti finished, it's time for a Choc Wedge and a story. Rory riffles through her pile of books and finally chooses *Orville: The Owl Who Was Scared of the Dark*. George calls on the spirit of Penny and reads with as much expression as he can muster. He does rather well, too, because Rory chuckles in all the right spots and then demands a repeat. Gratified, George obliges.

'... and Orville looked up at his friend the moon and knew he would never, ever be scared again.'

'One more time.'

George closes the book. 'Not yet. I've got something to tell you first.' He puts a tentative arm around her shoulder and she snuggles into his chest. It seems as though she belongs there. (*Don't get all sentimental, George.*) Swallowing, then clearing his throat, he begins. 'Now listen to me carefully, sweetheart. Mummy had to go away for a little while.'

'Will she be back tomorrow?'

'A bit longer than that. But,' he adds, as her lip begins to tremble, 'she's going to get some money so you can have a nice house to live in when she comes back.'

'We live *here*. This is nice. I don't want to go to another house.' She pulls away and he recognises the signs of an impending storm. Red face, clenched fists, green eyes smouldering to black.

Don't set her off, he pleads with himself as he launches into his spiel. 'Another house is a long way off,' he blathers, 'but while Mummy's gone, I'll look after you and we'll have a great time. We can go to the library every week and … and you can ride your bike in the park every day.'

She withdraws into her own world then. George has noticed this happens when something really affects her. When she screams and cries there is always an element of artifice. To a greater or lesser degree, it's a performance. But when she goes quiet, it means she's troubled, a reaction George fully understands. He's alert to the sound of her breathing and has her puffer to hand, just in case.

Patting her shoulder, he reassures her. 'Mummy loves you and she'll be back before you know it. In the meantime … Do you know how to keep a secret?'

Big-eyed, she nods.

'We won't tell anyone Mummy has gone. It'll be our secret.' George lowers his voice for effect and Rory looks impressed.

'Can I just tell Maryam and Kirsty?' she whispers.

'No one,' George says. 'Except maybe Slipper Dog and Elephant. Because they can't tell anyone else.'

To his surprise, this makes sense to Rory, who runs off to prepare for bed, shouting, 'If you're good, I'll tell you a secret, Slipper Dog. And Elephant, too, if you're extra-good.' She turns to George, who has followed her. 'Elephants have nice big ears for secrets.'

But George is trembling and it takes some time before he can go in and kiss her goodnight. She's lying on her back, eyes wide open. 'Mummy will be back soon, won't she, George?'

'Before you know it,' he assures her. Not believing it for a minute.

*

When he's certain Rory is asleep, he tries Angie's mobile again. (He has tried all day without success.)

This is Ange. Sorreee. You'll have to ring back.

George's body is rigid with anger and he grinds out his message through clenched jaws. 'This is George. Talk to me, you ...' He pauses. There's no point in abusing her. She might never ring back. 'Think of Rory,' he says, sounding weaker than he wants to be. 'She ...' The phone cuts out. 'Shit!' He swears; he paces the kitchen; he sets upon a futile search for a cigarette. All because there is no other way to release his feelings.

Energy expended, he slumps on the couch with a beer. In some ways, he has to acknowledge that he doesn't want

Angie to return anytime soon. He and Rory are capable of getting on perfectly well without her. He takes a swig from his can and jiggles his leg, absent-mindedly patting his shirt pocket. He hasn't felt such a need for a cigarette since Penny was diagnosed.

So does he want Rory to himself, and if so, why is he so angry with her mother? He has calmed down sufficiently to look at it straight. His anger is not on his own behalf, but Rory's. Abandoned on her fifth birthday. Kids and parents belong together. He, George, is one better than a foster parent, but her mother is her mother and that's the truth of it.

He's so weary. It's been a big day. Perhaps Angie will ring tomorrow and he can explain that Rory is her responsibility. He's more than happy to help, but (the argument just goes round and round) he isn't her parent.

On the way to bed, he picks up *Biggles Secret Agent* but puts it down again. He isn't in the right frame of mind to revisit his boyhood hero, so he spends some time in the Antarctic wastes before settling down to sleep. If Angie doesn't contact him tomorrow … what? What if she never contacts him? All at once he's wide awake, twitching and turning as he wrestles with an elusive Plan B. He feels his wheeze coming on and reaches for his puffer. Outside, an owl hoots a long, sorrowful note that stretches all the way to the newly sliced moon.

*

Returning home after taking Rory to school the next day, George sees the light flashing on his answering machine.

'You have one new message,' the robotic voice informs him. 'Message received today at eight-fifty-one.'

Of course it's Angie. 'Hi, George. Sorry I missed you. Catch you later. Love to Rory. By-eee.'

George clicks his tongue in disbelief. She rang at eight-fifty-one — perfect timing as she knows damn well. He returns her call and isn't surprised to find the phone switched off. But she won't get away with that. Tomorrow he'll be home between eight and nine-thirty. He'll ask someone else to take Rory to school. Redgum? No. A strange bloke is likely to cause alarm and unnecessary prying. Shirl? He baulks at that, concluding nevertheless that he needs a respectable grandmotherly type, like his sister, but less nosy.

When he goes outside, Mrs Nguyen is checking the mail. 'Morning, Mrs Noo-win.'

'Hello. Very nice,' she smiles, waving at the blue sky.

Mr Nguyen wanders out, and between the three of them, George's request is understood.

'Yes. Yes.' Mrs Nguyen's tiny, wrinkled face beams up at him. She's delighted with the idea of taking the little girl to school. 'Tomorrow we go.'

Pressed, George accepts a cup of green tea. (It's the least he can do in the circumstances.) They sit on the back verandah, a mirror image of his own, and instead of straining to make conversation, look out at the veggie patch and the trees beyond, their skin tingling with the frost that is soon diffused by a pale, wintry sun. There's a stillness in his companions that George absorbs without effort. He's never been any good at small talk – at keeping the conversational ball in play. Never got the hang of conviviality, animated discussion, or the easy exchange of confidences. Since Pen's death, he has kept himself to himself and, with the exception of a beer with Redgum and Shirl's popping in, he has all but forgotten the consolation of simple companionship.

He takes his leave with reluctance, accepting a small bag of apples straight from the tree. 'Tomorrow school,' his neighbours promise. 'Not late. Early.'

*

Gotcha! George picks up the phone at exactly eight-fifty-three.

'Oh.' Angie sounds startled. 'Hello, George.'

'Hello? Is that all you've got to say? Where the hell are you?'

She's all sulky and droopy. He can hear it in her voice. 'Just rang to see how Rory is.'

'Strange time to choose.'

'Yeah. No. Anyway, how is she?'

'Missing her mother, if you must know.'

'Yeah. Well. I'll be home in a few weeks.'

'A few ...'

The phone goes dead. George stares into the receiver as though, like an evil genie, the young woman might suddenly emerge. The immensity of her cheek! The breath-taking negligence! It's true what he told Angie. Rory is missing her, but as yet the kid has no idea of the seriousness of her plight. She went to bed last night believing that when she woke up, she'd find her mother flopped in an untidy sprawl in the bed opposite hers. How many nights before she realises she's been all but abandoned? For Rory's sake, he needs to find Angie but guesses that there'll be no more phone calls. Not on his terms, anyway.

Shaken, he stands by the bench, phone dangling at his side. Somewhere, in the soft jumble of his thoughts, is a hard core of understanding that he can touch only briefly before recoiling from its heat. He enjoys playing 'Poppy', but this isn't a game. A little girl is without a mother. He's not sure of his legal position, but the moral imperative is undeniable.

He begins to wipe down the bench, absently catching the toast crumbs in his hand. Then something familiar – a burgeoning dread that clutches at his stomach and sets it roiling in that alarming way it has in times of stress. Miserable as all hell, he sits hunched on the lavatory seat and a thought comes from out of the blue (or maybe from a god kinder than the one he had experienced so far). *Bree.* She is the one person he can think of who might know Angie's whereabouts. But he has no idea where she lives. Perhaps Rory will remember. It's unlikely, but he reels in hope on a slender thread and feels his stomach begin to settle.

Happy to have a plan, he goes outside to cut some of Pen's camellias for Mrs Nguyen. Funny how he still refers to Pen's roses, Pen's camellias. He probably always will. He soon has a nice bunch of just-opened buds. As Shirl is fond of saying, a small thank-you gesture never hurt anyone.

*

High on speed and freedom, Angie clings to Amp's broad back as trees and houses and pylons flash by. The fruit-picking didn't work out. Nothing much needs picking in May. Not that it matters. In a couple of weeks she'll be eligible for Newstart Allowance again – and anyway, Amp seems to have plenty of cash. That motel they stayed in last night must've cost a packet.

'Love you, babe.' She mutters this in his ear, knowing he can't hear her. Of course she doesn't really love him – and Amp isn't the sort to appreciate the sentiment. She just likes to be able to say it.

George had said that Rory misses her. Well, maybe that's a good thing. Maybe she'll appreciate her mother a bit more. It won't be always *George does this* and *George says that*. All the time George. It really pisses her off, that does.

9

In the three weeks since her mother left, Rory has been subdued. The after-school chatter all but dries up. She creeps around the house, eats her veggies without protest and it seems that every time George turns around, there's a small, anxious figure hovering nearby. She even waits for him outside the toilet, a habit he finds disconcerting, to put it mildly. Her upturned face looks as it had when he first met her. Eyes strained and mistrustful. Mouth tight with worry. *The face of a forty-year-old*, George thinks with real pain.

The situation has him on edge. If only she'd let him alone for a bit. Of course the kid is scared that he'll go away just like her mother – even he can see that. But what can he do about it? And why should it be his problem, anyway? The novelty of sole parenthood is beginning to lose its lustre.

One Friday, last to come down the school steps, Rory looks so miserable that George is alarmed. Recognising the inadequacy of his response, he can do no more than take her hand and remind her that there's a new packet of Choc Wedges at home.

She scuffs the dust with her shoe. 'Not hungry.'

She does look a bit feverish. 'Aren't you feeling well?'

'I'm all right.'

George takes her hand. 'Let's go, then.'

When they get home, she goes into her bedroom, leaving George to fret in the kitchen. He waits a jittery half hour, then knocks on the door. 'Can I come in?'

She's curled up on the bed with Slipper Dog and Elephant. 'Is Mummy coming back tonight?' She remains facing the wall and her voice is tentative, so soft it's almost as though she doesn't want him to hear.

Poor little bugger. She knows well enough. 'Mummy rang this morning,' he tells her. 'She was sorry she missed you.' He extemporises. 'She sent you a big cuddle and a kiss and said she was missing you lots and … um, lots.' George is silent a moment, listening. There it is. The asthmatic wheeze, sawing away in her chest. 'Where's your puffer?'

George strokes her back as she inhales the Ventolin. 'Take it easy, love. There we go. I'm here.' Thank God he was with her when it started. You hear of children needing hospitalisation when it goes on for too long. Never been that bad himself, but he understands how close you come to panic when each breath is a prize so hard-won. And she's just a kid. A five-year-old kid that he's now responsible for.

After a time, her breathing returns to normal, but George is shaken more than he cares to admit. The awful 'what if?' never really leaves him after that.

Colour (such as it is) returns to her cheeks but she still needs to rest. How better than with a story? So he reads her *Richie Finds a Bone*, watching her face as the story unfolds. That dreamy concentration, that living-in-the-pages sort of look – a visible manifestation of his own experience of reading. 'So the museum gave Richie a gold medal and twelve packets of Doggie Treats because it was the biggest dinosaur bone they had ever seen.'

He closes the book. 'Maybe we can go to the museum one day and have a look at the dinosaur bones. Would you like that?'

'Can Mummy come?'

'It can be a surprise.'

After dinner, she prepares for bed then comes to sit beside him with her backpack. 'George?'

Such a troubled whisper. 'Yes, love?' He hopes he sounds reassuring.

'Ms Hamilton gave me a letter for Mummy and I don't know what to do.'

So that's what she's been fretting about. With an uncertain gesture, she produces a crumpled piece of paper and gives it to him.

'Dear Parent,' he reads. 'Because of parent–teacher interviews, there will be no classes on Thursday, 14 June. Please complete the attached form and you will be allocated one of your preferred times. If possible, please leave the evening timeslots for working parents. Kind regards, Jessica Hamilton.'

'I'll take care of this. Off you go and I'll come and read you another story.' His reading aloud is beginning to rival Pen's. While Rory scampers off, he fills in the form. *If Angie's not back, I guess I'll have to be Mother for a day.* He finds a fresh envelope for the form and puts it in Rory's bag.

'Okay now?' he says, as he goes in to check that she's settled. 'Good-oh. What say we have that Richie story again? And—' He so wants to make her happy. 'This is due back at the library soon. What if I buy you your own *Richie Finds a Bone* book?'

*

Finding Bree's address is so easy, George nearly cries with relief. On the way to school the next day, he asks Rory if she can remember where Bree lives.

'In my pocket,' she says. 'Aunty Bree wrote her house for me in case I get lost.' She takes out a piece of cardboard with an address written in bold black letters. 'Bree Roberts, 25 Mill St Northcote'. *Not far at all.* George slips the small square into his own pocket.

'Give it back. It's mine.' Her voice is shrill with panic. 'What if I get lost?'

Startled, he takes in the stricken face, the brimming tears. 'Here,' he says, tucking it back in her pocket. 'So you always remember to take this? Every single day?'

She looks at him as though he's stupid. 'It's in case I get lost. Aunty Bree said I had to.'

*

Twenty-five Mill Street. The fence is sagging, the gate needs oiling, but a valiant azalea thrusts its way through compacted soil, defying, in its soft, curling blooms, all known laws of horticulture. The porch has been swept, and despite the dirty glass panels, the front door shows signs of recently applied paint. Sporadic, *effortful* effort.

As he steps up to the door, his tradesman's eye spots blisters and bristles in its bruised surface. *A bit like my face after a big night out.* Not that he has big nights out anymore. To be honest, he'd never had many of those at all. When he first started work, he gave his mother as much of his wages as he could. Then he married young, and Pen put an end to that sort of thing. He wonders, in a rush of self-pity, what he has missed in such an abbreviated youth, but shrugs off the thought. He had entered his teens ill-educated, directionless and fearful. Would nights out on the booze have corrected any of that? A dash of Dutch courage, maybe, but all the more reason to be fearful. He could have done a lot worse than let Pen shape his life. But now he has lived seventy-seven years, and without warning, he has to not only reshape his own life, but that of a vulnerable child.

Slovenly in pyjama pants and a grey hoodie, Bree squints at her visitor. 'So she did it.'

'Why didn't you tell me?'

Without makeup, she appears even older. Hands in her pockets, shoulders hunched against the morning chill, she regards him with weary eyes. 'I couldn't dob her in.

She's a mate. Besides, I never thought she'd really go.' Her mouth becomes ugly with disgust. 'Amp's a fucking bastard. I swear I'll kill him if he ever comes back.'

The doormat offers a frayed 'Welcome', but none is forthcoming from Bree, who continues to glare at some point over George's shoulder. He coughs. 'Do you mind if I come in?'

'All right.' She steps aside. 'I'm having a coffee. Want one?'

Inside, the house has the same duality as the exterior. Following her down the passage, George passes open doors then averts his eyes, but not before he sees the chaotic bedroom and the dark hole of a bathroom that smells of mould, stale perfume and wet towels. In contrast, the kitchen is shabby but light-filled and clean(ish), with an array of herbs growing in colourful pots on the windowsill. The sugar has hardened in the bowl, and not wanting to offend, George drinks the bitter coffee unsweetened.

'Do you know where she is?'

'No.'

'Would you tell me if you did?'

She hesitates. Pushes at her hair with an angry gesture. Plucks at a thread on her cuff. 'Yeah. Yeah – I would. I thought she cared about her – Rory, I mean. She's a good kid when you get her on-side.'

'She is that.'

'So what're you going to do?' Alarmed all at once, she bangs her mug down on the table. 'Not social services. You're never dobbing her in to social services.'

George is hurt. He'd put that thought away almost as soon as it entered his head. 'Of course not. I'm just going to struggle along for a bit and hope no one finds out.'

Anyone else (except Redgum, that is) would warn him of the consequences of concealing the desertion of a child, but Bree is all approval. 'Good for you, mate. I can give you a hand. You know, if you need one.'

The bitter coffee isn't all to blame for George's grimace. 'Take a good look at me, love. I'm a 77-year-old bloke who's never had a kid of his own. Reckon I might just need a bit of help now and then.'

The sweetness of her smile catches him off-guard.

'What about you come over Friday after school? I could give you a bit of a feed.' He refrains from adding that it looks as though a good feed is just what she needs.

'Done.' She shakes his hand like a man and sees him to the door.

*

His next problem is Shirl and her infernal popping in. He had managed all right when she came on the Monday after the party to pick up her cake tin. That was just a pop-in-pop-out kind of thing – he can handle those. The few times after that were during the day when she wouldn't expect Rory or Angie to be home. But his luck runs out when she arrives shortly before dinnertime on the Friday he's expecting Bree. ('Only popping in for a mo'. I found this nice jumper for Rory.') She stays long enough to accept a grudgingly offered cup of tea.

'So how's Angie's saving going?' A constant theme for Shirl – when would he be rid of the interlopers?

Lying is not George's strong suit and his sister has always been alert to the signs. 'Your eyes go all shifty,' she'd told him once. 'And there's something with the tip of your nose.'

George does his best with his eyes, but what can you do with the tip of your nose? He pulls out his handkerchief. (He's never held with tissues – girly things, tissues.) 'She's working extra hours.' A moment of inspiration. 'That's why she's late tonight.' He looks at his sister over his hanky. She seems satisfied, but with effortless transition turns her questing eyes to the fresh tablecloth and 'good' china.

'Expecting company?' She sniffs the air. 'Roast lamb, if I'm not mistaken. And all your own sister gets is a cup of tea.'

The doorbell. George is spared a reply, but when he comes back with Bree, Shirl does that thing with her eyebrows.

'Yes. We met at the party,' Shirl says in response to George's clumsy introduction. She dumps a plastic shopping bag on the table, with reckless disregard for the good china. 'I hope the jumper fits,' she says, frowning. 'I got it yesterday at the sales. Where is Rory, by the way?'

'Kirsty's mum's dropping her off later. They call it a playdate,' he explains, tossing off this new word with studied nonchalance.

Suddenly aware of the time, George almost pushes his sister down the hall, but not before she does her eyebrow thing again. This time it's accompanied by lips of string.

'A bit of a cow, your sister.'

George bristles. 'Shirl's all the family I got. You can say all you want about me, but Shirl's off limits.'

'Sorry.'

Surprised at his own outburst, George fusses with the roast. 'That'll be Rory. Let her in, will you?'

'Aunty Bree.' Rory bursts into the kitchen, dragging Bree behind her. 'Aunty Bree's here.' She stops. 'Where's Mummy?'

George shuts the oven door, wincing as he straightens his back. 'I told you, sweetheart. Mummy had to go away to work for a while.'

'But Aunty Bree's here.' Turning to Bree, the child repeats her question, this time with a perilous quaver in her voice. 'Where's Mummy?'

'She's had to go away for a bit.' Bree looks to George for guidance. It's not forthcoming.

'But *you're* here.' Rory grabs Bree's hand. 'So why isn't Mummy with you?'

George can't believe his stupidity. As far as Rory is concerned, Bree and Angie are a pair. He had thought a familiar face would cheer the kid up, but all he has done is emphasise her mother's absence. He rubs his chin. This is serious. The kid has gone all quiet and because there's nothing more to say, because he himself needs comforting, he squats down to give her an awkward hug.

'I want Mummy. I don't want to be here anymore.'

'Sweetheart.' But she melts from his grasp, and ignoring Bree, disappears into her bedroom. The small house overflows with the misery of her muted sobs.

Someone has to go to her. George looks at Bree, who looks back at him, eyebrows raised. 'I'll go,' she offers when he doesn't move. 'I suppose you've had a lot of this.'

George is grateful. 'If she starts to wheeze, her puffer's in her schoolbag.'

'No worries.'

Half an hour later, they appear at the table in time for the meal.

With the resilience George has come to admire, Rory tucks into her roast lamb, nattering all the while about Kirsty and Maryam, Ms Hamilton and a boy called Justin who pushes smaller kids off the monkey bars. 'I bit him,' Rory explains. 'He tried to push Maryam.'

''Atta girl.' Rory and Bree high-five and George whoops his approval before remembering that he's now *in loco parentis* and in all likelihood is breaking some parenting rule or other.

'Ms Hamilton mightn't like kids biting other kids.'

Rory's small teeth go to work on a piece of lamb. 'She doesn't know.'

Bree leaves without offering to help with the dishes. What's wrong with young women nowadays? In his day, if they went to someone's house for a meal, Pen always offered to help with the dishes. Even so, he's far from unhappy. After the initial kerfuffle, the visit went off pretty well and Rory was more cheerful than he'd seen her in weeks.

He clears the table, wondering if Angie will get in touch with Bree. Or if she already has, and Bree isn't letting on. He believed her when she said she would tell him if she heard anything. And she seemed sincere when she said that she'd contact a bloke she knew who was going out with Amp's sister's best friend. Good grief! He's falling into the trap of trusting Bree's contacts. It's all too much. George decides to soak the baking dish and have an early night. He's not getting any younger.

*

It was inevitable that Shirl would find out. 'Like a bloody ferret,' George tells Redgum. 'Nothing gets past her.'

As expected, her first response is to berate him. 'What on earth … ? Why ever did you … ? You can't possibly …' Culminating in a self-righteous, 'I told you so.'

'Finished?'

Shirl is taken aback. 'What? What did you say?'

'I asked if you'd finished,' he says. 'You've made it clear what you think, but I need to know what you'll do.'

'Do?'

'I can't do this without help. Angie might never come back. What if social services find out? They'll take her. We both know that.' Their eyes lock. 'You said you'd help earlier on, but this is different. I'm not even sure it's legal.'

Shirl looks frightened then. 'I can't be party to this. You'll have to tell them. You could end up in jail.'

'And Rory could end up in foster care.'

A shadow passes over her face. Then the practical. 'I hope you kept the letter she wrote.'

George scrabbles around in Pen's bits-and-pieces drawer. 'Yeah.' He's both relieved and surprised to find it. It hadn't occurred to him that the letter could be important.

Shirl clicks her tongue. 'Evidence.' (*For what?* he wonders.) 'I'll take it. Really, George. You can't be trusted to look after a piece of paper, let alone a child. Now.' She sits down, plonking a territorial handbag on the table. 'Make me a cup of tea while I think.'

So Shirl, model of integrity and good citizenship, agrees to aid (and abet) her brother, just as he knew she would. Bossy and scolding she may be, but George has known her longer than anyone else alive, and has never lost faith in her good heart. It's a lot to ask – he understands that only too well. Shirl has always hated muddle. You can see that in her grooming, her neat-as-a-pin house, her passion for organisation. But as always, when he needs her, she steps (albeit gingerly) beyond the right angles of her carefully ordered world into this new one of ambiguity and uncertain horizons.

Shirl picks up her handbag and, after presenting her cheek for a kiss, takes her leave.

George watches her retreating figure with renewed affection. Shirl has always been there for him. When he told her of Pen's diagnosis, he cried – it was only with his sister that he could reveal the full extent of his terror. 'Six months, Shirl. Maybe twelve with chemo.'

Shirl cried along with him. It had been many years since their awkward first meeting, but Shirl had come to love Pen. True, she could get a bit stroppy with her at times, but only as you would a younger sister. 'Penny's been good to the girls and to me,' she told her brother. 'And you, too. Let me take my turn.'

George didn't know what she meant but soon understood. Of course she cooked and baked and shopped for them, but so did Pen's sister and many of their friends. Shirl, however, went one step further. He remembers her wrapped in a large apron, cleaning away vomit and body waste as Pen became weaker and weaker. 'Go away,' Shirl would say. 'This is women's business.'

'You can come in now. I'm making her pretty for you.' With a lump in his throat, he watched the tenderness with which his sister took Pen's thin limbs and washed them down with lavender water. Then she'd wrap the sick woman's poor naked head in a bright scarf and add a bit of lipstick. Sometimes he'd see the two women laughing together. It did them all good to hear Pen laugh.

He'd never have managed by himself. Thanks to Shirl, Pen was able to die in her own home. George rinses the teacups, chastened as he always is when reminded of his sister's gift to them.

*

On the day of the parent–teacher interviews, Shirl agrees to mind Rory and briefs him on what to expect. 'Now don't forget your reading glasses,' she says. 'And remember – don't get all hot under the collar if she has anything negative to say about Rory. Although …' Shirl sounds almost affectionate. '… I must say the child has greatly improved since I first met her.'

'I was hoping to see Rory's mother.' Ms Hamilton, petite and pretty, stands up as George sidles into the room.

'Her mother had to go away for a bit. Her gran's not too good and she's got no one else.' Would this smart young woman swallow that? He and Shirl had colluded to devise the story and it seemed good enough at the time. But to George's hyper-sensitive ears, it has a very dodgy ring to it.

Murmuring vague sympathy, the young teacher sits down, indicating another chair for George. So he sits, hands dangling between his knees as though he's about to be punished for not doing his homework. *It's not my fault*, he hears his young self say. *Dad was shouting all night and Mum made us go to our room. My books were in the kitchen. It's not my fault.*

But no. The young woman (surely too young to be a teacher) is talking about Rory. 'She was becoming more settled in recent times. Then she seemed to regress. That must have been around the time her mother had to go away.'

George nods. A dumb show. What's he expected to say?

'I'll be sending home her first real reader soon. I believe you've been taking her to the library, too. I wish more parents would do that. A love of books is so important when a child is learning to read.'

Praise. From a teacher. George grins in a lunatic sort of way and nods again.

'So,' Ms Hamilton persists. 'Please make sure she reads the marked pages when she comes home from school. Every night without fail. More than once, if you have the time. I can't stress this enough.'

Another burst of nodding.

'I was wondering ...' She pauses, uncertain whether to proceed. 'Mr Johnson, we're starting a parent-reading program – where parents come to the school to hear the children read. So many of them work that it's difficult to find enough volunteers.' Another pause. 'I understand you're retired.' This on a rising cadence.

Is she asking me to help with the reading? 'You need volunteers?'

He tries to sound casual when he tells Shirl, but can't wipe the smirk from his face.

'It turns out they need someone to help with the reading. I'm doing Tuesday mornings.'

Shirl is warm in her approval. 'Good for you.'

Even more gratifying, Rory is so excited that, as soon as she gets to school, she shouts her news across the schoolyard. 'Kirsty. Maryam. My Poppy George is going to be a reading mum.'

*

George climbs into bed feeling pretty pleased with himself. Shirl is more or less on-side, Ms Hamilton seems to believe his story and Rory has been more settled and not so clingy in the last few days. Angie has been gone over four weeks and he feels that he's handled things remarkably well. He switches on his lamp, deciding to reward himself by starting his Biggles book. It's an easier read than he remembers and he's well into chapter eight when he hears a shriek from Rory's room.

'Marmee! George!'

'I'm coming, love.' Still wearing his reading glasses, George stumbles on the rug as he rushes into her room and switches on the light. Rory is sitting up in bed, eyes huge, clutching at Slipper Dog, her skinny chest heaving with great, almost soundless sobs.

'What's the matter?' George, who had been prepared (if necessary) to fight off an intruder, looks around the room.

'The wolves. They want to get in the window.' She flings herself at George. 'They've got red eyes and ...'

George is relieved. 'There are no wolves in Australia,' he says. 'It's just a bad dream. Come on. I'll show you.' He moves towards the window, but she buries her face in his chest. 'No. No. Not the window. They're waiting to get me.'

He puts her down on the bed. 'I'll have a look,' he says, pulling back the curtain. 'No wolves.'

'Stay with me. I'm scared.'

'I'll just go and get my dressing-gown.'

It's after midnight before George is satisfied that he can leave her. *Poor kid.* When he had nightmares as a child (his involved bats, he remembers), his father scoffed and called him 'Mary' and told his mother not to pamper him. So when he was scared, he'd climb into Shirl's bed. She was older and stronger and, she assured him, not the least bit afraid of bats. With these thoughts, George switches off his lamp and settles down to a sleep in which some part of him understands he must remain vigilant.

Night after night, the wolves appear in Rory's dreams and George's problems compound. By seven o'clock, he's already tired and dreads facing the battle now required to get her to sleep.

Rory mounts a go-slow strategy, taking longer and longer to finish her evening meal. After several nights of cajoling, George issues an ultimatum. 'No Choc Wedge unless you finish your dinner in half an hour.' He places the clock in front of her. 'You have to be finished when the big hand is on six.'

Rory is nothing if not resourceful. She earns her Choc Wedge then disappears into the bathroom for another half hour. When no more delay is possible she insists that George wait in her room until she goes to sleep.

'It's eight-thirty, even nine-thirty, before I get some time to myself,' he complains to Redgum. 'Then she wakes up with the nightmares maybe twice a night. I tell you, mate; a bloke is completely buggered by lunchtime.'

'Wolves, you say?'

'With red eyes.'

'Can't blame the kid for being scared.'

'I'm not.' George is hurt that Redgum would even suggest such a thing.

'Shirl'd know what to do, I reckon.'

Redgum is right on the money. But does George want Shirl to know he's not coping? After two weeks of broken sleep, he realises that he no longer cares.

'It's becoming harder and harder to get her to go to bed.' George is in Shirl's kitchen red-eyed and haggard, his voice whiny and aggrieved. 'I mean I try to understand. I used to have nightmares myself when I was a kid. Well, you know that. It's just that I'm not sure how much longer I can cope. I even yelled at her the other night.'

Shirl looks up sharply. 'That's not like you. What did she do?'

'She cried, Shirl. I made a scared little girl cry.'

'Most children have nightmares. Mine did.'

'I bet you didn't yell at them.'

Shirl grimaces. 'Sometimes I wanted to.' She changes her posture from sympathetic to practical. 'In the end, we made them dream-catchers.'

George has no idea what a dream-catcher might be, but the more important question is, did they work?

'Not so much for Marianne, but Claire's certainly did.'

'What do I do?' George is humbled and his sister gives a gratified nod.

'Bill made ours.'

Bill! George swallows hard. 'Would he make me one?'

'No. But he can show you how.'

*

'Now,' George says in what he hopes is an encouraging tone. 'We're going to make a dream-catcher.'

'No.' Rory looks really scared. 'Don't want one.'

'Why ever not?'

Rory looks astonished, as if she can't believe he could be so dim. 'I don't want to catch them. I want to send them away.'

The kid has a point. George tries to explain. 'You make a kind of net and hang it over your bed and the bad dreams get trapped.'

'Above your *head*?' The emphasis on the last word is more like a shriek. 'Your own head?'

'To trap them. They'll be trapped.'

'No way.' Rory folds her arms and channels Shirl. 'It's sheer madness, George.'

George is too tired to be amused. All that time he'd spent with Bill threading bloody beads and drinking non-alcoholic cider. It's enough to drive a man to drink. And it does. He goes to the fridge and settles with a can of beer, while Rory sits glowering at the television.

*

'So much for Shirl's ideas.' After another sleepless night George can barely keep his eyes open and peers at Redgum's figure as it ripples and sways, making him feel slightly drunk.

'Can't say I blame her.'

'Puts me back at square one, though.'

Redgum scratches his chin. 'Send them away. That's what she wants.'

It's at this moment that George, who had never had a creative thought in his life before Rory, invents the

171

scarewolf. 'Like a scarecrow,' he gloats. 'Only it scares wolves.'

Redgum raises his glass in homage. 'You're a genius, George.'

'I'll drink to that.'

By the time he picks up Rory from school, George has assembled all he needs. 'Now,' he says, as she finishes her milk and biscuit. (Milk good. Biscuit bad. He's not perfect.) 'Come outside. We're going to make a scarewolf.' Seeing her frown, he explains, 'Scarecrows scare birds called crows and scarewolves scare wolves. We'll put it right outside your window.'

George has already made the frame out of garden stakes he found in the shed, and Rory helps him stuff his old gardening pants and flannel shirt with wadding he bought from the craft shop. (He knows about the craft shop because he spent twenty dollars there on beads and feathers for the dream-catcher.)

'We have to give him a real mean face,' Rory says. 'Wolves don't scare so easy.'

'Would you like to do it? I've got some special markers.'

So Rory draws a mouth full of sharp teeth, black, red-rimmed eyes and several livid scars across its cheeks and chin. She looks over at George, who shivers in mock terror. 'Wow! Even I'm scared.'

'Now his hat.' George has bought a plastic Viking helmet with horns and he lifts Rory up so she can place it on the scarewolf's head. 'Just you wait, you wolves,' she shouts.

As bedtime approaches, her bravado wanes. 'It will work, won't it, George?'

'In all my born days, I've never seen a wolf go anywhere near a scarewolf,' George replies. 'Now off to bed and I'll be in to read your story in a jiffy.'

That night, there are no wolves. Nor the next night. Or the next. 'They hate scarewolves,' Rory tells Shirl. 'In my born days, I never saw a wolve go near a scarewolf.'

Shirl regards George with something akin to admiration. 'So you solved the problem all by yourself. Who would have thought?'

10

George closes his book. Biggles triumphs yet again. Speaks to him across the years. He sits back and savours the certainty, the *rightness* of his boyhood hero. He had gone to the bookshop to buy some more Richie books for Rory, keeping a promise he had made when she moved from the preparatory level of readers (red) to yellow. So far, she has eight of the series and is making a very good effort to read them for herself. She can pick out quite a few of the words, and now he's a reading mum, he's confident that with his assistance, she'll be reading them in no time at all.

The bookshop owner seemed to know all there is to know about books and George had ventured to ask about Biggles. All it took was a few keystrokes and she had the information he needed. A new presentation set was available, published only last year. A bit expensive, but then when did he last spend money on a treat for himself? 'For my nephew,' he explained to the saleswoman, as he registered the order.

'Of course. Your nephew.' Their eyes met. He knew that she knew but it didn't matter. Elation clutched tight to his chest, he left the shop like the respectable, elderly man that he is. That was a week ago and they rang today to tell him that his order had arrived. He staggered to the car, clutching the heavy box, and unable to wait, devoured the first book along with his lunch.

Three o'clock! And he's still sitting over his lunch dishes. He puts on his jacket and sets off for the school, turning up his collar against the chill wind. Where has the day gone? In recent times, where have any of his days gone? Since Pen died, he had spent every day in the same way – without motivation – stagnating in a morass of futile wishing. Enduring the solitary nights while the hour hand crawled its way up to ten, the time he could go to bed and forget for a little while that she wasn't there beside him. He hadn't thought of it before, but his days then, like a dead battery, were truly *spent*. And his life was no more than the sum of those worn-out, washed-out days.

But now – now that Rory was in his life, the days slipped by like minnows in a river. Like Shirl, he is always 'on the go'. And he enjoys it, this new routine. Sharing breakfast with the pyjama-clad Rory, making her lunch, walking her to school. Staying on Tuesdays for his reading-mum duties. On the other week mornings, he goes next door for a cup of green tea and watches while Mrs Nguyen paints her delicate watercolours or draws with black ink on wash. Mr Nguyen beams with pride at his wife's skill. 'She paint memories,' he tells George. 'See. That her house, the Mekong River, the market-place …'

George understands the longing in the soft colours, the nebulous ink-lines. Memories must be approached with stealth, gathered swiftly and savoured briefly before the 'now', with its insistent colours and sounds, destroy this tremulous communion with the past. Mrs Nguyen reconstructs her past on silk and lives her 'now' with equanimity – a state of grace that George envies and admires, and at times, aspires to.

When there's a child, however, the 'now' is at its most insistent, and after the daily tea ritual, it's time to head for the shops, or start the laundry or any number of the myriad things that having a child entails. He still has a beer with Redgum, but earlier in the day. 'Can't pick the kid up with beer on me breath.'

*

George makes himself a sandwich and a pot of tea and takes it outside to enjoy the early spring sunshine. It's going on four months since Angie left – in no time at all it will be a year since she came to his rescue that day in the lane. Her phone calls are becoming less and less frequent. On the rare occasions he manages to speak to her, Angie is guarded, almost hostile, and while still insisting that she loves and misses her daughter, has given up all pretence of looking for work. 'Need to do me own thing for a bit,' she says. Whining and wheedling. Explaining and excusing.

'I missed out on a lot, having a kid so young.' She sends a postcard from Adelaide and another from Albany. He doesn't show Rory the second one. The Adelaide card (with a picture of the casino – for a child, no less) had brought on another asthma attack and George feels justified in vetting the mail from then on.

It's happening less often, but some nights, out of the blue, Rory asks for the mermaid story – 'the first one about the wings'. Her reaction is always the same. When he's finished she says, 'I wish I had magic wings.'

'That would be great fun.'

'Not for fun, Poppy George.'

Her anxious little face all but breaks his heart. 'You won't need magic wings, sweetheart. She'll be back.'

'Promise?'

'Promise.'

There has been no repetition of the distress caused by Bree's first visit. She comes every Friday, expecting and getting a roast-lamb dinner. She's so thin that George wonders if this is the only square meal she gets all week. Her promised help consists of vague sketches of people who know people, but George has no more illusions on that score. He suspects that Angie is in touch with Bree more often than she lets on. There have been a couple of worrying slips and he's troubled by indications that, for Amp at least, drugs are now (or always have been) part of the picture.

His reverie ends abruptly when he find himself at the school gate and he nods distractedly at the young mothers who greet him with smiles. They probably just see him as a grandfatherly old man. He, however, sees in each of them, the archetypal mother. The mother that all children deserve. The mother Penny would have been. Should have been.

*

Doctor Fraser had been blunt. 'No way to make this easy,' he said. 'Your tests show a very low sperm count. The likelihood of fathering a child is as good as zero.'

As good? Nothing good about it. Shock. Then anger. Finally, despair. It was his fault there was no child. His fault that Pen would never grow and bloom, rub her back with that smug, rueful smile, or hold their baby to her breast. She would continue to act as babysitter, godmother, aunt; to knit bootees and read stories to other people's children. And he would stand back and watch, humble and shamed at the diminished life he condemned her to share.

The Mercy Street house, chosen (it didn't seem so very long ago) with love and hope, was as bleak as it had ever been since Pen left him drunk on the sofa. Too weary to make a meal, George sat in the darkening lounge room and allowed himself to cry. His heart (*Soft as butter*, his mother used to say) was flayed by knowing, and lay in his chest as open and vulnerable as a child's. Slow, fat tears scalded his cheeks. He had cried a lot as a youngster, but one day, after a particularly vicious beating from his father, he found strength enough to suppress the tears. The well from which they sprung was treacherous, but despite this, he was proud to be the obstinate little bastard everyone said he was. At ten, and nearly a man, he couldn't, wouldn't allow tears. Ever. Until now. Now he was twenty-seven years old, sitting in his own home, blubbing like a baby.

Wiping his eyes with the back of his hand, he understood what he must do. It calmed him, making a decision, but as distress drained away it was replaced with a terrible melancholy and his shoulders bowed under its weight.

*

That Tuesday so long ago, George took his blue suit to the dry cleaners. (His only suit – the one he wore at his wedding.) He picked it up on Thursday after work. On Friday night he scorched the collar of his white shirt so on Saturday morning he called at the shops to buy a new one before going to the barbers for a haircut. On Sunday morning he nicked his chin shaving. (His hand was unsteady and he wanted a really close shave.) After staunching the bleed and checking his unusually dapper image in the mirror, he set out at ten o'clock, twenty minutes earlier than he needed to.

Pen had agreed to meet him in the park. (Neutral territory – her sister had advised this.) He was early, and as he approached the park bench, he was surprised to see that she was there already, sitting in that neat, compact way she had, ankles crossed, hands folded in her lap. She wore her navy-blue winter coat, he noticed, and a thick fall of hair obscured her face.

'Pen.'

She looked up. 'George.'

'I've kept you waiting.'

'I was early.'

Their eyes met with startled brevity. George sat down beside her, careful to leave a space between them, his gaze finally settling on her gloveless hands. White knuckles, fingers tightly laced. He wanted to reach over and coax those fingers into repose. 'Thank you for coming.'

She inclined her head but continued to stare at the pond where a mother and toddler were feeding the ducks. 'Sue's picking me up in half an hour.'

Thirty minutes. He'd never had a way with words and had rehearsed what he wanted to say, but sitting there beside her, he failed to regain those careful, measured phrases. 'Pen. I'm so sorry for – everything.' He ventured to look at her again. Saw the thin, serious face; the pallor that accentuated every freckle. 'Look at me. Please.'

Her eyes were troubled and lined with fatigue. He had always thought of them as a soft blue, but realised for the first time, that they were mostly grey, a strange, shifting, sea-storm grey. He had asked her to look at him but could barely meet her gaze. 'I was so wrong. Wrong to—' (he choked on the word) '—*hit* you. I was wrong not to go for the tests.'

She bit her lip.

'Pen. I saw the doctor. It's me. It's me that can't have kids.'

Pen looked away, hair shielding her face. 'Poor George.'

George felt the thrill of her hand over his and thought he might cry with relief. But there was much more to say and he removed his hand in case his hard-won courage evaporated. 'I love you, Pen. I want you to know that.' He had said this so seldom in their married life. (Difficult thing for a bloke to say. Surely she knew. Women always seemed to know these things.) But today there could be no misunderstanding. He licked his lips and continued. 'That's why I have to do the decent thing. I'll give you a divorce. Then you can … find someone else. Someone who can give you babies.' She continued to look at her hands, clenched, now in her lap. With a gesture that was almost timid, he lifted her hair, revealing the long, sharp profile. 'Pen? Do you understand what I'm saying? I'll do whatever I have to. I just want you to be happy.'

'You'd do that for me?' Her voice was unsteady. Tears squeezed out from under her lashes and she shut her eyes for a moment before seeking his. The anguish and love in her face both shamed and heartened him. She touched his cheek. 'You're an honourable man, George.'

'I want to make things right,' he said.

'Walk with me.' They stood up and she took his arm. 'I miss you,' she said.

How could he have let this woman slip through his useless, blundering fingers? 'I miss you, too, Pen. I'll miss you as long as I live.'

She lengthened her stride, away from the lake and the family tableau. 'Do you remember our wedding day?'

'You looked real nice.'

'Thanks,' she said drily. 'But I wasn't fishing for compliments. We promised to stay together "in good times and in bad, till death us do part". You do remember that?'

He squeezed her arm. 'Yes I do.' Those words were engraved on his memory. They'd frightened the bejesus out of him not because he feared being 'tied down' as his mates used to call it. They (he and Pen) had said the unsayable. Even while sealing their pact, they had anticipated surrender to the enemy.

Stopping under a paperbark tree, Pen ran her hand over the soft, grey bark, tearing it off in long strips. 'You say you want me to be happy. Well, I was happy to be your wife. And I could be again. We can't have children. But that loss is not just mine – it's yours, too. We'd have to make a life that's a bit different from what we planned. It can be a good life, though. Just different.' She took his chin, forcing him to face her. 'I'm coming home, but if you ever hit me again …' He started to speak but she stopped him with her eyes. 'I'll leave you for good, George. I swear to that.'

*

It took George some time to broach the question of adoption. But finally he did one evening when they were babysitting Shirl's children.

Pen went to check on them. 'Snug as bugs,' she said, when she came back to the sitting room.

George cleared his throat. 'It's nice to have them to ourselves once in a while.'

182

Pen smiled, but only with her mouth.

It's now or never. 'We've never talked about adoption.'

'Don't imagine I haven't thought of that.'

'So why didn't you say something?'

Pen, it turned out, had a school friend who had become pregnant at seventeen. 'She wanted to keep the baby, but they took it away. She doesn't even know if it's a boy or a girl.' Pen twisted her rings. 'I couldn't take a child whose mother might want it.'

There were all sorts of arguments he could have used, but George knew his wife. This was her final word on the matter and he never raised it again.

II

George enjoys being a reading mum. He begins with four children in his group. (Not Rory. Apparently, it's not considered wise to assist your own child in this way.) After the first few weeks, he is given a fifth child, one who needs extra help.

'You seem to have the patience he needs,' Ms Hamilton says, smiling at him in that charming way she has. 'If you could stay with Joel, say, another half hour each day, I'd be so grateful.'

'No probs.' George has managed his other charges rather well, and has begun to wonder if he might not have made a very good teacher. He decides to start by reading Joel stories. (It makes sense, doesn't it? If you enjoy stories, you're more likely to want to read them for yourself.) Realising that early school readers lack something in the story department, he decides to bring some books from home.

The one-on-one reading takes place in a glass-walled area off the classroom, a space George comes to think of as his. He has begun his program with Joel and it seems to be going rather well. He has no idea what is causing Joel's learning problems, but the boy seems to enjoy their time together.

'So the museum gave Richie a gold medal and twelve packets of ...'

'That's mine!' Rory, face red with rage, snatches up the book and kicks out at George and the hapless Joel. 'I hate you. I hate both of you.'

'What on earth's going on? Rory!' Ms Hamilton flings open the door as Rory swings around.

'I hate you, too,' she sobs, and charges to the door, only to be barred by her teacher.

'Rory. Stop. Listen to me. What do we do when we're angry?'

'We take ten deep breaths.' She doesn't sound convinced.

Her narrow chest is rising and falling and George feels his own heart beating in time with hers.

Ms Hamilton talks her through it. 'That's right. One, two ... Good. And a big breath on ten. Now wait here with your Poppy. I'll talk to you later.'

Joel, bewildered by it all, and clearly scared of Rory, backs towards the door and Ms Hamilton takes his hand. 'It's okay, Joel. Rory's just a bit upset. And Rory ...' She opens the door, ushering Joel into the classroom next door. 'Have a think about your behaviour while I'm gone.'

Rory is frozen to the spot, her body taut like a string about to snap, and George experiences a violent quivering that pins him to his chair. He looks across at the distressed child, who clutches the book to her chest and returns his gaze with one of outrage and betrayal. His growing confidence in his ability to handle children has shrivelled in an instant, leaving him with an overwhelming sense of failure. How could he have been so insensitive?

He says the first thing that comes into his head. 'I think Joel is very upset.'

Her face is hard.

'And I think you're sad, too?' he adds with a tentative smile.

Her lower lip begins to tremble.

'I should've asked you if I could borrow it. It's your book.'

She's way across the room. Still out of reach. 'You like Joel better than me.' This she says in a whisper, as if she doesn't want anyone else to know.

George finds his feet although his knees won't stop shaking. 'Sweetheart, I ... like you better than anyone. More than all the other children in the school put together. You know that. I help Joel here but I wouldn't let him come and live with me. With us.'

He moves across the room and lifts her up in his arms. She's getting heavy and her body is rigid with resentment. 'I don't know about you, but I reckon we should say sorry to Joel and Ms Hamilton. What about it?'

'All right.'

Not exactly enthusiastic. 'You know you shouldn't kick people. Or shout at them.' He'll leave the rest to Jessica

Hamilton. From an outsider's point of view, Rory should be punished. So let the outsider punish her. He understands with sobering clarity that what Rory needs from him is the fierce, unconditional love of a parent. And it scares the hell out of him.

*

The incident shakes George more than he cares to admit, and it's only when he's leaning on the bar with Redgum that his thoughts, jagged and fragmented as they are, begin to coalesce.

'... so there she is, hanging on to me like – like paint on a wall. And me not knowing what to do.'

'Hard to get paint off.'

The metaphor has come out of nowhere, but George feels its veracity. How do you get paint off? You scrape it into flakes or dissolve it with some chemical. Either way, the paint is destroyed. And it can't be reapplied. Ever. Until now, he thinks with a jolt, he's been playing at being a parent. Enjoying all the good things. Crowing when he solved a problem like the nightmares. But all the while, this child who is not his has been claiming him as her own.

'What happens to her if I die, or become too sick to look after her? What happens if I get Alzheimer's? Or cancer or ...'

'A doc,' says Redgum, clearly relieved to discern a practical solution. 'Go and get a check-up.'

George is aware that this is only part of his problem, but he, too, is thankful that there's something he can do. *First things first*, as he always says. The other can wait until he sees the doc.

The doctor scans his computer. 'No history of anything sinister. You don't have any symptoms. What makes you think you need such a major check-up? There's such a thing as over-servicing, you know.'

George looks at him craftily. 'That your Merc outside?'

The doctor frowns. 'Yes. Although what that's got to do with your—'

'Bet you service it regularly – a fancy car like that.'

The doctor grins. 'Fair enough. Let's start with some blood tests.'

*

George's tests are ready. The doctor clicks through the results then looks up and smiles. 'Your blood pressure's a bit on the high side, but there's no real cause for worry at the moment. Your liver's a bit sluggish. How much alcohol do you drink each day?'

Let's see ... A beer with Redgum, two cans before dinner, two after Rory goes to bed ... 'One or two,' he lies.

'In my experience, that means four or five.'

'You got me there.'

'Ease off a bit. One or two at the most. And some exercise. Walk when you can.'

George, glad to get off so lightly, agrees with alacrity.

*

He'd been going to ask about Alzheimer's, but in the end didn't want to know. It isn't as though he's all that old and they say an odd memory lapse is nothing to worry about. So, fitness confirmed, he has no excuse. Has he, or can he, make a full (perhaps lifelong) commitment to Rory? The sort of commitment a parent makes without thinking? *I want to*, he tells himself. *Maybe I already have.*

Unsure whether he is able to judge for himself, he talks to Shirl. 'You warned me that I was taking on a lot. Is it too much?'

Shirl, for once, is silent.

Am I? Am I? He dredges the question to the surface. 'Am I ... the sort of person who can do this? See it through, even if Angie doesn't come back?' (Deep down, he doesn't believe that she will.)

Shirl doesn't harangue him. Doesn't say *I told you so*. Doesn't even give him *The Look*. George knows she doesn't expect Angie to return, either. So it's a big question he's asking and she answers with a question of her own. 'What if I advised you to take her to social services tomorrow? That's the alternative.'

George is stricken. 'You can't mean that,' he pleads. 'She believes in me. Trusts me. She might even – care for me a bit.'

'And you?'

'And me? It would kill me, Shirl.' George drops his gaze, looking at but not seeing his hands as they wring

189

and twist in his lap. 'I never had a kid of me own, but if I did …' He registers shock in a truth he's been avoiding. 'If I did, I don't reckon I could love her more than I love Rory.' George speaks quietly, sadly, aware that in asserting this, he is saying goodbye to Annie. Her insubstantial hand slips from his grasp and she disappears gently, in a puff of wind. For a moment, George is drawn into the twilight melancholy their parting brings. But he's no longer in thrall. He has chosen life and all the warmth and joy, muddle and heartache that life entails.

Shirl stands up and puts her hands on her brother's shoulders. 'You've answered your own question.' She plants a brief kiss on the top of his head. 'You'll manage, George. We all manage one way or another.'

That night, when he tucks Rory in, he tells her for the first time, 'Poppy loves you. You know that, don't you?'

She settles Slipper Dog into place on her pillow. 'Silly Poppy,' she says. 'Of course you do.'

*

George's renewed commitment is like Confirmation, a sacrament where the proxy vows of Baptism are confirmed by the adult believer. And like its sacramental equivalent, George's allegiance does not preclude backsliding. There are moments where he doubts his ability to stick with it; moments when he feels the burden but not the sweetness.

Rory can still be naughty, whiny and stubborn, and frankly, in the way. On Saturdays, George used to meet

Redgum at The Royal Mail, a hotel further away that's blessed with a TAB. They used to like watching the footy and races on the telly, betting their combined dollars on a hot tip, a quadrella or the Daily Double. As blokes do.

But not little girls. George resents this loss of freedom. On Saturdays now, they go to the park, or the zoo or the cinema. It's not that he doesn't enjoy these things. It's just that it's a piece of his life he doesn't own anymore. He feels guilty about this resentment, unaware that even the best of parents sometimes wish aspects of their old lives back.

There are battles at mealtimes. 'Just four more peas.'

Rory has been steadfast in her aversion to peas and plays with them sulkily, corralling the four negotiated peas (the smallest, by the look of it) to the side of her plate. She stabs at one with her fork. 'It's all squashed. I can't eat it when it's squashed.'

'There's more over the other side. Eat one of those.'

A tentative tongue grazes another pea. 'It's cold.'

George wonders why he keeps cooking peas. *Beans*, Redgum had suggested. 'They're green.' That made sense. Then contradictory advice from Shirl. 'Children like to make a stand when it comes to meals.' There's a combative light in her eyes. 'Never give in.'

So he cajoles and bargains. 'Just three, then.' Or 'No bedtime story if you're not finished in five minutes.' (He hates that one. Story time is his favourite part of the day.)

Mealtime has become unpleasant and exhausting and finally George has had enough. Quietly he replaces peas with beans. Rory frowns at her plate. 'Don't like beans,' she says.

'I'll get peas instead, then.'

Glaring, she shovels the beans into her mouth. 'They're all right,' she concedes.

Another problem solved. But there will be more. George has developed some understanding of this parent caper and knows that over the years he can look forward to many battles. Small things like peas and lipstick. Large things like study and boys. And each one will test his depleting energy. So he'll need to choose his battles and take a stand on the important things. 'Count your blessings,' Pen used to say, and when he hears the echo of her voice, he understands that despite the day-to-day frustrations, he is indeed blessed.

*

Rory comes flying out of the school gate with Maryam and Kirsty. 'Here we are, Poppy George.' He is briefly confused. Then it comes back. How could he have forgotten? Rory's friends are coming to play after school. Thank God he's on time. He's aware of that small, familiar stab of fear. What if his memory is failing? What if one day he forgets altogether to pick her up? What then? He braces himself against the fence and orders his thoughts. It takes only seconds but seems longer. Guilty that he had almost forgotten his promise to Rory, he feels the need to compensate.

'Maybe you girls need a treat.'

'Yay!' The three children scamper off, calling out to George to hurry.

He meets the eyes of one of the mothers and she shakes her head with an indulgent smile. 'They certainly keep you on your toes,' she observes.

'All in a day's work.' George quickens his pace and catches up with the children at the corner. An unseasonably chilly wind whips and snatches at their hair. 'Let's see,' he says, rubbing his chin. 'If it wasn't so cold, we could have an ice-cream.'

'We're not cold. It's boiling!' Three upturned faces, anxious to convince.

'Okay. Just because it's spring. An ice-cream for me. A big one. That's all we need, I think.'

The little girls giggle into their hands. 'You're so funny, Poppy George.'

Shirl arrives at his house just in time to supervise the hand and face washing while George makes the tea. 'It's good to see she has some friends,' Shirl says, as they set their tea things on the outdoor table. 'Nice type of girls, too.' She stirs in two teaspoons of sugar. (*We're all entitled to one weakness*, George thinks.) 'Have you heard from that mother of hers lately?'

'No.' If George sounds short with her, it's because he is sick of a question to which he has no answer.

'Tsk.' Shirl polishes her glasses. 'A lovely kid like that. Makes you wonder.'

George grins at his sister. 'Lovely kid? What happened to "sly little miss"?'

'She was given a chance,' Shirl says quietly. 'Thanks to you.'

'We're going to do a concert for you,' Rory calls out. 'But you'll have to wait till we're ready.'

Brother and sister watch as the children dance and whisper and push each other, half hidden behind the rhododendrons.

'Well done.' They applaud the capering children. But George is in a ruminative mood. 'I remember what you said when Rory and Angie first came here.'

Shirl looks surprised. 'I've said a lot of things. It's nice to know you listen sometimes.' She sits back. 'So what did I say?'

'About that Chinese proverb — if you save someone's life, you owe them. As far as I'm concerned, Angie has paid me in full. The life she saved wasn't worth much, but now it's ... a ...' (*He's so bad with words.*) 'It's a rich life I have now — a life full of riches.'

George expects advice or at least a commentary. Instead, Shirl stands up. 'I've got to go,' she says. 'Take care, little brother.'

*

George always walks Bree to the tram on Fridays. Amused at first, she'd protest that she's been getting around by herself for years. But she's stopped objecting and George is gratified when she allows him to treat her with the sort of courtesy and respect he likes to reserve for women.

The three of them, George, Rory and Bree, look forward to Fridays — lamb roast and a Choc Wedge then a DVD that Rory chooses on the way home from school. At 'interval' (Bree can only go so long without a smoke), George organises the microwave and they sit down for the second half of the movie tucking into fresh popcorn.

He times things to finish around eight-thirty so they can walk Bree to the tram and ensure that Rory is in bed at a respectable hour. The process has been so smooth that they are all surprised one Friday when a sudden deluge prevents Bree from leaving on time. The rain sheets down the window panes, drums like hail on the tin roof. Peering out the door, George sees a torrent running down his path to the gutter which is already overflowing. 'She's a beauty, all right,' he says. 'I better drive you home.'

'Just a shower,' Bree says. 'It's too dangerous to drive. I'll hang around here till it blows over.'

Rory looks gleeful at the prospect of a late bedtime, but soon falls asleep on the couch. George puts a blanket over her and he and Bree watch *Inspector Poirot*. It's a repeat and neither of them is much interested. Besides, they can hardly hear it over the racket on the roof.

'Beer?' George returns from the kitchen with two stubbies. 'I'll get you a glass.' (Pen would expect a woman to drink out of a glass.)

'Best straight from the bottle,' she says, twisting off the top. 'Cheers.'

Bree puzzles him. She seems self-sufficient, sometimes even efficient, but seeing her more often confirms his impression the day he visited her house. Here is a woman who paints her door but fails to clean the glass. Who keeps her kitchen clean and tidy but leaves a mess (an understatement) in her bathroom and bedroom. Who makes elaborate plans to help people but fails to deliver. Randomly directed bursts of energy, followed by periods of lassitude. What's all that about?

They have never really talked. 'How did you come to know Angie?' he asks.

She slurps her beer and wipes her chin. 'Diversion program. A few years ago it was.'

'Diversion program?'

'Yeah. You know, for potheads. Young offenders.'

'Drugs.'

'Just weed. You have to do rehab for the hard stuff. I was one of their so-called successes and they asked me back to talk to the newbies about "the dangers of drugs".' (She indicates inverted commas with waggling fingers.)

Turning away from the television, she fiddles with her bracelet. (One of those jangly things. Pen never liked them.) 'I usually don't tell people this, but I started smoking weed when I was in Year 7. Twelve I was then. Good at school, too. Got 'A's and all that in primary school. Mum and Dad wanted me to go to uni but I left school as soon as I turned sixteen and got this job in a bakery. Didn't last long. The weed did my head in. They reckon it stuffs up the connections when your brain's still growing. Probably right, too. All I know is sometimes I feel like hell.'

'Depression?'

'Yeah. Mood swings, memory loss – stuff like that.

Sometimes I don't get dressed for days. I'm good now, though.'

But George, though he pities this woman with the messed-up head, is wondering about Angie. Had she been affected the same way? *Amp.* Bree has hinted more than once that he was a druggie. 'Angie. Is she … still, you know, using drugs?'

Bree chooses to be offended. 'I'm talking about me, not Angie. I thought we were mates.'

'So we are.' George hadn't meant to upset her. 'It's just that I'm worried for Rory.'

'Ange always falls on her feet.' Bree sounds resentful. 'And I don't think she's been using much since Rory.' She begins to sniffle like a child. 'It's my life that's a mess.'

George takes her empty bottle. 'How old are you?'

'Thirty-five.'

'And the rest.'

'Forty-two. Honest.'

She looks even older sometimes. The rain stops as suddenly as it had started. He's glad to cut the conversation short. 'Help me get Rory into the car. I'll drive you home.'

The look she gives him is clear, even to someone as straight as George. 'I could stay the night.' She even puts her arms around his neck.

Alarmed, George feels a flicker of desire. She's an attractive woman, in her own way. Knows well enough what she's doing. But she's just told him she's messed up, depressed. What she wants, needs, is comfort, and George is too honest and too decent to take advantage.

'I'm flattered,' he says, disentangling himself as gently as he can. 'Really I am. But I'm close to twice your age. You can do a lot better than me.'

'Pity.' Bree is mildly regretful but not offended. 'Probably for the best. We still mates?'

'If I was twenty years younger ...'

She grins. 'Yeah. I'd have to wait in line with all your other girlfriends.'

He recognises bullshit when he hears it. All the same, he straightens his shoulders and stands somewhat taller.

*

As Christmas approaches, Redgum suggests a project that engages them for weeks. ('Them' includes Mr Nguyen. It seems only right.) They are building a cubbyhouse in the Nguyens' backyard, to be assembled at George's place when it's finished. Bickering amicably over materials and design, the three men hammer and saw and drill while Mrs Nguyen and Shirl choose material for curtains, and cushions for the table and chair set that Peta has outgrown. The cubby isn't finished yet and George is torn between wanting to see Rory's enjoyment and the long unfamiliar sense of belonging and purpose that the project has nurtured.

Despite the unseasonal wind that snaps and tears at his jacket, that numbs his nose and cheeks, George is cocooned in warmth that no mere weather can dispel. And wrapped up with him, generating and maintaining that warmth, is Rory.

*

Angie is unusually reflective. They've been gone for quite a while now – five, six, months? Time blurs by like the towns, the petrol stations, the railway sidings she sees from the back of Amp's bike. She's not quite sure how this happened, having told herself she was just getting away for a bit of a break. She deserves a break, she reminds herself. Five years bringing up a kid on her own. Trapped, that's what she'd been – trapped in the life of a single mother. No money. No help. No fun.

Now she's in Bunbury, on the other side of the continent, the Nullarbor Plain, that great, desolate wilderness, stretching wide between her and her child. She hasn't forgotten Rory. Not exactly. But she's a creature who has learned to live in the moment. And at the moment, she's experiencing life on the road – new places, the visceral freedom of the speeding bike and a man to provide sex and money. There is no lack of money and Angie doesn't inquire into its source. Amp knows some shady people. There are often packages stowed under the seat or elsewhere on the bike. Sometimes he even asks her to put a package in her bra. She's not so sure about this, but is reluctant to test their relationship by refusing his request. *If it is a request*, she thinks sulkily. *An order, more like.* There's plenty of cash, too. Used notes folded in a rubber band.

He's careless with money, is Amp, always rolling off a few notes when he wants some time to himself – 'Get yourself some boots' or 'a dress' or once, memorably,

199

'a tattoo'. Angie has never had a tattoo, and with much sentimentality and little emotion she decides to have Rory's name on a scroll surrounded by roses on her plump upper arm. She shows Amp when it's done.

'You stupid bitch. You want me to look like an idiot?'

She's puzzled. 'What do you mean?'

'For all anyone knows, "Rory" could be a bloke.' He gives her a backhander for good measure before stomping out to get drunk.

Angie has several hours to fret before he returns. She clutches at his arm. 'I'm sorry, babe. Didn't think.' She tries unsuccessfully to twine her body around his, wishing she were a better shape for twining. 'I can keep it covered. I will. Promise.'

Amp grunts some sort of assent before falling on the bed, fully clothed. Angie pulls off his boots and switches out the light. Snores like small explosions assail the darkness.

It's a couple of days before Angie can gather the courage to go out and buy Rory a Christmas present. The Toy Shed has just opened in Bunbury and she stands, mouth agape, intimidated by the racks laden with more toys than she could ever have imagined. A young woman is approaching her, and though she hasn't shoplifted anything, Angie is spurred into action, grabbing the first doll that comes to hand and fleeing to the register. Later, she wishes she'd bought a Barbie.

*

Christmas Eve. Over a year since George walked down that lane to be menaced by his young assailants. He hasn't seen them since, but if he had, he might have thanked them. *It's an ill wind that blows no good.* His mother used to say that, although God knows in her life, the ill wind seemed to blow without relief.

Rory takes a long time to get to sleep and it's after ten before he's able to call on Redgum and Mr Nguyen to help him assemble the cubbyhouse, supervised (unnecessarily, the men think) by Shirl and Mrs Nguyen. *Looks a treat*, they all agree, and it's after midnight before they sit down to enjoy a drink and some of Shirl's famous Christmas cake. George is ready to resume his relationship with fruitcake. Nothing like it, really – who can resist the smell of brandy-soaked fruit as the knife releases its fragrance?

After Redgum and the Nguyens leave, George and Shirl pack presents in the Santa sack. 'A bit more than we got as kids, eh?' No bitterness in this statement, just delight that it's different for Rory.

'Did *she* send a present?'

'No.'

'Nice to see a tree.'

'Yeah. When there's a kid ...' The tree is the first he's had since Pen died. And how she would have loved sharing Christmas with a child. It's a scrawny sort of tree, sitting there in its tub. The bright baubles wink and mock and glisten like tears.

*

Rory is awake the next morning at five-thirty, running barefoot into George's room with her pillow-slip of toys and books. The look on her face is priceless. Kids are so knowing nowadays and he hopes Rory can have another couple of Christmases believing in Santa. He hopes he'll be there to keep faith with her. He glances down at his hands. They're okay. Brushing these misgivings aside, he sits back and admires her treasures.

'Now,' he says as she munches on a chocolate frog found in the toe of her stocking, 'I believe Santa mentioned that there's something outside as well.'

Stopping only to put her shoes on, she runs out into the backyard. 'Ooooh. It's a cubby! Is it really mine?'

'Certainly is. Santa said so.'

'It's got chairs and a table. And a cupboard with drawers. I can put my new tea set on the shelf.' She pauses. 'What's my address?'

George is now a good improviser when it comes to children's questions. 'Seven-A Mercy Street,' he says.

Another present comes for Rory just before the New Year. 'From Mummy,' George says.

Rory tears off the paper. 'A doll.'

George tries to foster some enthusiasm, but he knows what her mother doesn't. As it turns out, her daughter isn't a dolly sort of girl.

12

Rory sets off for the new school year swearing she will hate the new teacher. 'I loved Ms Hamilton,' she mourned. 'Ms Bongiorno is going to be horrible.'

George is inclined to sympathise – he was comfortable with Ms Hamilton. In a few days, however, they are both reconciled when Ms Bongiorno is judged by the perfidious children to be 'totally awesome'.

In April, Rory meets George with the news that Grade 1 is having a footy-tipping competition. 'The prize is going to be a footy jumper. If you win you can pick what team.' Rory pauses mid-flight. 'Who do I barrack for, Poppy?'

George's own Poppy used to take him to Princes Park most Saturdays and his loyalty has always been with the Blues. 'I barrack for Carlton,' he tells her, 'but you can choose.'

She decides upon Richmond. 'It sounds like Richie,' she says.

That football season the two of them pore over the fixture every Thursday to work out who they'll tip for the week. It becomes their favourite time together, debating the likely winners. Back and forth they go.

'West Coast beat Sydney last time.'

'But that was in Perth.'

'You're right.'

'Luke Hodge might be carrying an injury. Don't forget that.'

Rory is ruthless in her assessment of each team's chances. But despite overwhelming evidence to the contrary, she always tips Richmond.

'Loyal to the bootstraps,' George tells Redgum.

A few weeks later, when Richmond plays Carlton, he takes her to the match. 'Now hold my hand,' he says as they're disgorged from Jolimont station. George worries that he might lose her in the cheerful, roiling crowd and reminds her of his instructions to find a policeman.

'You told me that.' She's becoming impatient with all this fussing. 'I'm nearly six.'

The crowd is dense so she does clutch his hand, but every few steps she executes an excited little skip.

At a yellow-and-black kiosk outside the ground, he buys her a beanie and scarf in Richmond colours.

'You'd better buy blue-and-white ones for you,' she says as she winds the scarf around her neck. 'It's only fair.'

The day is crisp but sunny and they rub their hands together in the breeze that blows cold across the oval. Foraging seagulls take flight as the umpires run on to the field.

'Booooo!' Rory cups her hands around her mouth and joins the crowd in this weekly demonstration of contempt.

The siren is a call to arms, players and spectators merged in one great will to win.

They eat hot jam doughnuts at half-time. Like most Richmond fans, Rory idolises Matthew Richardson. 'Richo's best of all,' she says, jam dripping onto her scarf. 'I'm going to have his number on my jumper. Do you think Aunty Shirl would sew it on for me?' (*They've become as thick as thieves*, George thinks.)

It's a close match and George finds himself hoping for a Richmond victory. A mighty roar lifts the crowd to its feet at each scoring shot, and Rory, red-faced and passionate, shouts herself hoarse, finding just enough voice to boo ferociously when Carlton wins by a point.

We are the navy Blues, sing the victors.

'I wanted to sing the Tigers' song – we only needed one more goal.' Eyes wide and tragic, she clutches at her *Footy Record*.

One lousy point. 'Never mind, love. Maybe next time.'

She's so despondent that they stop at a fast-food restaurant on the way home. It's a rare indulgence nowadays, but George feels personally responsible (and consequently, guilty) for his team's win.

*

Rory's sixth birthday comes and goes. A party, a cake and a late present from Angie – twenty dollars in a card. 'Happy birthday, Rory,' Angie has written. 'Ask George to buy you something nice with this.'

This is better than the doll, Rory tells him, but George isn't so sure. All the possibilities open to Angie and she chose to send money. Little wonder that within the year she's become a receding influence in her daughter's life. Rory no longer asks for the mermaid story, no longer speculates about when her mother might come home, no longer wheezes her distress.

'I don't know what to make of it,' George says to Redgum. 'It's like she's cut her mother out of her thoughts. Good in one way, I suppose. I just hope she's not, you know, pining inside.' *Like Shirl and I did when we were in care.*

Redgum shifts his bulk on the bar stool and thinks for a bit. 'A mother's a mother,' he says. 'I don't reckon a kid forgets its mother all that easy.'

George understands Redgum only too well, but it isn't what he wants to hear. After his initial anger at Angie's desertion, he's become more and more convinced that Rory's best interests will be served if her mother never comes back. He is Rory's family – all the family she needs, as far as he's concerned. So he ignores Redgum, buries his own childhood memories, and tries to be the best Poppy George that he can be.

*

Out of the blue, Angie rings George. 'Just thought I'd catch up,' she says.

'It's been a while.'

'Yeah. Well, things've been happening.'

'I suppose they have.'

'You know. Stuff.'

'Yep. Stuff happens.'

'How's Rory?'

'Good. Happy.'

'Does she … ?'

'Does she what?'

'I miss her, you know.'

'Ah well …'

Angie says a hasty goodbye and stares at her phone. George wasn't very talkative. And she wanted to talk to him. Amp is dealing speed – she knows that now for sure. Dealing's not so bad, but he's using, too. He's becoming more violent, but she knows it's just the speed. He does love her. She didn't get the opportunity to tell George all this. She rang him because she just wanted normal for a bit. She almost told him she wanted to come home. She would have, if he'd asked her. But this time he didn't ask, so she was left staring at the phone.

13

George's days have shape and weight. Rory is growing taller, her skin pink and healthy, her hair shiny, and the troubled little pucker between her eyebrows has given way to a smooth, high forehead. In her second year of school, she's flourishing. Her reading is improving by the day, and she's progressed to the Kookaburras. 'The top group,' George boasts to Shirl and Redgum. When they go to the library, Richie books are spurned for more prestigious 'chapter books'. Bedtime has become a war of attrition and George tells Shirl that he sometimes has to put his foot down. Rory still sleeps with Slipper Dog and Elephant, and when George goes in to kiss her goodnight, he feels like the luckiest man in the world.

In this second year, George is a more confident parent. He allows himself to feel frustrated at times and this no longer makes him feel guilty or ungrateful.

The Blues and Tigers clash for a second time. (The Blues win again. What's wrong with the Tigers?) It's then that George has a great idea for Rory's next birthday. He'll buy them season tickets for Richmond and take her to all the home matches. He almost blurts this out, so pleased is he with the idea, but decides to keep it as a surprise. The future, George believes, is looking better and better.

*

As the year passes, George begins preparations for their second Christmas.

Redgum has been wondering about a chemistry set. 'Seems like a good present from a scientist,' he says, obviously tickled that Rory still believes this. 'Trouble is, the box says not for children under twelve. I said she was nearly seven and as sharp as a tack, but the toyshop woman said, "It's too dangerous" and "What about an ant farm?" But I said I didn't like that idea and I wanted something with a bit of whizz-bangery. That's what I told her. I mean, what sort of scientist would give a kid an ant farm?'

'I'm thinking of getting her some fishing tackle,' George says. 'To take on our holiday.' They are going away on Boxing Day. *To the beach*, he tells the delighted Rory.

So many things to look forward to, so they make a calendar to mark off the days. George buys a big square of cardboard from the art shop and rules a grid. 'All ready, sweetheart. Go for your life.' So Rory is let loose with coloured markers, glitter glue (Shirl had put him on to this) and stickers. Tongue curled over her upper lip, Rory spends the rest of her Saturday labelling and colouring and decorating. She has a wonderful capacity to lose herself in a project. Barely stopping to eat, she fills each square with colour and sparkle, finishing with their holidays, where she draws shells and boats and sandcastles. (All from books or television. She's never been to the beach.)

'When I was a kid,' George tells her, 'I had a beach holiday with my Nanna and Poppy. We had a cabin just over from the water and it was sunny every day.' At least that's how he remembers it. Mornings holding a secret heat that was gradually released as the sun rose higher. The haze off the eucalypts. The smell of the sea, the shrieking of gulls and the frozen bliss of an icy-pole at lunchtime. Those two weeks were the best of his childhood and he and Shirl came back from the beach each day with sunglow on their brown bodies and that wonderful tiredness unique to a life of sun, salt and sea. Often, after their evening meal, they played Snakes and Ladders and Ludo and a card game called Twenty-one. Poppy helped him along, but Nanna played to win. (George makes a mental note to pack a couple of board games and a deck of cards – a new one. He had worn out the old pack playing Patience after Pen died.)

So he shares the anticipation of this holiday with Rory but keeps the fishing to himself. He doesn't want to spoil the surprise, which he hugs to his chest with the same faith and love Rory still lavishes on Slipper Dog and Elephant. Fishing with his Poppy had been the best thing of all. They sat on the pier, not saying much, but together. Like that was where he belonged. If it got cold, Poppy gave him an old jumper, so old it was hard to distinguish its original colour and shape. It smelled of sea and fish and Poppy's pipe tobacco, and when George took it off for bed, the smell lingered on his own body.

*

Rory marks off the eighth day before Christmas, which she has decorated with a bauble-laden tree. That afternoon, they had gone out in Redgum's ute and bought a tree from the Scouts, fussing and fretting the finer points of height and shape until they found one just right.

George, to his sister's surprise, organises a tree-decorating party and their friends all come with food and drink to watch and admire Rory as she decorates the tree to oblivion. She sings 'Away in a Manger' and the adults wipe their eyes and go all soft-in-the-middle, recalling Christmases past. Even the Nguyens, who are Buddhist, exchange delighted smiles.

In the next few days, George shops for presents, attends a thank-you afternoon tea for the school volunteers, checks what he needs for the holiday, and with some instructions from Shirl, makes a chocolate ripple cake for Rory's class party. He licks cream and stray biscuit crumbs from his fingers. 'Pretty impressive, Pen, eh?'

Shopping is the hardest task. Pen had always shopped for gifts. She seemed to have the knack of knowing exactly what everyone might want. For the first Christmases after she died, he had bought a bottle of Scotch for Redgum, cinema tickets for Shirl and Bill and put twenty dollars in envelopes for his great nieces and nephews. Until last year, Shirl had helped him, but this year he's on his own. So he acted on the advice of the reading mums. After much earnest discussion, they agreed more or less unanimously, that the best present for Shirl would be a Diamond Deluxe Pamper Pack from the exclusive Orchid Beauty Salon.

'Old Shirl has been there for me all these years,' he tells Redgum. 'So she deserves something a bit special, that's for sure.' But he isn't quite comfortable with the whole thing. 'I suppose they know what they're talking about, but it seems a funny sort of present – like telling someone they're not beautiful enough. She's never been a beauty, our Shirl, but you got to give it to her, she does her best and always looks *nice*.'

'A fine figure of a woman.'

'You're dead right there, mate. But it means I've got to go into one of those places with all those la-di-da women.'

'Wear a collar and tie,' Redgum advises. 'No one looks down on a man in a collar and tie.'

'Do you want the Basic Deluxe or the Diamond Deluxe pack?' The young woman with the alarming fingernails raises her perfect eyebrows, and despite his nice white shirt and tie, George feels looked-down-upon.

'Whatever's the best,' he says, not daring to ask the price.

'Lovely.' She smiles with her mouth and calculates with her eyes. 'Would you like the Dead Sea body scrub? It's extra, but all my ladies love it.'

George is impressed that the saleswoman has ladies she can call her own, but baulks at the thought of Shirl being scrubbed. 'Just the package,' he says, and his credit card is an extra two-hundred-and-fifty dollars in the red.

He buys the rest of his gifts without the reading mums' assistance.

'I want to buy a present for Aunty Shirl,' Rory says one evening. 'I've already got a surprise for you. Can we go to the shops after school tomorrow?'

They go to the Bargain Shop. *Lots of things to pick from, Poppy.* After discarding a bottle of nail polish (because, as she says, Aunty Shirl only wears pink), a bilious green scarf (George had to do some fast talking on that one), Rory finds a sparkly ballpoint pen. 'I'll get her the blue one,' she says and George takes out his wallet. 'No, Poppy. I want to use my own pocket money. It's from me to Aunty Shirl.'

They all come round for drinks on Christmas Eve. 'This is becoming quite a tradition,' Shirl says as she cuts into the fruitcake and passes it around. 'Cheers,' they all say, and Mrs Nguyen, after two glasses of bubbly, becomes a bit tipsy and dances Shirl around the kitchen. 'Happy Christ-a-mas,' she sings. 'I say Happy Christ-a-mas to you.'

The guests leave after supervising the Santa sack. Shirl has a big meal to prepare for tomorrow. In the past, Pen always cooked lunch for the whole family on Christmas Day. 'You're busy enough with the kids,' she'd tell her sister-in-law. 'Have a break.' Which Shirl gratefully did.

Since Pen died, Shirl has taken over and George and Redgum always go to her place for the festive meal. This year she's also invited the Nguyens and, somewhat less graciously, 'that Bree woman'. Fortunately, Bree was going to her sister's so Shirl manages to escape the consequences of her grudging generosity.

George, while enjoying the evening, isn't sorry to see his guests go. It's been a big week and tomorrow will be another big day. Tempted to leave the last of the cleaning up, he decides on another piece of Christmas cake and a fresh cup of tea. *Best wind down a bit before going to bed.*

He swears as the phone rings.

'It's me, George – Angie.'

She doesn't need to tell him. He'd know that voice anywhere.

'What do you want?'

'Just want to wish my Rory a Merry Christmas.' She pronounces her words with a drawn-out sibilance.

'Are you drunk?' He can hear someone in the background.

'Won't be long, babe. Not you, George. Just let me talk to Rory.'

'It's after eleven. She's sound asleep.'

'Okay, babe. Just hang on a minute. Never mind, George. I'll be seeing her in a couple of weeks. Me 'n' Charlie. We'll come and pick her up after New Year – around the eighteenth.'

'The eighteenth? Of January?' *That's hardly any time.* He can hear the panic in his own voice. 'What do you mean *pick her up*?'

'Me 'n' Charlie are gonna rent a place in West Wyalong.

We're coming down to Melbourne to bring her back with us. George? George? Are you still there?'

His voice echoes back at him. 'The eighteenth, you say? West Wyalong?' He's never heard of West Wyalong.

'Gotta go.' A girlish squeal. 'Stop it. I'm on the phone. Big hug for Rory. I'll bring her present when I come.'

'Who's Charlie?'

The line is dead.

*

West Wyalong. He doesn't like the sound of West Wyalong at all. He's fairly sure it isn't a suburb of Melbourne. Maybe down Geelong way? For the first time, he wishes he had learned how to use the computer. Pen had bought herself one a couple of years before she died. Whenever they needed to know something she'd say, 'I'll google it' and return flaunting the answer like she was Wally Carter, that bloke who won a million bucks on that quiz show they used to watch. For a while he called her Wally. Then the joke grew thin.

So, frustrated by his lack of computer skills, George prepares for bed and lies awake, focusing on West Wyalong, suppressing his panic at the thought of losing Rory.

On his way to Shirl's the next day, he remembers that Bill has a road atlas. It would be a few years out of date, but towns don't just spring up, do they?

Rory can't wait to give Shirl her present. 'I bought it with my own money,' she says. 'And it was only two dollars and fifty cents.'

Eyes glistening behind her glasses, Shirl kisses the upturned face, remembering with a smile the washcloth saga. 'It's a beautiful present, Rory. I'll use it to write all my birthday and Christmas cards.'

George stares in dismay at his plate, loaded with turkey and ham and God knows how many vegetables.

'Another roast potato?' Shirl is forever pressing food on people, but George feels like tipping it all in the bin. With a self-control that he marvels at later, he manages to refuse the extra potatoes and munches his way through food that might as well have been sawdust. Poor Shirl had gone to so much trouble so he munches and smiles and dutifully reads out his Christmas-cracker joke.

After lunch, while the others are loosening their belts and falling asleep in the lounge room, George goes into the bathroom with the atlas. His thick finger traces its way along the Newell Highway. *That's the middle of nowhere! Two days' drive at least.* All the energy, all the purpose of the last two years drain from his body. He's gutted – filleted like a fish, soft white flesh raw and exposed. It's so far away, this West Wyalong. He could drive up to see them, but eventually age and circumstances will put an end to that. Rory will grow up without him. She'll forget him. Is their short time together enough to bind her to him? It's a kind of death. The life-before-your-eyes you hear about was of his life with Rory – the defiant, snotty-nosed kid commandeering his couch; the freshly scrubbed little girl smirking in her new pyjamas; the sleeping child clutching Slipper Dog. The reel spools through his head as he sits motionless on the edge of the bath, finger still pointing to West Wyalong.

'Are you all right, George?' He jumps at Bill's voice, tactfully subdued through the bathroom door.

'I'm fine. Yes. Fine. Just need a breath of fresh air,' he assures his brother-in-law. Then stumbles out into the afternoon glare.

George is by nature a conservative man. Not one to buck the system. But it seems to him as he drives home that there is something terribly wrong with a system that allows a kid to be picked up and dropped and kicked from place to place like a football. He has loved Rory, cared for her, given her a home. She's doing so well at school – Kookaburra reading group, no less. He knows what that means – he's a reading mum. She has nice friends. And now Angie is coming to take her away to God knows what sort of life with God knows what sort of people. Who is this Charlie? Another addict? A drunken brute? What if he's a child molester? You read about it in the papers every day.

By the time they arrive home, his heart is thudding against his chest wall. He can feel it with his hand. This time the thought of a heart attack terrifies him. They'd give Rory to Angie for sure if he was laid up. He has to stay calm. A beer while he thinks. He opens the fridge then closes it again. Getting drunk will dull the pain but it won't make it go away (he knows that well enough) so, switching on the kettle, he all but collapses into a chair. He'll make a pot of tea and try to think straight.

He flinches when the phone rings. It's getting late. Angie again, maybe? With a new plan – maybe this time to come back and live in Melbourne. 'Yes?' His voice is eager. 'George here.'

But it's Bree. 'Angie rang. She's got this new bloke. They want to take Rory to some place in New South Wales.'

He struggles to speak. 'I know.'

'What're you going to do?'

'Not much I can do, is there?'

'I'm on my way. We're not going to let her get away with it. We need a plan.'

'Whatever it is, I hope it turns out to be legal.' (Not a joke. You never know with Bree.)

'Probably not.' With that, she's gone.

Half an hour later, she's in his lounge room drinking tea. 'I've been thinking,' she says. 'First you gotta go on as normal – Christmas holidays – all that stuff.'

'And then?'

'Suzie's brother plays footy with a copper. Says he's not a bad bloke. We could get him to arrest Angie.'

'Arrest her? What for?'

'Drugs, shoplifting, whatever. The coppers can always find something if they need to.'

George has led a sheltered life, and tends to trust authority. This is just another one of Bree's impossible schemes and he must rein her in. 'No.' He has to make it quite clear. 'I won't see Angie in jail.'

'Desperate times, George.'

Briefly tempted, he hesitates. What if this time Bree's plan actually works? No. Angie is careless and scatterbrained but doesn't deserve to be locked up. 'Absolutely not,' he repeats with uncharacteristic authority. 'She's the kid's mother, for Christ's sake.'

14

The first (and so far the only) part of Bree's plan is easy. Go away, as everyone expects, on Boxing Day. George packs everything he can think of, including the bike, filling his small car to capacity. Waving goodbye, the Nguyens joke that he reminds them of a turtle.

'Everything go with you.' They chuckle. 'Like a house on your back.'

A weak grin is all George can manage in response, but Rory, buckled into the back seat, surrounded by boxes and bags, calls out, 'I'll bring you back some shells and maybe we'll see a mermaid.'

It takes over half an hour to reach the freeway. 'Are we there yet?'

'It's a long way to the beach, love. You can open your potato chips now.' (So what if they aren't good for her? When you're on holidays it's okay to break the rules.)

Potato chips. George curses his lack of experience in the long-drive-with-child. Of course the salt means she needs a drink and a while later a toilet stop, where George hovers outside the women's toilets, trying too hard not to look shifty.

'No more chips,' he decides and allows her to sulk over an apple.

Usually, he enjoys Rory's prattle, but since talking to Bree, he's had no time to think. 'Piece of cake,' was her final pronouncement. 'Don't be there when Angie comes back – and remember it's just as likely she won't come back. You know Angie. Anyway, if she does, and you're gone, she'll be off again before you know it.'

Untangling the ifs and whens, George isn't so sure. Angie's is a careless kind of love, but it might be enough to bring her back for her daughter. And he hasn't seen her for well over a year. People mature in that time. He's an old man and yet, since Rory, he has changed. So how much more might a young person be able to grow in understanding? And change as a result of that growth? This could well be the case with Angie. So what on earth does he think he's doing?

'Not far now.' An automatic response to the persistent question. He flexes his hands on the steering wheel. All he's doing is taking Rory on the holiday they had planned. And coming back on the tenth, just eight days before Angie's threatened return.

*

Unused to long drives, George is tired when, nearly seven hours later, they reach The Famous Red Dolphin Caravan

Park. He had booked a van way back in June and when questioned, the proprietor agreed that as far as he knew, no one had ever seen a red dolphin. 'Plenty of Blue Dolphins,' he explained. 'But everyone remembers the "Red Dolphin", so we stand out from the crowd and become famous. A good business strategy, I reckon.'

Whatever the strategy, George is more than happy to see a red dolphin winking at them over the entry.

'We're here, love.' Two faces look out the window, then at each other with almost identical grins.

'Site twenty-two, row F,' the receptionist tells them. She's wearing the briefest shorts George has ever seen. 'Just down that way. Key's in the door.'

The caravan is sleek and modern and Rory dances about, her voice shrill with excitement. 'Look, Poppy, a little fridge. A stove. Is that my bed? A television. It's got a television.'

George feels like shouting himself. All these features had been listed in the brochure, but he can't quite believe the compact luxury of their on-site van. He tunes in to what Rory is saying. *Her bed?* There's only one bed that he can see, high off the floor. George has never stayed in a caravan before and is relieved when the proprietor comes by to explain how things work, unfolding the second bed, which fits snugly into the wall. 'Enjoy,' he says. 'Here are the keys to the toilets and showers.' George takes the keys, one marked *Gents*, the other, *Ladies*.

'I want to go to the toilet,' Rory says.

George hasn't thought about using shared facilities. He can wait for her when she goes to the toilet, but what about showers? She begins to hop from one foot to the other. 'I really need to go.'

So he takes her to the toilet block and stands outside until she emerges. 'Now we can have a swim,' she says.

'We need to unpack first.' For some reason (*the novelty?* George wonders) she's happy to oblige, singing to herself as they stow away their possessions.

While Rory puts on her bathers, George steps outside to have a look around. The Red Dolphin has, he guesses, been here for a long time. There are well-grown trees shading the vans and a cracked asphalt road winds between long rows of caravans and tents. A wooden sign, blistered by the sun, tells him that it's only ten metres to Sapphire Beach. George stretches limbs still cramped from the drive. The afternoon is hot and golden, the wayward bougainvillea a right royal purple. All in all, he could have done a lot worse.

The next two or maybe three sites are taken up by two caravans and a complicated series of tents and awnings. He has heard of shanty towns and this seems to be a likely candidate, but the more he looks, the more order he detects. Squinting into the sun, he's startled to see one of the tents moving with slow majesty, in his direction.

'You're the newbie,' the tent observes and George finds himself shaking hands with a woman in a canvas hat and an all-enveloping green-and-white-striped dress. She's a head taller than George, and it seems to him, three times as wide. Short curly grey hair framing a large weather-beaten face. Rough hands. Generous mouth. 'Stella.' She beams. 'Stella Parker. Looks like we're neighbours.'

'George.' He squirms as shrewd eyes appraise him, wrinkled and skinny, in his singlet and baggy shorts.

'Park's got the kids down the beach,' she explains. 'Happy hour's at six. Come over then and meet the gang.'

'Ready!' Rory, in her new red spotted bathers, jumps down from the caravan.

'Your granddaughter?'

Rory hangs back, shuffling her feet.

'Say hello to Mrs … ?'

'Stella, love. Or Aunty Stell, if you want. Do you like toffees?'

Rory sidles out from behind George and nods, while Stella's hand disappears into a large pocket. 'Here. And one for Granddad.'

'Poppy,' Rory says, unwrapping the sweet. 'He's my Poppy.'

It's quite a business, applying the sunscreen, but Shirl had been insistent when it came to skin protection. (And a number of other things, of course – but they're for another time.)

As promised, the beach is a short walk over a sand dune, and as they crest the hill, Rory slinks closer to him. 'It's a lot of water,' she says, dragging on his arm. George points out other children running and jumping in the waves, splashing each other, squealing with delight.

'Looks like fun to me.'

Rory sticks out her chin. 'I think I'll make a sandcastle,' she decides, and sits down well back from the water's edge.

He can't say he's not disappointed, but spreads out his towel beside her. 'I thought you wanted a swim.'

'Not anymore,' she says, and he resigns himself to a summer on the shore.

They return to the van covered in sand, sticky with sweat and sunscreen. The next thing is a shower and George is at a loss. He had hoped there might be one of those outdoor showers and had kept an eye out for one on the way up from the beach. If there isn't one in the park (and there are none in sight) he'll have to let her go by herself. Gathering her things, he reiterates his rules for the showers. '... and remember, don't talk to anyone. And don't let anyone in with you. And lock the door ...' Rory's attention drifts and the rules expand as George's imagination takes flight.

'Our Loris can take her.' Stella, now wearing a yellow tent, interrupts his lecture. 'I got ears like a vacuum cleaner,' she says. '"You slurp it all up, Stell" – that's what Park says. But I like to know what's going on. Nothing wrong with that, is there?'

She seems in need of reassurance, so George hastens to agree that eavesdropping is the most natural thing in the world.

'Loris!' Stella's voice, like everything else about her, is big.

A thin, brown-skinned girl appears from one of the tents. 'She's taken Dot and Bubs to the shower.'

'No worries.' Stella turns back to George. 'Scary Mary here can take your little girl.'

Scary Mary. *Just how scary are you?* Rory's eyes ask before turning to George for rescue.

Mary brooks no nonsense. 'Get your things and wait here.' As the girl returns to the tent, George grins.

'One in every family,' he observes. 'Reminds me of my sister.'

Stella's chuckle is low and throaty. 'Dunno what we'd do without her. She's so responsible it really is scary.'

Happy hour begins at six and finishes with a barbecue at dusk. Park turns out to be Stella's husband, a man even smaller and skinnier than George, with thick grey-black hair and the eyelashes of a movie star. In the course of the evening, George learns that they grow beef cattle on a property in western New South Wales.

'Long way from here.'

'Yeah.' Park swipes at a mosquito. 'I used to come here when I was a kid. Mum lives just up the road in Millingandi so we call in for Christmas and then come on down here. The kids hate the drive but love the place.'

George is too polite to ask how many children they have, but Stella tells him anyway. 'Nine kids,' two cars and two caravans.'

'This is Linda,' she says, presenting the chubby toddler playing at her feet. 'But we call her Bubs. Last one and all that.'

'Then,' adds Park, 'we had little Sam here, so we call him Ditto.' The Parkers all find this very funny and laugh as though it's quite new to them. Park pinches his wife's substantial buttock. 'Have to be careful we don't end up with a Double-ditto.'

George had never spoken this way to his wife; had never been part of a large family, so his laughter isn't as spontaneous as it might have been. Still. He can't help liking these people.

Park winks. 'She's a good sort, our Stell.'

'You're a lucky man,' George is inspired to say before his attention is taken by a delighted Rory running around with two boys and a girl about her own age – happy, Park remarks, as a pig in poo.

*

George almost weeps with pleasure. The easy camaraderie of the caravan park is foreign to him as well as to Rory, but Stell and Park, together with their tumbling offspring, have already broken down their defences.

After that first day, Rory is coaxed (by Scary Mary) and shamed (by Harry and Beano) to venture into the water. George hovers in the shallows, squinting into the sun as Rory becomes one with the squealing mass of children. 'Tomorrow I'm going on the boogie board,' she announces that night. 'Harry's going to show me how.'

For the first week it is sunny every day. Then out of nowhere the rain comes in a grey curtain that obliterates the horizon and sends the campers scurrying for shelter. 'Over here, love.' Stella's voice confounds even the thunder that's rolling in with the rain. 'We need more players. Charlie 'n' Brett are off with the Forbes kids.'

So George and Rory go to the Parker compound, as he likes to call it, to play board games and eat the doughnuts he'd dashed out and bought at the bakery. He feels awkward, proffering them to Stella; she's such a good cook.

'Perfect,' she says. 'Nothing like a jam doughnut, eh, kids?'

The Parkers fall upon the doughnuts as though it's their last meal, pleasing George enormously. Dry and warm, he looks out at the rain, now slowed to a drizzle. *A man could do a lot worse*, he thinks, pushing to the back of his mind that niggling reminder that it's all temporary. That sooner rather than later, Angie will return to claim her place as Rory's lawful guardian.

'Might take the tinny out tomorrow if it's fine,' Park says the next morning. 'You bring a rod, George?'

'Matter of fact I did plan on taking the young'un fishing,' George replies. 'But you won't have room for us. We'll go down to the pier.'

Park won't hear of it. 'My kids've been in the boat plenty of times. There's room for the two of you. We'll go before sun-up. Bloke at the pub says they've been catching whiting round Dinner Cove.'

They decide upon pipis for bait and the younger children set out on a pipi-seeking expedition under the watchful eye of Scary Mary. George and Park sit on the beach and enjoy the 'youngsters' as Park calls them, running and swooping on their finds. Rory returns with a wide grin and a bucketful of pipis. 'I found eleven of these myself,' she says, flourishing the bucket. 'Harry reckons pipis are like chocolate biscuits if you're a fish.'

George wishes that he could have taken Rory to find the pipis like his Poppy had with him, but is wise enough to see that for Rory, the best thing is being part of the Parker gang. He peers into the bucket. 'In all my born days I've never seen so many pipis in one place.'

At the first buzz of the alarm the next morning, Rory is out of bed, dressing in the warm clothes Park has advised. 'Come *on*, Poppy.'

In the pre-dawn chill, George helps Rory into her life jacket and the two men slide the boat into the water. The sky is pearl-grey, but by the time the boat is launched, the horizon is tinged with a salmon-coloured glow. They cross the sandbar into deeper waters. 'Careful,' George says as the little girl wriggles and fidgets and chatters in an excited treble. 'You'll scare the fish.'

The sun breaches the horizon, and smudged with pink, the colours of the sea emerge. 'Over there,' Park says. 'See that darker strip?'

'Looks like a deep gully to me.' George is pleased to show that he knows a thing or two about fishing. He turns to Rory. 'Fish like to hide in deep gullies.'

They show Rory how to make a trail of berley, using the stale bread she'd been saving for the purpose. George baits her hook with a pipi and the two of them drop their lines over the side. Park is happy to watch. 'Truth is, I just like being out on the boat.'

Rory finds it hard to be both quiet and still, but against all odds, a fish attaches itself to her line. 'Easy, there.' George helps her to reel it in and Park scoops it into the boat with his net. A fair-sized flathead wriggles and writhes in the mesh, its scales refracting the morning light.

Rory looks at the floundering fish in horror. 'It can't breathe.'

The men exchange amused glances. 'Fish can't breathe out of the water,' Park explains.

'Put him back. Put him back.' Rory's distress verges on panic. She clutches George's arm. 'I don't want him to die.'

'She gets asthma,' George explains to a perplexed Park. 'She knows what it's like. Not breathing, I mean.'

So they photograph Rory with the fish and put it back in the water, where it stops a moment before flicking away.

'I like fishing,' Rory tells Stella later. 'But I don't like hurting the fish.'

'We only caught the one.' George knows it's no big deal, but can't help thinking it would have been nice to come home with their catch. He had wanted to show Rory how to gut and clean it, like his Poppy had shown him. He had wanted them to fry it in butter and savour the special taste of freshly caught fish. 'She's always been a sensitive kid,' he offers by way of explanation.

'No harm in that.' Stella's tone refutes the implied apology.

'Of course not.' George is shamed, but can't help wishing that Rory had taken to fishing in the way he'd imagined. He feels she's let him down, something he hasn't felt in a very long time.

'I know it's childish,' he confides later to Park. 'But I had my heart set on the two of us spending time together fishing.'

Park is sanguine. 'All my kids disappoint me at times, but not in any way that matters.' He hitches up his shorts. 'And as far as I can see, you 'n' young Rory got a lot more going for you than fishing.'

Of course we have. Late in life, George is beginning to understand that you can't mould a child in your own image. *And who'd want to be like me, anyway?* He returns to the caravan, and in the absence of a fish fry-up, makes Rory's favourite pancakes.

*

One night towards the end of the holiday, Stella, with lazy generosity, suggests that she and the older children will see to the younger ones while George and Park head for the local pub. 'Blokes need time at the pub,' she says. 'And you can get us some fish 'n' chips on the way back.'

George demurs (he's afraid of imposing) but Park hisses in his ear. 'Don't often get a leave pass, mate. Let's get a move on before Stell changes her mind.'

George hasn't been to a pub with anyone but Redgum for years and feels a brief pang of disloyalty to his old mate as he downs the cold lager Park brings over from the bar.

'Cheers.' He savours the bitter taste and the way it slides down his throat in double quick time. The day's heat has percolated through every corner of the small town and the usual sea breeze is late. Hot and sweaty, George flaps his T-shirt for relief. 'Another one?'

Park empties his glass in one gulp. 'Touches the spot, eh?'

It's no time at all before George is pronouncing his words with excessive care. It is important (he frowns in concentration) that Park understands his thoughts, the insights achieved over seventy-eight years *on the planet*. 'What I'm saying, mate, is that you can't trust any of them. From the prime min–is–ter down. They're all in it for their own … their own … own …' He waves an all-encompassing hand.

Park, George is impressed to see, is a man who recognises a profound thought when he hears one. 'Know exactly what you mean, mate. Snouts in the trough.'

'Exactly. Wallowing in it, the lot of them. Another beer?'

Park looks at his watch. 'Jesus. The missus'll kill us.'

As one, they bolt across to the fish shop. The queue is long and while they're waiting, a phone rings close by. George frowns down at his pocket. 'I think it's mine,' he says, surprised. Shirl had convinced him that he needed a mobile phone when Rory came into his care, but it rarely rings. He takes it out with two fingers, carefully, as though it might explode, and stares at it, wondering who might be ringing him here. *At this time of day.* 'Dunno who it can be.'

'You could answer it.'

It's Bree. 'Angie's back early,' she says. 'Wants to know where you are.'

George sobers in an instant. 'You didn't tell her?'

'What do you take me for? I told her you're somewhere down the beach way but you'll be home in a few days so … George. Are you still there?'

George opens and shuts his mouth like the fish they had so lately pulled from the sea. When he reaches for his voice, there is an obstruction, deep in his larynx. He clears his throat with difficulty. 'Yeah. I'm here.'

'Bad news?' Park's face swims through his field of vision. George nods.

'Stay put,' Bree says. 'I'll be there sometime Friday.'

Fish and chips wrapped and paid for, the two men walk back to the caravan park. George has regained some of his colour but says little. What could he say? It's all over. Bree isn't a bad sort of woman, but when it comes to the crunch, she's all talk – like those bloody politicians rabbiting on, promising this and that … His eyes slide sideways to meet Park's puzzled stare.

'Nothing I can't handle,' he lies.

*

George does his best to join in, but his mind is engaged elsewhere. He sees Stella raise her eyebrows at Park. *What's the matter with him?* they signal, and Park indicates his perplexity with a shrug.

He needs to get away and think. The children are arguing about who has the most chips and Ditto, red-faced and tired, roars his indignation. How long before George can reasonably leave the noisy feast? His head pounds, and as he nibbles disconsolately on a fish stick, his stomach begins to churn. 'Crook in the guts,' he mutters and runs towards the toilet block.

'Are you all right, mate?' Park's voice comes to him through the cubicle door. 'Stell says I oughta check on you.'

Tears spring unbidden to George's eyes. He is drowning in a wash of fear, and the kindness of his new friends unmans him. He sits, pants around his ankles, and begins to howl like a snotty-nosed kid. Like the weak sort of kid his father despised. He's seventy-eight years old, crying like a girl. There have been two great loves in his life and he's already lost one. Now he's losing the other.

The door shudders beneath Park's fists. 'George. George. Say something.' The handle rattles, none too gently. 'Do you need a doctor?'

George opens the door. 'Let me be for a bit, mate. I'll go back to the van – talk to you when the kids are asleep. Promise.' He could see by Park's expression that he doesn't look too good at all. So he adjusts his features into a less-than-convincing grin. 'I'll have a cuppa and you'll see – I'll be right as rain.'

By the time Rory and the Parker children are asleep, it's after ten o'clock. The night is warm and mothy, and a nearly full moon washes puddles of light over the camp ground as small groups cluster and drink and speak softly to each other so as not to wake their sleeping children. Stella and Park are waiting for him, two dim shapes under the tree between their compound and his van.

'Beer?'

'Not at the moment, mate. Stomach's still a bit iffy.'

'Tea? I've just boiled the kettle.' Stella disappears for a few minutes and returns with three mugs of tea. 'So ...' Her voice is softened by the night. 'Can we help?'

He doesn't mean to tell them, but the strain is too great — there's just no way he can deal with this alone. Voice subdued, he cups his hands around the warm mug and begins his story. Stell and Park listen without comment until he tells them how Angie had left Rory with him.

'Leaving her own child!' Stell and Park turn towards the tents where their own children lie sleeping, then draw together. 'Some kids have a bugger of a life.'

George isn't sure who's speaking, but knows in effect that it's both of them.

'So for going on two years it's just been me and Rory.' George's voice, without resonance, is swallowed by the dark. 'And after all we've been through together, her mother is coming to take her off to West Wyalong.'

'Bloody hell!' Park is indignant, but George can see that Stella is conflicted. Her instincts must tell her that a child should be with its mother. Well, one part of him thought so, too. But such a mother. Stella's large expressive face screws up in an effort to understand.

'Drugs, you say?'

George has to be honest. 'She was a user earlier on, I think, but she was clean by the time I met her. At least, I think she was. Dunno if she still is. Bree – that's her girlfriend – she reckons the bloke Angie ran off with is a dealer and the new one's been arrested for possession.'

'That poor child.' Stella wipes away a tear. 'Whatever will happen to her?'

'Dunno. She'll probably end up with social services.' He heaves himself up and squares his shoulders. 'Sorry to bother you with all my problems. Her mate Bree's coming tomorrow. She's got some plan but I'm not holding me breath.'

The generously fleshed woman and the compact little man look almost comical, sitting there side by side, but George senses the strength that comes from shared values and the united front they present to the world. Scary Mary might be the manager of the family, but Stella and Park are its heart.

15

'Aunty Bree! It's Aunty Bree.' Rory runs towards the two figures walking down behind the vans. 'And Redgum! It's Redgum! Come and see me on the boogie board.' She dances round them, shouting for her new friends. 'Harry. Mary. It's my Aunty Bree and Redgum. He's the scientist I told you about.'

'In a moment, love.' Bree kisses her on the cheek. 'We need to talk to Poppy George first.'

'Come in.' George is surprised to see Redgum but glad of the opportunity to call on the big man's uncomplicated common sense.

Despite the seriousness of the problem, George plays at host. 'Another nice day,' he says, switching on the kettle and fishing in the cupboard for some biscuits. He turns to the fridge. 'What's the matter with me? I'm turning into an old woman. After that long drive, you'll want a beer.'

'Too right.'

It's hot in the van, so they set up under a neighbouring tree.

'Have you spoken to Angie?'

'Told her you might be a couple of days late. With the good weather and all.'

George is grateful for crumbs but forces himself to face reality. 'Still set on West Wyalong, is she?'

'Silly bitch.'

'I guess that's a "yes".' George, head bowed, hands between his knees, is remote from the holiday buzz and bustle. 'I'll see if we can stay another couple of days. Then I suppose it's home to face the music.'

'Not if we can help it.' Redgum puts down his beer and turns to Bree. 'We've got a plan, haven't we?'

'Redgum and me, we reckon Rory shouldn't go back unless Angie agrees to stay with you.'

'Easier said than done.'

Bree lowers her voice. 'This is the plan …'

So far, it sounds almost feasible. George wants it to be feasible. 'So I take Rory somewhere till it blows over one way or another? But where?'

'We haven't got that far yet,' Bree has to admit.

'Perhaps we can help.' Stella and Park appear, it seems, from nowhere. 'Nice to meet you,' Stella says as George introduces them. 'Ears like a vacuum cleaner,' she explains to the puzzled newcomers. She addresses herself to Bree, who has assumed an air of authority. 'They can stay at our place. No one around for miles. Except Rabbit, but he won't be a problem. We'll be here till school goes back – that'll allow them another four weeks.'

'I can't let you …'

'Of course you can. But we have to be careful in case they come looking. Let me think, now.'

Park explains. 'Stell watches every police show on television. Mark my words – she'll know what to do.'

Stella's eyes gleam. 'We've got a couple of things to sort out first. They'll be able to trace your car. And your credit card and phone.'

Bree, who's been looking annoyed at being gazumped in the planning stakes, smirks. 'Ahead of you there,' she says. 'We drove up in separate cars while it was still dark. Redgum's is parked out on the road near town, and the other one's hidden in bush a few k's back. I got it from a friend of a friend. *Untraceable*, that's what he said.'

'How much … ?' George begins but Redgum interrupts him.

'You don't know how much you'll need,' he says quietly. 'I'm in no hurry. What else have I got to do with me money?'

George blinks behind his glasses. 'Ta, mate.'

'So,' Stella sums up, earning another glare from Bree. 'George leaves in his own car tomorrow as planned. Then he picks up the other car and drives out to our place until what's-her-name gets tired of waiting or Bree talks her into staying.'

'He'll need cash in hand.' Park is eager to contribute to the plan. 'I'll take him round to the bank. He can tell them he needs cash to pay a bloke for a car. That'll explain the large withdrawal. Private sellers always want cash.'

Redgum pulls an envelope full of notes from his backpack. 'Some readies here, too – just in case.'

'They'll need at least one overnight stop on the way,' Stella warns. 'And we don't want them recognised.'

'Easy-peasy.' Bree's back in the game. 'We'll shave George's head and buy him some sunglasses. And ...' She's all fired up. 'We can cut Rory's hair and dye it dark brown.'

Stella hugs herself with excitement. 'We'll disguise her as a boy. She's the same size as Harry – close enough, anyway.'

While they plan around him, George listens in a kind of daze. He has never contemplated kidnapping Rory. He just wants a few more days with her. Then enough time to persuade Angie to stay in Melbourne. How is it possible that all these apparently responsible adults are planning what has to be a crime? Or even if it isn't a crime, is it the right thing to do? Not from Angie's point of view – that much is obvious. But in the overall scheme of things, what's in Rory's best interests? He tries to imagine her in five, ten, twenty years' time. Will she be an addict, or homeless, or reliant on some sleazeball for support? Will she be another Angie, small child in tow, her best not nearly enough to rescue her child from the same fate? George sees them, one generation after another, plodding through life, heads bowed, or racing reckless to the same end. He, George, can offer her so much more. Stability. Education. (He sees her, clear as can be, in a cap and gown, Doctor Aurora-Jane

Wilson – in this scenario, even her name sounds dignified.) And love. His love will never waver. She can rely on him every inch of the way. *As long as I can keep it together until she grows up.* This thought, submerged for some time, bobs up to the surface like a drowned man, a clamorous corpse that, if he's to go along with this preposterous plan, needs to be buried deep in the earth.

'George, are you listening?' His reverie broken, George looks around at the four conspirators – all of them his friends. 'I can't let you do it,' he says. 'You could end up in jail and – wait—' A thought strikes him. 'Shirl. Does she know anything about this?'

Bree shakes her head. 'Only told Redgum 'cos he had the key to your house.'

Stella nods her approval. 'Excellent. *A need to know.* That's what they call it.'

George is relieved. He isn't sure how Shirl would react, but it's hard to imagine that she'd condone kidnapping. Best keep her well out of it.

'Accessories,' Stella confirms. 'That's what we are. If you're caught at our house, we'll tell them you did it all off your own bat. That you knew the house would be empty and used it without us knowing.'

'No reason to suspect us, either,' Bree says. 'We came in from the beach. No one knows we're here.'

'But all this cloak-and-dagger stuff. Isn't it a bit over the top?'

'You haven't spoken to her,' Bree says. 'She's very jumpy and aggro at the moment. I thought I knew her, but

I don't know what she'll do if Rory's not back by Monday. We need to play it safe.' George looks so alarmed that she hastens to reassure him. 'She wouldn't call the cops or anything. Lover boy's got too much to hide. But he does have some nasty mates.'

Unsure whether it's crazy or courageous, George agrees to go along with their plan. How else can he keep his little girl? His stomach betrays his anxiety, but he has to be firm. Angie, with her wild ways, has lost the right to be a parent.

*

How many years is it since he'd stood behind Penny, holding a lock of the rusty grey hair that fell, soft and full, just above her shoulders? In his other hand were scissors. 'I don't think I can do this, Pen.'

'I need you to do it. It's better than losing it in clumps.' She smiled without conviction. 'I suppose this is the price we pay for vanity.'

He began – lifting each strand, brushing it with his lips, then cutting, sculpting, until all that was left were short tufts.

'Now the shaver.' Her voice was so steady – and there he was, his hand shaking so much that he could barely hold the razor. He turned the dial to zero and began at the back. Her eyes were closed; he could see them in the mirror. Shadows lay across her skin like bruises. He screamed without sound – *God Almighty*. Then resumed his task, unsure if he'd just uttered a prayer or a curse.

As the razor did its work, he cupped her head in his free hand. And through his fingers, with awful clarity, he came to understand her mortality. Shrouded in a thin layer of flesh, a skull was biding its time. Shorn of its protective fleece, it laid bare sinuous curves, delicate undulations. *Remember, man that thou art dust* ... Life was so fragile. He wanted to stand there forever, holding her mortal skull; shielding her from life and death.

*

'Hold still.' Bree is shaving around his ears. 'I'm giving you a number-one. Don't want you to look too bald.'

It's such an intimate thing, shaving someone. Pen had shaved him a couple of times when he had the flu. He can't have been too sick because they made love afterwards. Bree rests his head on her stomach as she finishes the front, and George finds, to his embarrassment, that he's aroused. And he'd just been thinking of Pen. He closes his eyes and shifts in his seat. It's all too difficult.

*

Rory is not at all happy with the thought of having her hair cut. From a straggle of light, yellowy brown, it is now a deep honey colour and falls thick and shiny, long enough, as she demonstrates, for a ponytail. No wonder she's appalled at the prospect of a boyish crop. 'Me and Maryam and Kirsty are growing our hair as long as Rapunzel,'

243

she shouts at the scissor-wielding Bree. 'We measure it every single day with our rulers. And …' She pauses to emphasise the outrageousness of her situation. 'I'm already ten centimetres behind the others. I'm not a boy,' she continues, clutching her head. 'And I don't want to look like one.' Having said her piece, she makes a sudden dash for the door, only to be blocked by the diminutive figure of Park, who catches her by the shoulders and squats down so they can talk face to face.

'Hey there, Rorykins. Slow down.' His voice is conspiratorial and, though poised for flight, she listens as he continues. 'It's like this. We're playing this huge joke on everyone in the whole world and I reckon you're just the girl to help us out.'

Rory is intrigued. George can tell by the way she stops, head to one side. With any luck she'll go into negotiation mode. They'll have to up the ante here. The situation is way beyond Choc Wedges. With inspiration born of two Rory-filled years, he picks up the first available container. 'We'll pay you, of course. Every time someone mistakes you for a boy, I'll put a dollar in this lunchbox.'

Rory's inbuilt calculator whirrs. 'How many dollars to buy a dog?'

Despite the seriousness of their situation, George can't help but grin.

'About seventy-nine, I think,' says Park. 'You'll have to pretend very hard.'

Rory looks at George. 'Is that true?'

'Park should know,' he tells her. 'He's got a couple of dogs of his own. We can meet them when we go to his place.'

So Bree and Stella dye Rory's hair a dark brown and cut it as short as she (and they) can bear. 'It'll grow again in no time,' Stella whispers.

'No wearing pink,' Bree warns her. 'That'd be a dead giveaway.'

Rory is still inclined to sulk, but when the dependable Scary Mary comes in and asks who the new boy is, she gleefully holds out her lunchbox. 'One dollar, Poppy George.' She giggles. 'Only seventy-eight to go.'

*

Bree and Redgum plan to slip away after dark. It wouldn't do for strangers to be seen around George's caravan. Stella brings them some meat and salad from her barbecue and George eats inside with them, while Rory shouts and tumbles about with the Parker children.

George looks out the window. 'She'll miss them. Growing up with all these other kids around, down here, at the beach … It's the sort of *healthy* life I'd like her to have.'

'That's for sure.' Redgum wraps a sausage in bread and he, too, looks out at the clamour of children. 'Sometimes a man wishes he'd had a kid or two of his own.' He adds tomato sauce to the sandwich and savours his first bite. '"Course, little tackers come with a missus and who'd have an old bloke like me?'

'Could do worse.' Bree busies herself with the salad, and won't meet George's quizzical gaze. He glances across at Redgum, but his big mate is refusing the proffered salad. 'Lettuce,' he declares, 'is for rabbits.'

After dinner, Rory and George walk Redgum and Bree to their car via the beach. They stop at the path leading to the road and the two men shake hands, their clasp lingering a fraction longer than usual.

'All the best, mate.'

'Yeah. I owe you one. That's for sure.'

Bree hugs a startled George and kisses him on the cheek. 'Good luck. And don't forget – ditch the mobile before you leave. I'll ring the Parkers' place from a phone box in a couple of days.'

They hug Rory in turn. 'See you later, alligator. Be a good girl for Poppy.'

As they disappear into the dusk, George is chagrined to see Bree take Redgum's hand. The track is rough. That's the obvious reason. Although, there was that look she gave him when he spoke of children. The thought of them together bothers George – it isn't all that long ago that she'd come on to him. This pang, it must be jealousy – is it for Bree or for Redgum? Redgum is a nice bloke, but what would a woman over thirty years his junior see in him? *Security*, he thinks. *She wants security.* Well, she'd get that in spades with Redgum. He sends a silent message through the dark. *If you're after my mate, girlie, you just better do the right thing by him.*

'Come on, Rory.' They turn back towards the caravan park, but as their feet whisper across the sand, George feels a deep reluctance for the venture ahead. At that moment he truly understands his situation. After tomorrow, he and Rory are on their own. She snuggles into his side, and with absent-minded affection, he tousles her hair. His fingers understand before he does. From now on, he has a grandson.

16

George and Rory leave the Red Dolphin after an early breakfast and Park follows them to where the untraceable car — a roomy station wagon — is hidden. The men quickly transfer the luggage from one vehicle to the other and Rory climbs into the back seat. 'Bye, Uncle Park.'

The men shake hands. 'Can't thank you and Stell enough, mate.'

'No worries. Safe trip.'

As Park stands on the verge, waving them out of sight, George has to suppress a creeping panic. It's all up to him now.

With so many years of moving from place to place, Rory has learned to face most changes with equanimity and, as they turn north, she chatters on about the farm and the dogs and wonders aloud if there'll be a river to swim in.

George drives with a nervous eye on the road behind, and is relieved when a dark-blue sedan that has been following them for miles turns off on the road to Canberra.

How on earth had he allowed himself to be talked into this? It was madness, pure and simple. There's a U-turn bay ahead – it isn't too late to change his mind. But then Rory, who's been quiet for a while, sits back and sighs with a long, contented exhalation.

'Can we go to the caravan park again next year?'

George doesn't know how to answer her. 'We'll see,' is the best he can do.

'Please. Please. Please. Promise. It was the best holiday anyone has ever had in the whole world.'

It was. And if everything goes according to plan, they'll go back year after year and stay beside the Parkers. Year after year, until she grows up. Then his job will be done and he'll sit back, an old man (a very old man) and enjoy watching her children. He sees them, a boy and a girl, sitting by his side as he tells them stories. 'I remember when your mum was a little girl ...'

The alternative, that the plan fails and Angie has her way, is too awful to imagine. He turns to Rory, who is waiting for his answer.

'Will you remember this holiday, do you think? I mean, when you grow up?'

'Of course,' she scoffs. 'I got the best remembering in Grade 1.'

'Can't say fairer than that.'

'Soooo. We can go back?'

George makes the best promise he can. 'I promise to try my best to go back with you next year.'

'Yay!'

Rory hasn't noticed the equivocation, the fence he placed around his promise.

*

The drive to Parker's Run takes two days, thankfully uneventful. But what is happening back home? George, who had once resented the sound of a phone shattering his solitude, begins to wish he hadn't thrown away his mobile and needs to make an effort to console himself. His co-conspirators are drama queens. Even the police have to go to court to track phone calls. Or was that in England? Or even the US? He's sure he's heard it somewhere. So Rory whines (*Are we there yet?*) and George chews over these unsettling thoughts as they drive through scrubby bushland punctuated by sparsely populated towns and hamlets. A night in an indifferent motel, more driving and they're within fifty kilometres of their destination.

'Here we are,' says George. 'Half an hour to Patterson's Creek then only twenty minutes to Park's place.' They stop in the small town to buy a newspaper, cold drinks and a few perishables.

'Passin' through?'

This simple (or is it a deceptively simple) question elicits a stammered reply. 'Yeah. No. Stayin' at Park's place. Me brother. Park's me brother.'

'You're the one from Adelaide!' The woman behind the counter has bleached hair and black, spiky eyelashes, which she bats at George over the cash register.

250

'Yeah. Something in your eye?' he asks with what he hopes is that country concern for neighbours you read so much about. 'Hold the lid like so.' He demonstrates on his own eye. 'Then blink.'

'Gawd help us.' The woman gives him his change without further discussion. George notices that her eye seems to have improved without his help.

*

'That must be Warren's place.' George slows down and turns to Rory in the back seat. 'Mr Warren's looking after the dogs.'

The shack looks as though it's held together with sellotape and string. Greying timber walls, a sagging verandah and a series of sheds and lean-tos hunker down on a graceless, barren block of land. A few chooks peck their way through the dust and George is surprised to see that their coop is sturdy and well maintained.

Feeling nervous, he knocks on the door. 'Anyone home?'

'Who's askin'?'

George jumps. The voice, coming from the side of the house, is accompanied by the barking of dogs.

'You must be Pat Warren,' George says. 'I'm Park's brother, Jeff.'

The man approaches with a stiff, bow-legged gait. 'Yeah. He rang.' He holds out his hand, eyes unsmiling. 'Rabbit. They call me Rabbit.'

It's difficult to estimate Rabbit's age. His skin is hard and brown like dried mud in a claypan, and the hand George takes is like an old rooster's claw. 'Takin' the dogs off me hands, are you?'

Restrained by Rabbit, the dogs continue to growl and George steps back. 'Not too friendly, are they?'

'We don't like strangers.' George doesn't know what to say and the other man decides to relent. Observing his struggle, George almost expects that the effort will cause the hostile old face to crack into a thousand pieces. 'But I'll introduce you, like.' He spots Rory peering from the window of the car. 'They love kids, but. They'd have to, wouldn't they? Livin' with Stella and Park.'

'My grandson, Roy,' George says, then raises his voice. 'Stay in the car, Roy, while I see about the dogs.'

Rusty is a labrador, ancient, fat and arthritic. He responds to George's overtures with benevolent disdain, while the border collies, Minnie and Dog, dance over to sniff at his hand.

'Dog'll keep you busy. He's only three months old.' Rabbit delivers the news as though it was yet another of life's many tribulations. 'Park's been lookin' for a good home.'

Park had mentioned Dog, but not that he's a pup. One more thing to worry about – first a child, then a pup. And a pretty lively one at that. George looks at the capering Dog with some misgiving. 'Not sure we can manage a pup.'

Rabbit snorts. 'From Adelaide, aren't you?' *That says it all*, he implies.

Suitably squashed, George calls to Rory. 'Come on, love – mate. Mr Warren says the dogs like kids.'

'Go slow,' Rabbit tells her. 'Let 'em smell your hand. That's right.' Rory is soon hugging and kissing the dogs, who respond with delight. It's obvious that they miss the Parker children.

Rabbit turns to George. 'Your boy's playing with them dogs like a flippin' girl.' His scorn is as vast as the landscape.

George freezes. 'That's city kids for you,' he says, bundling Rory back into the car.

Rabbit looks even more morose. 'Can't say I like kids much meself – but city kids? They take the cake.'

*

'This is it.' The sandstone house, framed in the car windscreen, is long and low, stretched across the flat horizon as though it had grown, fully fashioned, from the soil. A wide verandah on all sides and several large gum trees provide shade from the searing heat. And it is hot. George feels the sweat saturating his collar, running down his face, sticking his shirt to his back. The dogs, with no such city reservations, set up an excited bark, paws scrabbling in the back of the station wagon.

Inside, the house is cool (or maybe just cooler). The curtains are drawn and even when they pull them open, the verandah prevents a direct solar assault. Before unpacking the car, George and Rory sit in the flag-stoned kitchen and wolf down two each of the icy-poles Stella has stored in the freezer.

'I reckon those dogs must be pretty thirsty by now. How about you give them a drink.' George points to the bowls by the sink and Rory is delighted to see them slurp up every last drop.

'That can be your job,' George says. 'If you want a dog of your own, you'll have to learn how to look after them.'

'I will.' She's already refilling the bowls. 'C'mon, Rusty, Min, Dog. Let's play.'

Rusty walks out onto the verandah and lies down, head on paws. George has a good deal of sympathy for the dog that continues to ignore Rory's entreaties. 'Let him be, sweetheart. He's a bit like me – all worn out.'

Min and Dog, however, are ready to play, and Rory's only too happy to oblige.

George refuses his weary body's call to rest and finishes unpacking the car. When the phone rings, he feels his stomach lurch and almost doesn't answer. After all, it could be anyone. On the fifth ring, he picks up the phone and almost whispers, 'Hello?'

It's Park. 'Just checkin' you got there okay. Everything orright?'

'Good, mate. Good. Got the dogs from Rabbit.'

'Miserable bugger, but he knows his dogs. By the way, how's Rory getting on with them?'

'Running them ragged.'

'That's the stuff. See how she goes with Dog. She can have him if they get on.'

'Geez, you don't have to do that.'

'Up to you. They got lots of energy, border collies, but they're great with kids. If you decide to keep him, let Rory name him. Can't be called Dog for the rest of his life.'

*

They are out in the middle of nowhere and George is surprised that there's plenty to keep them busy. Rabbit drops by to show them how to feed the homestead chooks and collect the eggs. Together with care of the dogs, Rory takes on the hens as her special chore. George, meanwhile, busies himself with some small repairs around the house, and before it gets too hot each day, tends the kitchen garden. He enjoys sitting on the verandah, too, either reading or just looking out to where land meets sky, not really thinking of anything at all. In later years, he will recognise this as contentment.

Park had told them about the swimming hole, and on the second day they drive a short distance to the creek. George spreads out their things under the shade of the river gums, while Rory and the dogs run to the water.

'Wait till I check the depth,' George yells. 'Remember your water drill.'

By the time he is organised, the dogs are swimming out to the middle and Rory capering on the edge. 'Hurry up, Poppy George.'

The brown water ripples over their sweaty bodies and George splashes and ducks and snorts like a kid. As Rory says, it's the best fun. Min and Dog chase the sticks they throw, while Rusty, after a brief swim, shakes his fur and settles in the shade. When George joins him, the dog puts his head on his lap and drifts off to sleep. George fondles the silky ears. 'We can't keep up with those young folk for long, can we, boy?'

It's the question that, since his precautionary visit to the doctor, George has refused to tackle head-on. He has skirted the edges once or twice, but that's all. At home, at the beach with the Parkers – even driving up here – he always had something to divert his attention when the nagging thought arose. But out here, where life is simplified, it presents itself with an insistence he can no longer ignore. He's an old man and that's a fact. In no time he'll be eighty, and Rory will still be at primary school. He does some fuzzy calculations. She'll need him for at least another eleven, twelve years. What if he dies, or has a stroke? What if he develops Alzheimer's? Afraid to face his ageing, he stopped checking his hands for tremors a while ago. Though the air feels as hot as anything he experienced in his time as a boiler-maker, George shivers. *Someone's stepping on your grave.* That's what they used to say when they were kids.

He begins to worry about what's happening at home. Has Angie been persuaded to stay? That's by far the best outcome – all of them living together in Mercy Street. Over time, he could get Angie on track, so that if anything happened to him, Rory would be secure. He begins to feel anxious that they aren't where they can hear the phone. They've been here two days and there's still no word from

Bree. According to his original plans, he is now three days overdue and Angie must be wondering what has happened to them. 'Five more minutes,' he calls. 'We have to go back soon.'

'Not yet. I'm teaching Dog how to do a duck-dive.'

It's a good forty-five minutes before they're ready to drive back to the house. George, happy to settle with his book, is relieved to see that Rory and the young dogs have worn each other out. 'Quiet time,' he says. 'You can draw or read, maybe.'

'I'll draw Aunty Bree and Redgum a picture of Dog,' she decides. 'And one for Aunty Shirl and Mr and Mrs Nguyen. And one for Maryam and one for Kirsty.' She comes over and kisses his bald head. 'And a special one for you.'

'That's the way.' George opens his book at page twenty-four. By page twenty-seven, he's asleep.

*

Turning the corner into Mercy Street, Angie experiences the unfamiliar sensation of coming home. She has some awesome presents for Rory – a Barbie with a glamour wardrobe and a backpack shaped like a koala. She even got George a present – a tea towel saying 'Mermaid Beach' with pictures of the sea and stuff. He went somewhere up there with his wife. Not bad – remembering a thing like that.

The front windows are shut, the blinds drawn. *Like it was the first time I saw it*, she remembers. *Not very welcoming.* After they had been living there a while, somehow the blinds were always open in the daytime. *Much more cheerful, if you ask me.* Angie hesitates at the gate, hoping that George doesn't get all preachy. She's reluctant to admit it, even to herself, but she misses him sometimes. A dad like George would've been a pain, but he did what he thought was best. Like he cared what happened to her.

She frowns at the straggly lawn. Unusual. George is so fussy about his lawn. The front door is closed. Should she knock or use her key? Her key is somewhere in her anarchic backpack so she knocks several times before deciding to check with the Nguyens.

Mrs Nguyen gives her the evil eye. 'They go on a holiday.'

Angie is shocked. She had expected to come back and find Rory waiting right where she left her. They had plans, she and Charlie. He lived in this West Wyalong place when he was a kid, and he reckons they can set up there on the cheap and keep clean. No drugs there when he left twenty years ago. They'll have this nice house and Rory can go to school and George can come to visit. Though, admittedly, the last was more her plan than Charlie's, but George was all right and the kid liked him. He'd be pleased with her, would George. In some obscure way, this is important to her. *I have a plan*, she sees herself telling him, all responsible and mature. *When we get to West Wyalong, we'll have a house and we'll be a proper family, Charlie and Rory and me.*

But where has he taken Rory? Now she's here, she realises that she wants to see her daughter more than she ever imagined. At a loss, she looks up and down the street, as though George and Rory might appear from somewhere around the corner. 'Let's try Bree.' Angie gets back on the bike, which has been revving for some time. Charlie's scowl tells her his patience is wearing thin. Fortunately, it takes no time at all to get to Mill Street.

'It's me, girlfriend.' Angie throws her arms around a surprised Bree's neck. The other woman pulls back and, piqued, Angie cuts to the chase. 'Where's George taken Rory?'

'Down the beach,' Bree tells her. 'Don't know where.'

'There's a nice homecoming for you.' Angie glares at Bree. 'Me kid gone and me bestie sounding like she's got a broom stuck up her arse.'

But she's back, and she wants to see Rory. Soon – sooner than soon. Is that too much for a mother to ask?

*

George and Rory are playing Uno when the phone rings. It's Bree, who tells him she's ringing from a public phone. (Where she managed to find one, George can't imagine.)

'Angie's getting restless. And so's Charlie. He pretends he wants Rory, but I reckon he just wants to get going.'

'What about those mates of his?' Suddenly nervous, George sees a phalanx of leather-clad hoodlums roaring into town, turning his harmless lie into a terrifying reality. Has he covered his tracks well enough? He's read loads of detective thrillers and knows there are ways and means. He blanches as he pictures what the means might be.

Bree is quite blasé, considering. 'Don't worry about that. He's not making any threats. If we're lucky, he'll get tired of waiting and go. With or without Angie.'

'You must get her to stay.' George can't impress Bree enough with the necessity of this solution and imbues his voice with as much urgency as possible. 'Get her to stay but encourage him to leave.'

'Like I've got any say.' Bree sounds annoyed. 'She's driving me crazy with questions, but there's no way she'll listen to any advice I give her.'

George is fearful, not far from panic. 'So what do we do now?'

'Give me a bit more time. I don't think Charlie'll last much longer. Then it'll be easier to work on Angie.'

George returns to the game, but his concentration is shot. Putting down his wild card, he calls the wrong colour.

'Green. You should've said green.' Rory gives an exasperated sigh. 'I don't want you to let me win. I'm in Grade 2 now and I can win all by myself.'

'I'm trying very hard. I really am. It's just that I'm not very good at this game.'

'Mummy was.'

George flinches. This is the first time she has mentioned her mother in months and he has an awful feeling that he's a long way from winning the endgame.

*

'You mean we can keep him? Take him home?' The delight on Rory's face is matched only by George's. He has consulted Rabbit, who is helping them train Dog (now known as Richie) and the man agrees, with a few caveats, that Rory is worthy.

'He's not such a sissy after bein' out here for a bit. Long way to go, but.'

George still sometimes forgets Rory's new identity as his grandson, and wonders for a moment who Rabbit is referring to. 'Yes. Of course. Roy.' It's pathetic, but he wants full endorsement from this dour old bushie. 'The kid seems to have a way with dogs, wouldn't you say?'

'Wouldn't go that far.' Rabbit scratches his chest where a few grey hairs escape the confines of a grubby singlet. 'All dogs is different. He's lucky this fella's got a good temperament.'

Old bugger. Why can't he admit Rory's done a good job? George is annoyed but can't afford to antagonise the man. 'Yeah. It all goes into the mix. Thanks for your help, anyway.' He indicates a box on the verandah. 'A slab. Fourex okay? For helping the kid with the dog.'

Rabbit goes off with a brief nod and George and Rory high-five in the way she has shown him. 'Here's to you and Dog – known forever after as the mighty Richie.'

17

The kitchen calendar hangs right at eye-level, so George can't ignore it. Every day it brings them closer to the end of the month when Stella and Park are due home and he and Rory will have to leave. If things aren't sorted by then, where can they go? Richie, who is having an identity crisis and still answers to Dog, flops at his feet and George's head begins to ache. You can't just wander the country with a school-aged kid and a dog. George curses under his breath as Richie licks his bare foot. Why on earth had he complicated things by taking on a dog? Even as he asks himself the question, he knows the answer – they now own a dog because he had anticipated Rory's delight and that was good enough for him.

The phone rings at about four o'clock. It's Bree, with an urgency in her voice that fills him with dread. 'Don't let Rory watch the news tonight. Angie's gone and told the police.'

George dredges his response from somewhere beyond his day-to-day experience – a fictional world, inhabited by fictional characters who commit fictional crimes. 'The police, you say? Why? What about Charlie?'

Bree's voice is grim. 'Charlie left yesterday and Angie went out and got drunk. I mean really, really drunk. When the cops picked her up, she blubbed all over them and said her daughter had been kidnapped – George, are you there?'

'She left Rory with me – asked me to look after her. How's that kidnap?' Something prevents George from taking in the situation. 'Kidnap? There's no logic in that. Once they know the truth, the cops'll understand.'

Bree continues as though he hasn't spoken. 'Stay put for the moment. No one knows where you are except the Parkers, Redgum and me – and we're not telling. When Angie has time to think, she'll tell them the truth. Trouble is, it might take a while. They're kind of making a fuss of her – the cops, social workers, telly news reporters. She's enjoying all the attention.'

George can't fasten on the facts and is incapable of making a decision or even formulating the question. 'We can't go off half-cocked. Ring back after nine,' he says. 'Rory'll be in bed by then.'

Five forty-nine and Rory is watching some animated rubbish about a pig. 'What about you hop in the bath and have a nice play while I watch the news.'

Rory looks up, surprised. He'd often told her that they had to be careful with water, but as she prefers a bath to a quick shower she doesn't argue, and George closes the bathroom door just in time to catch the beginning of the news. The first item is about the floods up north, followed by a horror smash on the Princes Highway. Then a not-too-recent photo of Rory appears on the backdrop.

'*Police are seeking the whereabouts of schoolgirl Aurora Jane – Rory – Wilson. They are concerned for the welfare of the six-year-old from the Melbourne suburb of Fairfield, who was last seen at the Red Dolphin Caravan Park, Pambula, in the company of one George Johnson ...*'

Rory's likeness morphs into a photo of George standing in the kitchen at her birthday party. No sign of the food, the cake, the Happy Birthday sign. Just an elderly man. An odd-looking elderly man with a faint smirk and a stain on his shirt.

George feels sick. What do they mean 'concerned'? She's with her Poppy George. Angie knows that. Even so, he's heard of reporters getting the wrong end of the stick, deliberately or not, pumping up a story. When Angie actually listens to what they're saying, she'll put them right. He needs reassurance. *She will, won't she, Pen?*

He returns to the screen in time to see the Crime Stoppers number and hear that anyone knowing his whereabouts should make contact. Then, a minor sop to his outraged feelings: '*The man is not believed to be dangerous, but police advise that he should be approached with caution. Stay tuned. After the break, we have Bonza, the young koala found after the bushfires in Victoria's Grampians region ...*'

Checking in the mirror over the mantel, George is relieved to see that he's pretty much unrecognisable as the man in the photo. He has kept his head shaved and over time grown a grizzled beard, which he thinks makes him look distinguished. (A look he had never dared aspire to in the past.) So he's okay, but what about Rory? He can't remember seeing the lighter roots he was supposed to look out for. How long does it take? Thank goodness Bree had given him a good supply of hair dye. It's comb-through stuff, so he'll manage without help. He has to, doesn't he?

When Rory comes out from her bath, shining and pink, George switches off the television and peers at her head. So far, so good.

'Are you all right, Poppy?'

'Yeah – yeah. I'm fine.'

'You look like you've been crying.'

'Just the onions, love.' George blinks. 'Come and give your Poppy a big hug.'

Skinny arms twine around his neck. And at that moment, George becomes a confirmed outlaw. He can't, he won't let her go.

*

Their new bedtime ritual includes a quiet time, cuddled up on the lumpy verandah sofa. On one of the untidy bookshelves, they had found an astronomical atlas, and every night regard each other with delight as they identify the evening star, the Southern Cross, the Saucepan, the Milky Way – all burning intense and white in an unpolluted sky.

Tonight, George's storytelling takes on a mythic quality. 'There was once a beautiful princess,' he tells her, 'and she lived in a blue and white palace with a man who wasn't a prince and who wasn't handsome, but she loved him anyway.'

'Was he rich?'

'No. He wasn't rich, but he loved his princess more than anything, so they married and were very, very happy. But one day, she told him that she was a sky-princess and that it was time for her to return to the stars. "I'll come, too," he said, but she smiled a sorrowful smile and said that she had to go alone.'

'Was he sad?'

'He was very sad. But before she went, she told him that he could look up at the stars every night and she would be there, watching over him.'

'We should look for her, too.'

'So we should. But guess what? Because the man who wasn't a prince was so very lonely, she sent him a sky-child, all the way from the stars.'

'Did he love her, too?'

'More than anything else in the whole world. She was his special gift from his lost princess – the most beautiful sky-child of all.'

Rory kisses him goodnight and George is left alone, looking up at what is, after all, an ultimately unknowable vastness. No wonder humans need stories to make sense of it all – stories that, no matter how elevated, are no more than narrative dross compared to what they endeavour to explain. He and Rory had tried to find the princess star but agreed in the end that there were too many to choose from. Funny how that story came to his mind unbidden.

He had never thought before that Rory might be a gift from his dead wife. Never believed in an afterlife. When you're dead, you're dead. That's it, as far as he's concerned. Nevertheless, as he steps out under the dome of stars, he finds a prayer on his lips – not a prayer to a distant god, but a prayer wholly domestic, wholly earthbound. *Don't let them take her away. Please, Pen. I couldn't bear it.*

*

Bree rings back as promised. 'So what do you think?'

'I'm not giving her up.' George is surprised by his own vehemence. 'Angie forfeited the right to Rory when she ran off. It's going on two years, Bree. And in all that time we got twelve phone calls. Twelve! I counted them. And for most of those she was drunk or stoned.'

'It's your decision, George.'

'My oath it is.' But Bree is wavering. He can hear it in her voice. Rattled more than he cares to admit, he speaks to her sharply. 'You're not going to let us down, are you?'

'No. But I can't get involved any more than I am. With my record I'll end up doing time for sure.'

She sounds really frightened and she's already done more than he could have reasonably expected. 'You're right,' he says. 'It's my problem. As it happens, I've got a plan but it's better you don't know.'

'I'll only ring if there's something you really need to know – and George?'

'Yes, love?'

'Good luck.'

'No worries. And keep Redgum out of trouble, won't you? He's not a very good liar.'

George puts down the phone and opens a can of beer. He has never been a good liar either, but now lies slide from his tongue without the impediments of consciousness or conscience. He has no plan, just resolve. And resolve, though a start, is not nearly enough. He still has a week before Park and Stella's return. Tomorrow he'll organise things so, if forced to, they can leave in a hurry, but he has no idea where to go. That's the best he can do for now – it's time to prepare for bed. But as soon as his head hits the pillow, he's wide awake and his brain continues to buzz, ideas forming, collapsing and reassembling like fragments of glass in a kaleidoscope.

What if … ? How about … ? We could … We could!

He sits up and clutches at the momentary hope a random reassembling has produced. He'd read about it somewhere – people managing to live cheaply and anonymously in places like Thailand and Bali. Riding the wave of this thought, he sees them in some remote tropical village where his pension would be enough to live on, with Rory attending an English school (miraculously operating in this insignificant place) and … He flops back on the pillow. What on earth is he thinking? He'll have to do a lot better than that. His overwrought imagination crumbles into dust under the implacable force of reality. They don't have passports. As a fugitive, he'd have no pension. Sudden weariness prevents him from further planning, fanciful or otherwise. He turns over, determined to sleep. Things always seem brighter in the morning.

*

Rory is training Richie Dog to beg. None too successfully, but at least it keeps her busy while George makes his preparations. He's pleased that he filled up with petrol last time he went to the township, and estimates that, with good preparation, they could be on the road within an hour if necessary. He works on this most of the morning, which leaves him a couple of hours to worry before taking Rory for the promised trip to the swimming hole later in the day.

So he frets and dozes while Rory makes a rainbow snake out of penne pasta and string. She's an enterprising little kid. Artistic, too. Her activity makes George feel guilty, so he takes out the road map and tries to focus. Which way would they expect him to go? He has no idea himself, so why would they? 'They' loom in his imagination as social workers with judgemental briefcases, and SWAT teams and lawyers and judges in wigs. He worries at the map and finally settles on a place, a largish town by the look of it. They'll stop there and head for Sydney the next day. Hide in a crowd. He's beginning to feel very exposed out here.

*

George douses his head and comes up snorting and blowing. Rory's water confidence has improved with regular practice and she duck-dives and swims and jumps off his shoulders, squealing her delight. Rusty and Min, after a quick swim, retire to watch from under the trees, but Richie Dog, too young or too silly to stop, frolics along with Rory well after George has had enough.

Watching child and dog, George is at once envious of their carefree play and nostalgic for these simple pleasures that he knows are coming to an end. Let them stay a while – finish in their own time. The sun is low and he feels strangely enervated. A haze, faintly blue, rises from the gum trees. There's an end-of-day smell of dust and eucalypt. George tips his hat over his eyes and listens to the splashes and shrieks and Richie and Min's short, sharp barks. There's a remnant of daylight left. Let them play while they can.

*

There's a message on the answering machine when they get home and, while Rory has a shower, he listens to Bree. Her voice is sharp and flustered. 'George? Don't let Rory watch the news. Angie's going to be on, making an appeal. Then there's going to be a piece on that Channel 14 show – *As It Happens.* I don't think they'll be on your side. They didn't want to talk to me or Shirl. And George? Don't forget to delete this.'

There is an old video recorder with the television and George tests it, relieved to find it works. He sets it to tape the news programs and after dinner is quite short with Rory in an effort to get her to go to bed. As soon as he hears her little snuffles and snores, he closes the door and rewinds the tape. 'Let's see what they have to say,' he mutters, sitting down with the remote, preparing to fast-forward through irrelevant items. Not necessary. They are headline news now.

Newsreader, face suitably grave: *'Police are still appealing to George Johnson to give himself up and return six-year-old Aurora-Jane Wilson to her mother, who is fearful for her child's safety. Today, Ms Wilson made her own appeal to the kidnapper.'*

Cut to Angie, looking distressed and respectable in the outfit Shirl had organised for her job interview. *'George, if you have a heart, please bring my Rory back.'* She's close to tears and looks young and vulnerable. *'You mustn't hurt her, George. Please don't hurt her.'*

Newsreader: *'More from Ms Wilson at six-thirty.'*

George is stunned. Why would Angie say that? She must know there's no way he'd hurt Rory. Fingers trembling, he fast-forwards to *As It Happens.*

At short notice, the producers have gathered a formidable array. First Detective Inspector Harrop is introduced as the chief investigating officer. George sees a middle-aged man with kind eyes and an austere mouth, who may well be a father himself. *'As each day goes by,'* he says, *'we become more and more concerned. Given his past actions, there is no reason to believe that this man would harm young Aurora, but …'* He looks directly into the camera to emphasise the point that sets George reeling. *'We must always bear in mind that abused children are most often victims of family members or family friends.'*

Hand shaking, George tries to find the stop button but drops the remote control and sits in sick fascination as Mr and Mrs Nguyen appear, distressed and nervous. '*George. Our neighbour. He a good, good man. He take care of Rory while mother run away.*'

George looks with affection at his elderly friends as they blink uncertainly at the camera. They are standing outside their house and he can see Pen's roses dipping and swaying over the side fence. A yearning for his old life in Mercy Street hits him with a force that is almost physical. He reaches out but Mr and Mrs Nguyen turn away from the camera. *Bless them.*

Barely acknowledging the Nguyens, the reporter indicates the house now behind him – George's own. '*This is the ordinary house in Mercy Street, Fairfield, that George Johnson left nearly six weeks ago, claiming he was taking Aurora-Jane Wilson on holiday.*'

Claiming? Claiming? George doesn't hear the rest of her presentation as the word spins and swoops around him in stomach-churning loops. He tosses his head, squeezes his eyes shut and bats at the word as though swatting a fly.

Here's Angie, looking tired and confused. '*No. I didn't say that he'd hurt Rory. Just that I hoped he wouldn't.*' Beside her is another older woman the presenter identifies as Angie's grandmother. She doesn't look like the frail, ailing granny of Angie's story. *Early sixties*, George estimates. But that must seem ancient to someone of nineteen.

Back in the studio, a woman with hair that looks a bit

like Pen's, and broad shoulders weighed down with gravitas, responds to the first question.

'*Doctor Philips, you have vast experience in psychological profiling, what would you expect this man to do next?*'

'*What next? You may well ask. The outcome is difficult to predict and until I've had time to construct a full profile of the kidnapper, I can only say we must assume the worst and hope for the best.*'

The kidnapper? The man? Where is he, George, in all of this? Mr and Mrs Nguyen were the only ones to call him George. His eyes leak self-pity.

The reporter senses something untrustworthy in Angie. '*And is it true that you left your four-year-old daughter with this man, a stranger?*'

'*She was five.*'

George almost feels sorry for her.

'*Anyway, it was just till I found a job.*' Predictably sulky, she pursues justification. '*He seemed okay. I didn't say he could take her away.*'

'*Time for a break. Meanwhile, we all wait for this man to give himself up and return the little girl. The police will find you sooner or later. Give yourself up, mate. It'll be better for everyone.*'

Mate? That weasel-faced dickhead wouldn't know a mate if he fell over one.

The next segment shows some dumb husband with his foot stuck in a tin of paint. His wife looking exasperated, then radiant as she remembers 'Paint-off', which it seems even works on graffiti. How can they show such rubbish when worlds are falling apart — groaning under the strain

273

of wars, poverty, climate change – and his own little world, the one he has created out of a child's need? Under threat, his own need has become voracious. One thing at least is clear. It's time to move on.

*

Shirl rings Redgum. She and Bill have just watched the news, their first intimation that anything is wrong.

'George is a mate. A man has to help his mates. Didn't want to worry you, Shirl.'

'Worry me? What do you think it's like to see your brother on the news, being called a kidnapper and – worse?'

'Sorry.' Redgum's voice seems to float from a long way away.

'So where is he?'

'We can't tell you, Shirl. A promise is a promise.'

Shirl snorts her derision. 'Schoolboy stuff. This isn't a game, for God's sake.' She pauses. 'We? That Bree woman is involved, isn't she?'

Not waiting for a reply, she ends the call and turns to Bill. 'I'm off to see that Bree woman.' She doesn't say *I have ways of making her talk*. The words remain unspoken but, in Shirl's world, it's a given.

Shirl waits on Bree's porch, fingers itching, twitching to clean the grubby glass and sand the badly applied paint.

Bree responds to the first knock. 'Thought you'd come.'

'You were right.' Without waiting for an invitation, Shirl strides down the hall, taking in the chaotic bedroom with one disdainful glance.

'Coffee?'

A curt nod.

She looks tired, Shirl thinks as the younger woman prepares the coffee. She pauses now, wishing she'd taken the time to think things through, to formulate a plan of attack. 'So,' she begins, as they face each other over the kitchen table. 'What do you know about all this?' She puts down her mug. 'He's my brother,' she says softly. 'I'm worried sick.'

'We never thought Angie would tell the police.'

'That's as may be, but she did, didn't she?'

'Got herself drunk when Charlie left. Cops picked her up.' She parodies Angie's whine. '*He kidnapped my little girl.* Just a way of getting herself out of trouble, if you ask me.'

'Where is she? I need to talk to her.'

Bree shrugs. 'You gotta be kidding. No way she'll talk to you. She's at her gran's, and the old cow's guarding her like a Rottweiler. Won't even let her talk to me.'

'So where's George?'

'I don't know.'

Shirl raises a sceptical eyebrow.

'It's true. He was on a farm somewhere in New South Wales but he would've left by now. He wouldn't say where he was going.'

Shirl sees fear in her eyes.

'If it gets out that I helped him, I'll end up back in jail.'

Despite her exasperation, Shirl can see that Bree is telling the truth and that, in her own misguided way, she had tried to be a friend to George.

'Pull yourself together, woman.' Shirl's manner is all at once brisk and business-like. 'No one's going to jail. I just need time to think.'

*

Angie wonders why she ever left her gran's in the first place. She has had a nice meal, a hot bath and is tucked into those crisp, clean sheets that her skin remembers from her previous life with Gran. Charlie's defection still stings, but long experience has taught her that to adapt is to survive and already she has a new plan. When she gets Rory back, she'll stay here and get a job. Maybe train as a hairdresser or a nail technician. Rory could go to her old school. Gran's is close enough. And who knows? The kid could grow up to be a doctor or a beautician. Not a teacher or a lawyer. Angie has never had much time for teachers or lawyers.

She reviews her television experience and decides that she likes the fuss everyone is making of her. She has never really thought that George would harm Rory, but that cop said kids were mostly *abused* by family and friends. *Abused.* She rolls the word around in her mouth. It tastes gross, but that was the word he used. So she panicked at the end and asked George not to hurt Rory. The TV dudes were happy about that. But alone and safe in Gran's spare bed, she experiences a small flicker of remorse.

18

The rooster crows, and George, who's been wide awake for hours, suddenly falls asleep. An all-night talk-back radio station had been discussing the 'missing child' and callers were both outraged by Angie's neglect and convinced that George is most likely a paedophile. The latter had sent him scurrying to the toilet, where he first vomited and then sat in an agony of stomach cramps as his bowels heaved and yarked his distress. No wonder, then, that when Rory and Richie Dog come sneaking in, the sun is already sending its slatted rays through the half-open shutters onto the rumpled bed. George groans and turns over to look at the clock. *Good God. It's nearly eight.*

Rory is in her pyjamas and George finds himself suddenly uncomfortable. He hadn't felt that way yesterday or all the days before. Why now? In watching those television programs, listening to the radio he, like Adam, has eaten from the tree of knowledge. He's never thought much about that story he first heard at Sunday school. It had been all about an apple then. Later, in one of the few times he attended church as an adult, he discovered that it was about much more than a piece of fruit. Knowledge of evil is contaminating, and in this new manifestation, it makes him pull back from her hug.

'Poppy?'

Small eddies of anxiety ripple over her face. 'Poppy. Richie Dog and me have made you breakfast ...' Her voice trails off, uncertain.

With some effort, George rallies. 'How's that for luck? I'm hungry as a lion.' He waggles a finger at Richie. 'I hope you aren't giving me dog biscuits for breakfast, young pup.'

Rory giggles. It's a sign she feels safe, that she hasn't done anything wrong after all. 'You're so funny, Poppy.'

In the kitchen, George spoons up the cornflakes from their inundation of milk and *yums* at his undercooked toast.

'I didn't make the tea,' she says. 'Richie and me are a bit young for boiling water.'

She's so serious, so anxious to be responsible. George grins. 'Very wise. I'll make the tea and you can have a cup, just for making such a nice breakfast.' He pours her a milky tea and stirs in two teaspoons of sugar.

Rory's eyes gleam. This is an unexpected treat. 'What about Richie? He helped, too.'

'I might share my toast with him,' George says, tearing off a substantial chunk. He chuckles to himself as the dog wolfs down his portion. *Talk about killing two birds with one stone.*

'Best breakfast I've had in years,' he says, swigging the last of his tea. 'Now we'll clean up here and get ready to go.'

*

'I like it here.' Rory sits on the front step and folds her arms. 'Who's going to look after the chooks? And Min and Rusty?' (They have already established that Richie is coming with them.)

'I told you, sweetheart. Stella and Park will be home in a couple of days and Rabbit'll take over the chooks and dogs like he did before we came.' After two years, she seems to have forgotten her early life of constant moving and change, and now wants to stick where she is. As though the past is irretrievable and the one guarantee of a future is to cling to the present. If only he could tell her that they were returning to Mercy Street, to her schoolfriends, to Bree, to Redgum and Mr and Mrs Nguyen. Even to Shirl. After a shaky start, Rory and her Aunty Shirl have taken quite a shine to each other.

No. All he can promise her is a new town with new faces. And for how long? Sooner or later they'll be discovered. Or maybe they'll move on, never more than one step ahead of their pursuers. So the stable life he had envisaged for her (for them) is receding, and he can't see a way out. He could take her back and face the consequences, but would her life with Angie be any better for that? In no time at all she'll be a teenager and then God help her with the men her mother takes up with. No. He'll have to play this out to the end. Pray that the end will mean Angie meeting some other no-hoper and taking off for good. Is it over-optimistic to imagine that in such an event, he and Rory could return to their old life? The life she (and he) deserve to live? He squirms at how easily he's been able to sacrifice Angie.

He turns his attention back to the diminutive figure on the step. 'Stell and Park have all those children. There won't be room for us as well.'

'Can we come back for a holiday?'

'Sure can. Now let's get ready. First we'll run Rusty and Min back to Rabbit's.'

They have almost finished packing the car. Five minutes later and he'd have missed the call. It's Bree. 'I know I said I wouldn't ring again, but I wasn't sure you'd get the newspapers out there.'

George closes his eyes. *Please. Not another problem.*

'It's your photo. They've Photoshopped it.' George nods rather than speaks and Bree feels the need to ask if he's heard of Photoshop. He has. (It came from spending time at the school.)

'So they've got photos of what you would look like with a beard and a different haircut and a shaven head … and are you there, George? One of them looks a lot like you did when you left the caravan park.'

George manages to hide his panic. Just. 'Thanks for the heads-up. I'll bear that in mind.'

'A lot like you. You've got to be careful – this is serious stuff.'

George puts down the phone. He thought they'd be safer on the road, but after Bree's call ... Understanding that he has no choice, he goes back into the house. The Parkers are due back in a couple of days.

He rummages through his bag and finds his fishing hat, pulls it low over his eyes and looks in the mirror. He fingers the collar of his polo shirt. He's always worn a shirt with a collar, once a symbol of the line he liked to draw between his working self and his home self. As time went by, it became the way he dressed. Maybe Angie noticed this quirk. Maybe the police are already issuing a statement to that effect. He has kept the door to the Parkers' bedroom closed, but this is an emergency, so with a shamefaced apology to the absent couple, he rifles the drawers for collarless T-shirts. He takes four, the oldest he can find. Two are plain white and baggy. The other two are captioned – *It's Always Beer O'clock* and *Sydney Olympics 2000*, the latter with a picture of the Harbour Bridge and what could possibly be a wombat. He prepares to write a note of apology but stops himself in time. Instead, he puts on the Beer O'clock T-shirt and bundles child and dogs into the station wagon.

Rabbit asks no questions. It's clear that, apart from Park, he prefers animals to people. Rory (George is proud of her good manners) holds out her small hand. 'Thank you, Mr Rabbit for helping me with Richie Dog.'

'I'll be buggered. You're a funny kid, that's for sure. Wait.' He turns back to his shed then emerges with a strange contraption which he hands to the puzzled child.

'Yabby catcher. Designed it meself. Never know when you might need one.'

Even as they thank him, he has returned to his shack and is closing the door.

*

George is carrying the last of their stuff to the car when the phone rings again. This time it's Stella. 'Everyone here is talking about that program. They reckon the police are on their way from Melbourne – CID by the sound of things. The local police have already questioned us.'

George hadn't considered what effect the program might have had on his neighbours from the Red Dolphin and hesitates before asking. 'You didn't believe all that rubbish – you know, about – about me?' Not only does he need to know they won't give him up, but that there are ordinary people, good people, who believe in him.

'I was a primary teacher before I had all these kids. Kept up my quals and did some training in the – um – subject at Armidale Uni. So I watched you together and had a little chat with Rory after you told us she wasn't yours.'

George gives a kind of yelp.

'Don't take it personally. We'd only known you five minutes. We liked you, but we had to be sure. You don't really think we'd help you if we had any doubts about—' She's still avoiding the word. '—about that sort of thing.'

George can't help being hurt, but has to acknowledge that he'd have done the same thing himself had their positions been reversed. 'I know what you mean,' he says. 'But what they're saying – it's killing me. You're a good person, Stell. What would you do?'

He can hear her breath, a deep inhalation. 'I think you should go back and clear your name. You can't keep her from her mother forever.'

'I can't – I just can't. I told you. She's not a fit mother.'

'But she is her mother. She's a bit older now. And maybe wiser.'

'Not exactly a rolled-gold guarantee. Thanks for the advice, Stell, but we're moving on.'

'Fine. We won't say anything about where you've been. But bear one thing in mind, George. When you're making these big decisions, Rory's needs should be front and centre.'

'It's never been any other way.'

George closes the door on another chapter of his life, an interlude, really. One which, until last night, had shown him other possibilities for childhood. He pauses and looks across the paddocks and thinks of the narrow streets and mean, tumbling house he grew up in. *Water under the bridge.* He bundles a skittish Richie into the back of the station wagon, checks Rory's seatbelt and takes off down the dusty track. It is probably just the sun glare, but he can't for the life of him see the road ahead.

*

The trip is taking a lot longer than he'd anticipated. The road is dodgy and he hasn't banked on a kid and a dog needing toilet breaks, food-and-drink breaks or just breaks. It seems that Richie can't stand being in the car for more than half an hour at a time. His displeasure is evident in a cacophony of barking that upsets Rory and drives George crazy.

'Rabbit says dogs need to run.' Rory pouts when he refuses to stop for a fourth time. 'You're just mean and we both hate you.'

'Too bad.' George, his nerves already on edge, turns up the radio so he can't hear all the kerfuffle in the back. 'We'll stop when I'm good and ready.'

After about twenty minutes or so, he relents and lets them loose in a park in a town so small he'd missed it on the map. A young woman with a child in a stroller sits down beside him on the park's only seat. 'Big day on the road?' she asks him, indicating his loaded car.

'Yeah. Just passing through. Have to let them burn off some energy.'

She begins to unbuckle her child. 'Tell me about it. This is my youngest. I've got two more at school. One eight and one nearly seven – the same age as that poor little girl who was kidnapped in Melbourne.' She places the child on her knee and puts on a pair of velcro-fastening sneakers. 'There. Let's hope they get him. Hell's too good a place …'

Thank God she's been looking at the child the whole time. If she'd looked at him, George is sure those photos would have given him away. 'Can't be too careful,' he manages to croak, pulling his hat further down over his eyes. Standing up (not too hastily, he hopes), he checks his watch. 'Nice talking to you but we got a few k's to go yet.'

'Safe journey.'

By four o'clock he realises that he's a long way short of his planned destination and decides to stop at the next town. He hasn't driven so far in a day for years and his back is aching and his temper short. They drive past a sign indicating that Rainbow Creek is only five kilometres down the road. *Five, four, three, two ...* The end is in sight. For today at least.

'You can't wait until we get to a motel?'

'Noooo. I got to go now.'

George pulls over on the outskirts of town. 'Quick. Hop behind those bushes.' While he waits, he reads the sign. Unaware that they are about to harbour a fugitive, Rotary, Lions and the population of one thousand and twenty welcome them to Rainbow Creek.

Still rattled by the two phone calls, he sends Rory into the newsagency to buy a paper. Several versions of his face are on page two. Bree's right. He can only hope that the hat and T-shirt will fool them and wonders if he should shave his beard – leave a moustache, maybe.

'Hurry *up*, Poppy.'

There are two motels in town and he chooses the Outpost Inn because the sign says 'Pets Welcome'. An added bonus is a pool.

'You don't have a credit card?' A young woman with sceptical eyebrows examines the fifty-dollar bills like an archaeologist with a collection of exceptionally baffling artefacts.

Stell had prepared George for this and he's word perfect. 'My father never had a credit card and did very well for himself, as it happens. And as for me, I've got along just fine without.'

He and Rory spend the next couple of hours in the pool, and when it's cooler, take Richie for a long walk. There's nowhere much to go. The highway bisects the main street and the rest of the town consists of a small grid of residential streets, a red-brick school, a service station and a sports oval with a modest playground. They see only two other people (also walking their dogs), who look at them with no more than idle curiosity and say g'day as country people do. When they get back they eat in their room, ordering from the room-service menu. What with petrol and all, it has been a fairly expensive day and George drifts in and out of sleep, attempting to calculate how long his supply of cash is likely to last.

The next morning, just before six, he tells a sleepy Rory that he's going to check the car. He slides behind the wheel and turns on the radio. He's expecting it, but jumps when he hears his name. *'Police are still seeking the whereabouts of the missing six-year-old child who is believed to be in the company of George Colin Johnson, a retired pensioner from a northern suburb of Melbourne. It is now believed that they may be interstate. There have been possible sightings in a number of cities, including Adelaide and Newcastle, but all have so far been discounted. Police are encouraging the public to ring Crime Stoppers with any information.'*

The next voice is strangely familiar. *'Our best hope remains with the public and we ask that you contact us with any information, no matter how slight. We have spoken to his known associates and believe that they know nothing of his whereabouts.'*

'*That was Detective Inspector Harrop of the Melbourne CID. In other news …*'

When had they started to use his middle name? They only do that with criminals, don't they? What's more, when had his friends become 'known associates'? He imagines poor Shirl – indignant, mortified and tearful – showing them the letter that proves Angie left Rory in his care. At least he hopes that's what she's doing. And what about Redgum? Mr and Mrs Nguyen? Maybe Ms Hamilton, panicking at the thought that she'd invited him into the school. They all suffer, are all tarnished by their friendship with him. He turns off the radio, deciding that he won't listen to it again. It's a wilful throw of the dice. If fate means him to survive this ordeal, well and good. If not, he's tried. And it's all for Rory. He must never lose sight of that.

19

Neither child nor dog wants to get into the car. Over breakfast, George had made a sudden decision to head for Newcastle – a diversion from his original plan, but if there have been 'sightings' there already, maybe people will be reluctant to come forward again in case they make fools of themselves. In the past, George was never known for his cunning. *With George, what you see is what you get.* That's what everyone used to say. Being a fugitive – does that foster a criminal way of thinking?

'Just get in,' he tells Rory. 'Richie won't get in without you.' The dog, nose on paws, hindquarters in the air, is mounting a one-dog mutiny. Exasperated beyond endurance, George kicks out at him, barely connecting, but the animal jumps in and glowers at him as he shuts the door.

'I'm never ever speaking to you again,' Rory says. 'People who kick dogs are like – *murderers* or *crooks* or …' Overcome with his cruelty, she is lost for words and begins to cry. 'I want to go home. I don't want to be on holidays anymore.'

Dismayed, George gets in beside her but she shrinks away. 'I'm sorry, love. I really am. Poor old Richie. It's not his fault. Or yours. I'm just a bit tired and cranky.' He turns her chin so she's facing him. 'Forgive me?'

'You'll never kick Richie ever again?'

'Cross my heart.'

'And we can go home – back to Mercy Street?'

A secret thrill quells his earlier despair. For Rory as for him, Mercy Street is home. She has no idea how much he wants to be home, too. He pats her hand. 'Not right away, love. But we will as soon as we can. I promise.' He becomes aware of the sawing in her chest. 'Get your puffer. Calm down, there's a good girl. Use your puffer.'

She takes it from her backpack and puts it to her mouth. Her eyes, wet from the recent tears, look over it at her Poppy.

'Hold it firm. That's right.' George's voice is gentle. 'We'll take it easy today. I'll stop at the first nice place we find after two o'clock.' He hesitates. 'You're not cross with me anymore, are you?'

She snuggles up to him. 'I only get cross when you do something naughty. But I love you just the same.'

She's too young for irony but George has to grin. How many times has he said that to her?

*

Even though they have reached the highway, the kilometres no longer slip by. It's like driving through sludge. Too tired

289

(and not confident enough) to pass, George sits behind a truck and is overtaken by any number of impatient drivers. He checks the rearview mirror. Here's another one, sitting on his tail, horn blaring. George sweats and squints and tries to roll his shoulders. He's getting past this sort of driving.

They stop for morning tea (an ice-cream for Rory; coffee for George). They stop twice more to give Richie a run. The dog obviously isn't one to hold a grudge and fetches his beloved tennis ball with the joy of a prison escapee.

They are only an hour or so beyond their last stop when George is suddenly aware of the frantic tooting of a car and the long, drawn-out blast of a truck's horn. *Christ almighty.* He's drifted onto the wrong side of the road. In his panic, he swerves, almost over-corrects, and when he pulls up on the blessedly firm shoulder, his hands are locked to the wheel, while witnesses to this sobering drama drive on, cursing him for propelling them all so close to the abyss.

'Is this it?' Rory must have been asleep, but Richie's barking is hysterical.

'Not yet.' George's voice comes from way back in his throat. 'Poppy just needs to stop for a bit.'

Rory seems to sense something's wrong and, instead of setting up the usual whining, sits quietly, her fingers reaching through the grille to reassure Richie. 'Good dog,' she whispers. 'Quiet now. Good dog.'

How long has he been here, hands on the wheel? Only minutes, surely (*five, ten?*), but it seems like hours. He shakes his head to marshal his thoughts. They clatter and clunk but won't come together. He rests his forehead on his fingertips. *Steady, George – think.* But it's too hard. All he knows is that, while he's in no fit state to continue driving, they can't stay here. The map shows that they are only ten kilometres from the middling town of Owens Gap, so taking a swig of water, he adjusts his seatbelt. *Thank God for seatbelts.* In the old days they'd have gone through the windscreen, stopping so suddenly. 'Nearly there.' He sounds more assured than he feels. If he had his druthers, he'd never drive on a highway again, but what choice does he have? 'When we get to Owens Gap, we'll have some lunch and find a place to stay.' He only hopes the town is large enough to have accommodation, because ten kilometres is his absolute limit. And it's barely eleven a.m. At this rate, Newcastle might as well have been the moon.

George pulls into the first motel they see, and after turning on the television and air conditioner, flops back on the bed. 'We'll get some lunch soon,' he promises. 'See if there's a can of soft drink in the fridge. You can have that with your apple.'

An hour and a half later he's woken by an impatient shake. 'Poppy. I'm hungry. When are we going to get lunch?'

Lunch is a pie and chips, eaten on a seat under a tree at the local cricket ground. The snack she'd had earlier must have taken the edge off Rory's professed hunger because she leaves most of her pie and picks desultorily at her chips. The obliging Richie polishes off the remainder of the pie and capers around, ready to play.

George proffers the car keys. 'Do you want to get his ball?'

'No.'

He looks at her, surprised. 'You don't want to play with Richie?' She shakes her head and he notices the sharp contrast of her freckles against the pallor of her skin. He puts his hand on her forehead. 'Hot?' Of course she's hot. It's at least thirty-five degrees out here.

'Can we go back?'

George is confused. 'Back where? To the farm?'

'No. Just to our motel. I'm tired.'

'Not a problem. It'll be nice and cool in there. You can watch a bit more telly.'

Richie can't believe that they're leaving a park without a game of fetch, but it seems that he's hot too, so with no more than a formal objection, he jumps into the car.

They stop at a newsagency on the way back, so George can buy a newspaper. He glances quickly at the headline – *Rabbitohs Coach Sacked*. Chagrined, he turns to page two. Surely a missing child is more important than a football coach. There it is on page three – thank God, no photos, but a column and a half saying that police are following a number of leads. He doesn't believe that for a minute. As long as his friends hold true, there can be no leads. It seems that he's home free. But where is home now? And what price freedom? At this point, he doesn't care. All he knows is that he's earned the right and he'll never give her up.

With these thoughts, he drives the short distance back

to the motel, where Rory lies on her bed and is asleep before he can find the cartoon channel.

*

George wakes in the fuzz of afternoon sleep as Richie, who they had smuggled in, whimpers and nudges at his hand.

'What is it, boy?'

The dog pads over and puts his head on Rory's bed.

What's that noise? George is suddenly wide awake. 'Rory. Your puffer. Where's your puffer?'

'Under my pillow.' She scrabbles for the puffer, holds it to her mouth and takes a breath. 'I used it before. It isn't working very well.'

'It sure isn't.' *This is the worst I've seen her.* She's fighting for breath and George struggles to conceal his anxiety. He pours some cough elixir into a teaspoon, which he offers to the sick child.

She tosses her head and pushes the spoon away. 'Stop. I hate that stuff. Mummy doesn't make me take that stuff.'

Mummy? She hadn't mentioned her mother in months. Now a second time in a couple of days. 'Just one teaspoon, sweetheart. Just until your chest clears.' He feels his own chest tightening and turns away to use his own puffer. *Please. I can't afford to be sick, too. I have to look after Rory.* He's lucky. Whoever he's addressing gives him a reprieve and his airways begin to relax. 'I'll get the nebuliser.'

He runs out to the car and brings in the equipment, blessing Bree for the thoroughness of her packing. He sets

293

it up with shaking hands, and is relieved when Rory gives up her opposition and lies holding the mask to her face. Her eyes are still a little wild. Tears slide off her cheeks and onto the pillow as her narrow chest strains and labours. George holds her hand. 'It's okay, love. The medicine will kick in soon and you'll be as right as rain, won't she Richie?'

The dog woofs quietly and licks her other hand. Rory manages a small smile as George strokes her head. 'Any better?'

She nods. 'A bit – and, Poppy?'

'What, sweetheart?'

'When's Mummy coming home?'

'Let's worry about that when you've had a nice rest.' George grips her hand as though she might be taken from him at any minute and stays beside her bed long after she falls into a restless sleep.

He gnaws at his thumbnail. Angie again. Rory is happy with him – he's certain of that. So why ask for her mother now? Surely he's enough. She is surrounded by a geography of love that reaches well beyond the boundaries of blood, beyond, even, the law. All he needs is time – in a year or two her mother will be a wraith, a wisp of memory and he, George, the solid centre of her world. His throat tightens. To be the centre of her world. As she is his.

He had planned to leave the next day, but rings reception to see if they can stay another night. 'Just a precaution,' he says. 'My grandson's a bit crook. Odds are he'll be okay in the morning.'

'No worries, love. Do you need a doctor? Number's in the folder on the bedside table.'

'No. No, I don't think it's that bad. He just needs to take it easy for a bit.'

But what if she does need a doctor? What if the nebuliser fails to open her airways? It seems to be working at the moment, but ... The consequences frighten him. A doctor would soon find out that his 'grandson' is a girl and then what? He watches the sleeping child. Listens to her breathing. A bit easier, perhaps? She wouldn't be able to sleep if she really was struggling to breathe.

It's a while now since he invoked his dead wife. *Don't tell me to make a list, Pen. I wouldn't know where to start. All I know is I don't want to − I can't − lose her, too. You say what if she's seriously ill? Maybe there's a pharmacy in town. I could explain about her asthma and get some stronger medication. I know, Pen. I know what I should do, but she's had asthma before. And got over it. Fit as a fiddle the next day. That's what kids are like. Up and down, then up again in a flash.* He hates himself but he has to make her understand. *I'm sorry, Pen. I know what you'd say, but I've had experience bringing up a kid.*

His wife is dead. Unable to hear him, but he knows what her reaction would be and cringes from her hurt and judgement. *Sorry, old girl. That was a cruel thing to say. With any luck, it won't come down to a choice.*

By dinnertime, Rory is somewhat better, though she continues to cough. The receptionist is kind enough to offer to 'nick down' to the shops for him when he inquires about room service. 'So's you won't have to leave the kid,' she says. 'We don't have a restaurant here but I can get you some chicken and salad from the supermarket.'

George is so grateful he feels tears spring to his eyes. You can meet unexpected kindness wherever you go. Pen was always saying that, but it's only since his time with Rory that he has lived the experience. He needs to talk to Redgum. Or Shirl. Until all this happened, he's never understood how much he's relied upon his sister's sleeves-rolled-up brand of common sense.

*

Shirl's common sense has all but deserted her, and she's hell-bent on confronting Angie. One way or another, she'll make that girl tell the truth.

Bill used to work as a printer with the *Herald Sun* and has kept some contacts. He hangs up the phone and hesitates. 'Are you sure you know what you're doing?'

Shirl is taken aback. Bill never questions her judgement. 'I know you don't like George,' she retorts. 'But as his only living relative, it's all up to me.' If pressed, she'd be unable to explain what 'all' referred to, and thankfully, Bill doesn't ask. He gives her the address and escapes to the garden.

It's really just a question of physics. *What happens when an irresistible force meets an immovable object?* Shirl and Gran meet head-on at the front door.

'My name is Shirley Adams. I'm George Johnson's sister.' Shirl enunciates each word with care. She's dressed in a nice skirt and blouse. And carries a black leather handbag over her arm. That's why she's stunned by the response.

Gran gives a little yelp and begins to close the door. A furious Shirl sticks out her well-shod foot to wedge it open.

'You've got a cheek,' shrieks Gran. 'Get out of my doorway. You lot have done enough damage. Where's Rory? Where's that evil brother of yours?'

'Evil? Evil, you say? You don't even know my brother. What about your Angie? What about a mother who deserts her child?'

Enraged splutters accompany a struggle with the door, and Shirl pulls her foot out just in time. 'How dare you?' She swings around to encounter a microphone centimetres from her face.

'Can you tell us who you are and why you're here harassing these poor people?'

Face flaming, Shirl pushes her way to the car and drives off, tears of humiliation and anger vying for precedence.

That night they carve her up into bite-sized pieces. There she is, on Bill's giant television screen, banging at the door like a madwoman, while the voice-over identifies her as George Johnson's sister, postulating that it might be as well for the stricken family to take out an intervention order on the whole clan.

Battered but not beaten, Shirl contacts the independent broadcaster (Angie, it seems, has contracted her appearances to a pay-TV network). Shirl fares better in this more controlled environment and has Angie's letter with her.

'She just took off and left Rory with George. He's taken care of her ever since. We all have, in a way.'

While the conventional press are avid for detail, social media slaver at the possibilities. The twits tweet, the bloggers blog, and Facebook friends like and dislike in almost equal numbers – all reconstructing the past two years with prejudice, ignorance and innuendo. Twitter feeds, engorged, consume themselves within a couple of days, but *Mothers for Rory* and *Women for Angie* take root and brandish slogans and shout at each other across cyberspace and once in the flesh outside Parliament House.

Shirl, meanwhile, tells George's story at every opportunity, but after a while, opportunities become fewer and fewer. And because there's nothing more she can do, she rages and frets until Bill becomes concerned for her health.

'Take it easy, love. There's nothing more you can do.' He puts out his arms and holds her while she sobs into his chest. 'He'll come back of his own accord. You'll see.'

*

Redgum, dazed by it all, blames himself for the part he played. The day after the first television broadcast, he goes to the pub as usual.

'That was never your mate on the telly last night?' One of the old codgers comes out of his corner to peer over his glasses at Redgum. 'Looked a lot like him.'

Redgum isn't going to deny his friendship with George. 'So what if it was?'

'Good on him, I say. Me missus got the kids when we split up. Women get all the sympathy, whether they deserve it or not.' He turns to his cronies. 'I'm right, aren't I?'

There's muttered assent from the corner, but the barman, at least fifty years their junior, sees fit to chime in. 'The point is, he's not the kid's father. He could really be a paedophile for all we know … No offence,' he says to Redgum. 'I'm sure he's okay, but you can never be sure of anyone.'

The other patrons, with the exception of the corner-dwellers, side with the barman.

'I've come to this pub for nigh-on fifty years,' Redgum says. 'If I was even ten years younger I'd take on the lot of you.' He slams down his beer. 'I'll tell you this much for nothing. I'll never set foot in here again.'

After this he takes to drinking at home. Sometimes he's joined by Bree. *Misery loves company*, his mother used to say.

*

Angie sits in her grandmother's family room and tears at her remaining viable fingernail. Things are turning nasty. Sure, there are a lot of people on her side, but there are others who say she's a bad mother. They don't even know her, these people. She knows she's not too bright. *Not the sharpest tool in the shed*, her stepfather used to say. And maybe she was a bit slack, leaving like that. But she's not bad. That's an awful thing to say about someone. Her nail is bitten down to the quick. It hurts.

20

There's a time in the hours after midnight, before the birds begin their morning chatter, that George always thinks of as the fag-end of the world. A time, he had heard nurses say, when souls slip away from bodies too weak to resist. A time for anxiety, when solutions dance and weave and dissipate like smoke between your outstretched fingers. A time for tossing in tangled sheets, longing for morning when things once again become ordinary.

Bone-weary and soul-weary, George lies awake in those hours before dawn, and wrestles what is not, after all, an ordinary problem. He stares into the dark and listens to Rory cough. Tenses for the onset of a wheeze. He had gone to bed with a feeling of unease – some instinct (a parental one?) tells him that Rory's asthma isn't going away so easily this time. There's something in her breathing, the nature of her cough … She mutters in her sleep and his body is instantly alert. Straining into the darkness, he listens for the signs. She settles eventually, but George is no longer sleepy. It's as though his eyelids are glued open. He stares at the ceiling, the strip of moonlight that slices through a gap in the blind. Then, more for something to do than from necessity, he gets up, pulls the covers around the little girl's shoulders and tucks Slipper Dog in more firmly.

Richie pads up and George lets him out for a pee. The air is hot and still and smells of dust. *How do they stand this weather day after day?* George whistles softly and the dog returns, growling a warning at some nocturnal creature scurrying about its business.

'Inside, Richie.' The dog lies down near Rory's bed while George returns to his. Eyes too grainy to close, he once more stares into the darkness. His mind – it used to be so tidy – is in such disarray that, try as he might, he fails to recapture a single thought or plan or possible solution. Surely just minutes ago ingenious and robust ideas had presented themselves to him.

He becomes aware that the room is no longer black. A subtle shift in tone reveals dim shapes – not yet recognisable, but a sign that the night is ending. A distant rooster crows just as George collapses headfirst into an exhausted sleep.

He lurches to a sitting position, dragged into a woozy sort of consciousness by Richie, who is whimpering and pawing at the bed. How long has he been sleeping? He squints at the clock, still only half awake. It isn't quite six but the sun is up and the birds have set about twittering the business of the day.

But it's the sound from the other bed that shocks him into consciousness. While he slept (surely not for long?), Rory has been struggling for breath. A second time, God

301

help him, he has slept through his watch. Pen said that you shouldn't take a child from a mother who might want it. Are these the consequences of such an action?

Red-rimmed eyes look back at him from a face with a frightening, bluish pallor. 'I'm scared, Poppy.'

'Sweetheart.' The pounding of his own heart fills his chest. (*So this is how hearts break.*) 'I'm calling the doctor,' he tells her, rummaging through the folder and pressing the buttons with clumsy haste. The phone rings and a click signals connection. *Please. Not an answering machine:* 'Surgery hours are eight to five weekdays. For out of hours, a doctor is in attendance at the Base Hospital in Muswellbrook. In an emergency, call triple 0.'

George looks across at Rory. She's blue around the mouth and her eyes now seem to be all pupil. *0-0-0.* He holds her hand as he gives the operator the details, trying to focus. The motel. What's it called? His head is going to explode. *What's the name of the fucking town?* He is about to run outside to check when he remembers the folder. 'The Kookaburra,' he tells her. 'Main Street, Owens Gap.'

'An ambulance is on its way,' the operator tells him. 'It should arrive in about twenty minutes. I'll stay on the line with you while you wait. Keep calm. That's the most important thing. Talk her through it ...'

George does as he's told. 'Breathe,' he says. 'Slowly. That's right. Another one. The ambulance will be here soon. Breathe in. Slowly. Easy now. Breathe.'

Even as he speaks, George marvels at the calm that overlays his panic. It could be the reflected composure of the emergency operator. Or perhaps he has drawn on a personal store of strength that has lain dormant these many years. 'Easy,' he says. 'Breathe. That's the girl. You're doing well.' He mustn't let her see his fear. 'Breathe. Easy does it. Breathe.' With an almost feminine gesture, he smooths her hair back from her forehead and faces the sobering truth. He has taken someone else's child into his protection only to find, in this place so far from home, that his care is wanting and his love insufficient to protect her.

Rory is trying to say something. 'Richie.' George can barely understand her and has to ask her to repeat what she said.

The blasted dog. 'We can't take Richie in an ambulance, can we? Shh. You mustn't get upset. Tell you what – we'll take Slipper Dog and leave Richie with the nice motel lady. She'll look after him. You just have to get better so you can play with him again. Breathe in, sweetheart. That's right. Slowly …'

There's a strange vacuum of silence just before George hears the sound of an approaching siren and the crunch of tyres pulling up on the gravel. He has never experienced such relief. It pours out of him like sweat. Patting Rory's hand – 'I'll only be a minute, love' – he goes to the door to meet the paramedics, a young man and an older woman. Without greeting them, he steps aside and indicates the child. 'Asthma. We usually control it with Ventolin.' He hovers at the foot of the bed, folds and unfolds his arms and finally takes hold of the small, bony foot in what he hopes is a reassuring grasp. They're connected. The crisis is out of his hands, but after all they've been through, he won't let her go. They must stay connected.

The woman unpacks their equipment while the young man sits down beside Rory. 'Hello. My name's Ben and this is Laura. That's a nice toy. What's his name?'

Rory's voice is no more than a whisper. 'Slipper Dog.'

'Great name. You hold on to Slipper Dog there while we make you a bit more comfortable. So what's your name?'

Her eyes slide across to George. 'Roy?' she says.

It's all over. All the running, all the deception. All the sharing and laughing and crying. All the learning and the joy.

'It's Rory,' George corrects her with uncharacteristic brusqueness. And moves aside to make room for Laura and her equipment. The paramedics exchange a glance. *What does that mean?*

As he lets go of her foot, frightened eyes follow him. *Poor little bugger. She's only a kid. A baby, really.* 'Don't worry, sweetheart. I'm just going to see about Richie. I'll be back in a tick.'

The receptionist ('Call me Chrissie') is already at the door. 'Heard the ambulance,' she says. 'Is he all right?'

George stops for a minute. He? She already knows about Richie? Then he remembers. 'Not too good – maybe a bit better since the ambos came. Look. I know we shouldn't have, but we sneaked a dog in and ...'

'A dog?'

'I'm sorry. Could you look after it while we go to the hospital? I wouldn't ask, only the kid's worried about it and I've got to go with her.'

Chrissie puts a warm, brown hand on his arm. 'No worries, love. Lucky the boss is down in Sydney – he's got a strict no-pet rule.' She takes Richie's collar. 'What's his name?'

'Richie.'

'Come on, Richie. We'll tie you up out the back till I finish my shift.' She turns to George, who is impatient to get back to Rory. 'If you're not back by then, I'll take him home. Here.' She scribbles on a supermarket docket retrieved from somewhere about her person. 'My phone number. Take it. Give us a call when you're ready for the dog.' She tugs at the mutinous Richie's leash and waves George back inside. 'He'll be fine. I'm used to dogs.'

Laura looks up as George comes back in. 'We've got her on oxygen, but she's still not stabilised.' She mutters something to Ben. 'We'll have to take her to the hospital. Are you ready to come with her?'

Rory looks so tiny on the stretcher. 'Richie's all set, love. I'm coming with you. We're going to have a ride in an ambulance.' George's over-bright voice makes it sound like a ride on a merry-go-round. He scrambles on some clothes while they wheel her out. He hadn't wanted it to end like this.

*

The ambulance travels at speed. No siren, but he's sure there are lights – those insistent, red-and-blue lights that demand right of way for the sick, the injured, the dying. It's familiar, this space, with its tubes and wires and machines. In a space such as this he had held Pen's hand on each of their journeys to hospital, while he prayed to a distant god and watched the paramedics ply their trade in a manner both professional and deeply intimate. Here, now, he holds a smaller hand. Prays for another someone who is dear to him. Watches as Laura regulates oxygen flow, checks blood pressure and listens through her stethoscope. All with gentle hands and a soothing murmur. George, humble, watches those hands, listens to that murmur, and believes.

'She'll be all right.' It isn't a question.

Laura looks up. 'Nearly there,' she says. 'It's a good hospital.'

Belief is fragile. 'She *will* be all right?'

The ambulance stops at the hospital entrance and Rory is taken, still attached to the oxygen tank, through reception to the large swinging doors of the emergency ward.

The space is small, just six cubicles, all of them empty. The medical team begin their assessment, and George, agitated and clumsy, gets in the way. A nurse appears at his elbow. 'Just come out here for a moment, sir. We'll get some details while Doctor sees to the child.' She has a lovely Irish accent and a broad pleasant face.

'I'll just be outside,' he tells Rory. 'Be good for the doctor.'

Rory's eyes are glued to him. They're so big and so scared that he can't let go of her hand.

'Come with me,' the nurse says, taking George's arm. 'I'll leave the curtain open so you can see each other.'

George goes with her to the nurses' station, turning every few seconds to give Rory a reassuring wave.

'Name?' George and the nurse (Niamh – *You pronounce it Nee-iv*, she tells him) are sitting at the desk squeezed into a corner of the ward.

'Name,' George repeats, as though it's a medical term he doesn't quite understand. 'Of course. Yes. Name. Johnson. George Johnson.'

She looks up with searching eyes then her shoulders lift in the slightest of shrugs. 'Patient's name, George Johnson.'

'No.' George's voice is so subdued that she has to lean forward to hear him. 'My name is George Johnson. The little girl is Aurora-Jane Wilson. We call her Rory.'

The nurse is immobile. But she knows. She knows. And there's fear in her eyes.

'I won't hurt you,' George says. 'And I haven't hurt Rory, I swear.' Doubt flickers across her face and George presses his slight advantage. 'Do what you have to do, but you must let me call her mother. And ...' His voice is breaking with the terror of it all. 'Please. Please, Niamh. Don't let them take me till her mother gets here.'

She hands him the phone. 'Her mammy first. But I make no promises, mind. After that it's the police.' Pol-ice. She puts the stress on the first syllable.

He rings Bree. Without his phone, he has no idea of Angie's mobile number. 'She's at her gran's,' Bree tells him. 'Nowhere else to go. I'll ring her there. And, George?'

'Yes?'

'Rory is all right? Only we didn't hear from you and they were saying such dreadful things.'

'I swear,' George says. 'I swear I've never hurt her.' It kills him, the thought that even his friends are beginning to doubt him. In the end, he has no choice but to see it through.

'I'm in the hospital at Muswellbrook. Tell Angie to come as soon as she can. Maybe the cops or the television people can help.'

'Hospital? Why is she in hospital? What have you done to her?'

'Nothing. I've done nothing. It's her asthma. I only took her because Angie was going to take her away from me. You know that.'

George can't take any more. He hands the phone to Niamh and begins to cry. He doesn't sob or wail. From deep inside he feels the tears well until they roll, in an unstoppable stream, down his face and onto the desk in front of him.

*

That's how the young constable finds him, in tears. Unmanly. Unmanned. They have let him back with Rory, who is separated from him by the walls of an oxygen tent. 'She'll be okay,' the doctor tells him. 'We're only letting you back in because she's fretting.' Niamh stands by in the corner of the cubicle and a security guard takes position after frisking him for a weapon. Shattered, George accepts these precautions as inevitable.

Rory's eyes are closed. She had relaxed once her Poppy was back. Her hands are tucked beyond his grasp, behind the plastic tent, but she sneaks one out and George takes it in his. She has been his life for nearly two years – but this is the moment when he begins to let go, curiously impatient for it all to end. He is already thinking of life with her in the past tense. As a tale fondly told. *She really loved our trips to the library. Cheeky little bugger – she used to call me a 'reading mum'.*

It had been like that in the end, with Penny. He loved her, but waiting for the inevitable had torn him apart. He hadn't wanted her to die. He hadn't. But the wait was cruel for both of them. He was ashamed when he fell asleep as she lay awake. He was ashamed that he sometimes had to go for a walk, just to escape the knowing. To breathe in air that was fresh and redolent of an early spring. She must have understood that this was to be her last spring. She must have. He filled her room with daffodils. She loved them, but he found their joyful yellow trumpets obscene. So sometimes, in that fag-end of the world, overcome with weariness and grief, he'd pray that she'd let go. Finalise this awful process and leave him to his memories of long, happy years.

So it is with Rory. Her colour is returning. She isn't going to die. But she is going to leave him. Regardless of his wishes or (he hopes) hers, their life together is finished. He needs to lash out and looks up at the young constable, hovering in the doorway. 'A bit of a feather in your cap, son. Arresting me.'

The boy (he still has that golden fuzz on his face) places his hand on his gun. 'Shut your mouth or I'll make you sorry you messed with a little girl.'

'Poppy.' Rory is awake and trying to sit up. 'Don't go.' She begins to wheeze again and Niamh slips into the tent and lays her head back on the pillow.

'There now, cushla. It's grand. You'll be grand, darlin'. Your Poppy's here.' She turns to the young policeman. 'Now, Tony Martin. You'll be waiting for the sergeant, you will, while I'll be looking after this child. She wants her Poppy and we don't want to upset her.'

Constable Martin is clearly in two minds, so George tries to help out. 'I won't escape. On my mother's grave. And …' He looks the lad in the eye. 'If I had hurt the kid, would she want me here?'

The constable decides to ignore George and addresses Niamh. 'All right, Mrs Connolly – if you think there's a medical reason …'

'Good lad. That I do. And how's your mother's tennis going?'

The 'lad' shuffles and glares at his feet. George (strangely perceptive at such a time) can see him thinking – *The next vacancy and I'm out of this hole.*

The sergeant and the social worker arrive within minutes of each other. The small cubicle is beginning to feel like a train carriage at peak hour. The doctor returns and demands that they leave her patient in peace. 'I think my authority has precedence in these circumstances,' she tells the sergeant. 'You can all wait outside. Not you,' she says to George, as he stands to go. 'She won't settle without you.'

So George gains a few more precious minutes and uses them to explain to Rory why he has to go. 'Your mummy is on her way,' he says. 'Nurse Niamh told me that she's coming in a helicopter. Isn't that exciting?'

'Can we go in a helicopter too?'

'I don't know. We can ask. But, sweetheart, I can't come with you. I have to … They think I …' There's no simple explanation. 'I have to collect Richie from the motel.'

'Give him a big kiss from me.'

'Sure will.'

'And, Poppy?'

'Yes, sweetheart?'

'Promise you'll come back really fast?'

'Promise.'

'Can Mummy stay with us?'

'Mums are very special, aren't they?' He seeks her hand. Finds it. 'And Rory? Don't forget your old Poppy, will you? Remember he loves you more than … a double ice-cream sundae. With chocolate and sprinkles.'

She giggles. 'You're so funny, Poppy.'

She closes her eyes and George's head begins to nod. His lack of sleep the night before is compounded by emotional turmoil and the craving for sleep overwhelms him. He wakes to the sound of voices and the shock of a decent thump between his shoulderblades. 'Prison's too good for you,' a woman's voice screams. 'You should be drowned in boiling oil and put through a mincer.'

Alarmed, George springs to his feet as a second thwack knocks him back into his chair. His assailant is a small, fair-haired woman with Rory's pointy chin, wielding a large handbag like it's a broadsword. The grandmother! She's followed in quick succession by Angie who, not notwithstanding the oxygen tent, throws herself with youthful drama onto her daughter's bed.

Angie screams. 'My baby!'

Rory tries to sit up.

Niamh calls for assistance and two policemen, a security guard and a cleaner wielding a mop explode into the room.

George, who has been fending off Gran and her handbag, is grateful when the security guard pulls her away, less grateful when the policemen grab either arm and pull his hands up behind his back, wrenching his shoulders in their enthusiasm.

'That'll teach you,' yells the mop-wielding cleaner, bobbing around behind the policemen.

'Settle down!' Niamh (who would have thought it?) yells like a navvy. 'Think of the child, yer feckin' eejits.'

'Where's George going? I want George.' Rory, frightened, is trying to reach for her Poppy. 'Where are they going?'

Angie flusters and blusters. 'Don't worry about that. You got me. I'm here.'

Amid the fuss, George is led out, none too gently, by Constable Tony, the sergeant and the security guard. They all want a piece of him – to be within his ambit at this time is to be within a hairsbreadth of glory. He opens his mouth to say goodbye. To remind Rory that he loves her. But what's the point? Her mother and great-grandmother are there for her, one each side of the bed like bodyguards. All he wanted, he tries to explain to the sergeant, was to give her a shot at a better life.

'Poppy!'

He'll never forget that cry. *I let her down, Pen. I promised to be with her and I let her down.* His arms are twisted tighter and he hears the snapping of handcuffs. 'Shut up,' the sergeant says. 'Or you might have a nasty accident.'

21

The solicitor advises George that the most serious charge he will face is abduction. Serious enough – but at least the authorities have satisfied themselves that Rory has not been subjected to any kind of abuse. 'Although,' the solicitor adds, 'that doesn't mean everyone will believe the evidence. There was a lot of shit flying around when you went missing. People don't like their prejudices challenged. Look at Lindy Chamberlain.'

George mumbles a response. He has reason to feel bad about Lindy Chamberlain. He had been one of those who'd refused the evidence even when it became irrefutable. *Dingo, my eye. It was one of the family – mark my words. A dingo couldn't take away a baby. I don't care what they say.* Now he understands. There has been hate mail, and his house – his and Pen's modest refuge in Mercy Street – has been egged.

Bail is set at two-hundred-and-fifty-thousand dollars, surprising even the prosecutor, who concedes that George is unlikely to either abscond or re-offend. And before he can gather his thoughts, an 'anonymous businessman' pays his bail.

George steps out to temporary freedom, puzzling about his unknown benefactor. Shirl is driving him to the flat she's organised. (Under the circumstances, they've been advised not to take him home.) 'It's Mr Nguyen, you idiot,' she says. 'He owns three Vietnamese restaurants and imports Aussie flags and kangaroo keychains and that sort of thing from Vietnam and China.'

George shakes his head. 'He seemed like such a nice, ordinary bloke.' He feels cheated by this new knowledge. It will take some getting used to – the discovery that he'd been hobnobbing with a millionaire and didn't even know it.

'He's the same person,' Shirl snaps. 'A bit of gratitude wouldn't go astray.'

Sheepish, George slides down in his seat. 'Fair enough.'

*

So for the months leading up to the trial, George stays in a rented flat not far from Shirl's, while the press feeds on speculation. Having an eye to the laws of libel, they can no longer suggest that he may be a paedophile and turn their attention to Angie. Within a few days (for those outside Angie's 'media group'), he is a hero who rescued a child from a drug-addicted mother and her series of nasty boyfriends; and George, though relieved to be vindicated, pities poor Angie, who looks more miserable and defensive with each appearance. *Don't talk to them, Angie. When they smell blood, you can't win.*

Her story is confused, and confusing. 'No. Well – yes.' She did leave Rory with George.

'No.' She didn't expect him to kidnap the child.

'Yes.' She had been frantic.

'Yes.' Even though it took nearly two years to come back for her.

Surely as a mother … Didn't she ever think he might harm Rory?

'Yes. No. He bought her pyjamas. Two pairs. He seemed kind … He *was* kind. I think – thought he was. And puppy-dog slippers. She liked those …'

*

As the date set for his trial comes closer, the media, both social and conventional, ignite with renewed passion, so much so that the press are warned not to jeopardise the integrity of the trial. Print and television media pull back, assessing each news item against possible contempt of court.

Not so the social media. *Mothers for Rory* are not as focused as *Women for Angie*. While they're against Angie, they are not quite sure what being 'for Rory' means. Does it mean that they believe that Rory should be raised by a man well into his seventies who is no blood relative? At the extreme end, some do. Others want to use the story as an example of how society fails vulnerable children. Most, however, are good-hearted women who, appalled at

Angie's desertion, do the cyber equivalent of milling about, uncertain of the outcome they want.

When Angie's grandmother applies for custody, a relieved cohort form a splinter group – *Mothers for Jeannie* – while others mutate into the *No Jail for George* movement.

Fortunately for George, none of his friends (except Bree, and she's not telling) has any idea how to access these websites, and for a while he enjoys an ignorance, if not exactly blissful, at least not as troubling as it might be.

He's the inert centre of all this controversy and sits in his flat watching television in a kind of stupor that frustrates Shirl beyond telling. 'One interview, George. Let me give your side of the story.'

'Let me be, Shirl. Just this once, let me be.'

She's appalled by the misery, the quiet desperation in his eyes, and without further nagging continues each day to minister to his physical and mental comfort. She talks of other things – reminding him of the good times in his life, the amusing incidents, the stories that are part of their shared history. This comforts him more than she can know and he feels the need to offer something in return. So he sets the record straight about Penny.

'She didn't go off with another bloke. It was me that made her leave. It was a terrible thing to do – telling you that.'

'I know, George. I've always known.'

He doesn't know how she found out, but it doesn't matter. It's like he's dying and has to tidy up his life.

Shirl brings him books but he can't be bothered. He has read the first three pages of *Biggles Flies Again* several times but can't remember a word. He eats the food prepared and delivered by Shirl and Mrs Nguyen (delicious) and Bree (barely edible), but all dishes taste the same. He has known bereavement – and this is very like.

*

George becomes aware of the *No Jail for George* group when he answers the door one morning to two middle-aged women. 'Hello?' He scans their faces. He's almost certain he hasn't met them before. 'Do I know you?'

'Paula Henson,' the tall one says. 'And this is Maria Katsakis. We've come to help you with your Twitter account.'

George has heard of Twitter, of course, but has only just begun to use email, so what could this have to do with him? 'Twitter,' he says. 'I see …'

Encouraged, the women step past him and he stares at them blankly while Maria turns on the kettle and Paula arranges some biscuits on a plate.

Feeling like a guest in his own living room, George is invited to sit down. 'Did Shirl send you?'

'No.' The short reply, through pursed lips, indicates that they had perhaps met Shirl.

Paula waves George to a seat while Maria brings in the tea on a tray. 'As you know, I am the founder …' Maria bangs down her cup. 'Or should I say, we are the founders of the *No Jail for George* movement.'

'The what?'

'*No Jail for George.* The one on Facebook.'

318

'I'm sorry,' he says. 'I'm not very good with computers. My wife …'

'Not even Facebook?' Maria looks at Paula in dismay. 'We've had over six thousand "likes".'

The women explain that their mission is to keep George out of jail and they want him to assist with daily (at *least* daily) tweets to keep up interest in the cause. 'After all,' Maria says, 'you're the victim here. All you did was try to make a little girl's life easier. You sacrificed your peaceful retirement to take on a difficult child and …'

They didn't understand. 'It was no sacrifice,' he says. 'I love her.'

'Wonderful. All you need to do is tweet that sort of thing. And how Angie deserted her.'

But George will not be persuaded. 'I wouldn't want you to think I'm ungrateful,' he says, 'but I'm too old for this Twitter thing. Besides, I've already decided not to make any public statements – on my solicitor's advice.' This is true, as it happens, and it's proved to be a godsend. He doesn't have the energy to argue.

*

'Traumatised,' the women agree as they walk back to their cars. Maria's son-in-law knows someone who works at Channel 5. 'We need to counter all that rubbish Channel 14 are putting out,' she says.

*

A few days later, Angie's grandmother appears. (The whole world, it seems, knows his hiding place.) George takes a step back and she smiles faintly. 'Don't worry. I've come to say I'm sorry. Bree told me where you're staying.'

Still doubtful, George ushers her in. The flat is small, the furnishing minimal and impersonal. They stand. He hasn't offered her a seat, and waits instead for her to speak.

'I'd love a cuppa.' She peers past him to the kitchenette.

George makes the tea in silence and brings in two mugs, which he puts down on the dusty coffee table. 'No biscuits,' he says, but doesn't apologise.

She indicates his book lying on the couch. 'I see you enjoy *Biggles*. I'm rereading the *Billabong* series. There are some books you can enjoy, whatever your age.'

George unbends a little. 'Classics,' he says. 'Not just for kids.'

Gran (he's fairly sure he doesn't know her name) takes a sip of tea. 'I hope you'll understand my behaviour at the hospital. There was so much in the press … And the police kept on questioning Angie about your … suitability. I have to admit I thought the worst and it nearly broke me. The only thing that kept me going was the thought of making you pay.' She gazes out the window and speaks as if to herself. 'You see, when Angie and Rory came to live with me, I believed that I could save at least one generation, maybe even two.'

George is listening intently. 'Go on.'

'I could never control Rosemary. That's my daughter – Angie's mother. A wilful child, if ever there was one. She ran away at fifteen and had Shiloh to some mongrel who left her high and dry three days after she came home from hospital. Angie was born fifteen months later – a different father, of course. I begged Rosemary to move back in with me, and she did for a bit, but she was off again in a matter of weeks.'

This woman has been grieving for years, George thinks.

The hand holding her mug is thin and trembling slightly. 'I hardly saw my granddaughters as they were growing up, but when Rosemary and that brute of a stepfather threw Angie out, she came to me.'

'And you took her in.'

'We were managing – I was even getting closer to Angie, then I had to go into hospital for bypass surgery. I'd only been home a couple of weeks when they left.'

'Just when you needed help.'

'I don't blame Angie. She was very good for a while, in her own way. Rory was a cranky baby – kept her busy.'

'She told me you were too frail to have a screaming baby in the house.'

'She may well have thought that. Or she might have become tired of me telling her what to do. Or maybe it was a combination of both.' She puts down her mug. 'Rory is my last chance to give a child the right sort of life. I see now that's what you wanted, too, and I'm sorry about what happened at the hospital. I'm not saying you did the right thing, mind … if anything had happened to her …' She's looking at him straight. He likes that in a woman. 'But what you did was understandable. I just wanted to tell you that.'

George inclines his head. 'Thanks. It was natural – what you did. Not knowing me and being her great-grandmother and all.' He hesitates. 'Have you heard of a group called *No Jail for George*?'

'The one on Facebook?'

Was he the only dinosaur left in the world? 'That's the one. They want me to tweet stuff. You know, about what happened. I think they're good people, but I've always been a private sort of bloke. And I don't want to trash Angie. She's had a tough trot, one way and another.'

The woman regards him with genuine respect. 'There's another group called *Mothers for Jeannie*. I'm going for custody and they've come out in support.'

'Custody. You'll take care of Rory?'

'And Angie, too, if she'll let me.'

She picks up her handbag, smiling as George pretends to duck. 'One more thing – do you know where her dog is? She's pining for him dreadfully.'

He's hurt. *Not pining for me, then.*

Reading his expression, she puts a hand on his arm. 'Of course she misses you, too. A lot. But you must realise it's impossible at the moment.'

No contact. A condition of his bail. His instinct had been (still is) to confront Angie, to explain to Rory why he had to go, make some arrangement – it couldn't be too hard. But he's law-abiding by nature and his one transgression has left him with no options.

'Richie – I left him with the motel receptionist at Owens Gap. God knows where he is now.' He thinks for a moment. 'Tell you what. I've got a mate who might be able to drive up and get him if I can contact the woman I gave him to.' He knows he can do this. He has guarded that scrap of paper with her phone number like it was a cheque for a thousand dollars. Mortified by his plight, he looks away. 'Can't go meself. Judge said I have to stay in Melbourne.' Suddenly angry, he strikes the door with his fist and the woman jumps in alarm. 'Sorry. Sorry,' he says. 'It's just that I'm not a criminal. A fool, maybe. But not a criminal.' His anger dispels as swiftly as it had come. He feels very old. 'Anyway, I'll give her a call and let you know.'

'Thank you.' She puts out her hand. 'I'm sorry for taking up so much of your time, Mr Johnson.'

'George,' he says.

'Jeannie.'

'Give Rory my love, Jeannie. Always.'

'I will, George – and good luck.'

22

As the date for the trial approaches, George finds it more and more difficult to concentrate. His thoughts are erratic and slide away or crumble when he tries to hold on to them, shape them into coherence. He watches his hands shake as he pours his tea. It no longer matters. All he wants is to stay cocooned in his tiny flat where those who come are on his side. (More or less. The solicitor is paid to be on his side and Shirl has again begun to gnaw at the issue like Richie worrying a bone.)

Mr and Mrs Nguyen come bearing green tea and chocolate teddy bear biscuits. They greet him with customary politeness and talk of trivial things that assume mass and dimension because they are part of a life he can no longer share. *We cut back your roses yesterday.* They hand him some blooms wrapped in newspaper. Smiling, he finds an empty coffee jar in the back of the cupboard and puts Pen's roses in water.

Autumn leaves are falling. My wife is painting the colour. Mrs Nguyen looks modestly at the carpet.

Then the information that pierces the thin membrane of his hard-won equilibrium. 'Rory's gran brought her to visit us. To meet her Richie dog.' He can see them trying to read his face. 'She happy with her gran.'

Of course he wants her to be happy. He does. So why does the news make him so unhappy? He smiles as he knows he should. Lucky children are fleet of foot. Move lightly. Peel off one life then glide away without a backward glance. That's how the smart ones survive.

But I can't shake off the past so easily, George thinks, showing his teeth as he hoists his lips into a smile. *It has burrowed into my bones. It's who I am.*

The Nguyens are waiting. 'Rory's happy – that's the most important thing,' he says, knowing that however painful, he's telling them the truth.

*

For the duration of the trial, there are no earthquakes, no terrorist attacks, no political exposés. Shane Warne's Twitter account is strangely silent and there's not even a Grand Final or Ashes Test to divert the press.

So they concentrate on the trial, and it's as if banality is a seasonal hazard. There is no drama and certainly no unforeseen revelations. When questioned, Angie is sullen and uncooperative and the cameras have to make do with shots from outside the court – George in his suit and tie, Angie with her gran. At first Shirl was good for a pithy quote, but as the trial progresses, she sweeps past, looking to neither right nor left.

In the absence of real news the media spend their time crossing to a reporter outside George's house, or the steps of the Supreme Court and even Rory's school, until Ms Fontana threatens to call the police.

Despite some tempting offers for a photograph, Rory is nowhere to be seen.

*

George pleads guilty. That's his instruction to his solicitor and he brooks no argument. 'I took her,' he says, again and again. 'It's as simple as that.' It isn't, of course, but he refuses to discuss it. Despite the consequences, he can't stomach the thought of Rory being called as a witness. (Although there was never any suggestion that she would be.) He sees her, small and scared, in a room full of strangers with fusty wigs and black gowns, hovering like crows. *You must tell the truth*, they threaten the cowering child. And what truth are they seeking? What questions will they ask? He can't bear the thought that a child would be asked to condemn her own mother. But, worse, what does Rory think of her Poppy George now? He'd left her, after promising he'd stay. Unwilling to face an accusation of betrayal, he stands by his guilty plea.

And, anyway, what could he say under oath? How much of what he did was for Rory and how much for himself? He is still not capable of answering this question with any certainty.

So the arguments are mainly in mitigation. It is noted that George did return Rory voluntarily, although, as the prosecutor points out, this was as a result of her illness. *There is no evidence to suggest that he would have returned her had the asthma attack not occurred*, she concludes.

He put her health above his own needs, George's barrister responds. *More like a caring relative than a child abductor.*

Shirl, Redgum, the Nguyens, Stella, Park and even Shirl's Bill and Marianne all attest to his good character.

Angie is allowed a victim statement and reads one workshopped by the convenor of 'Women for Angie'. 'When I came home to find my daughter had been abducted,' she reads, 'I was dev-*devasted*. I took care of her for five years and when George agreed to mind her while I looked for work, I was relieved and happy. I thought I could trust him, but he let us down. And when I knew he'd taken her, I couldn't stop crying in case he hurt her. The shock made me sick – ill.' She looks at the prosecutor with real dislike and strays from the script. 'But I don't want George to go to jail. He's too old for all that.'

*

Justice Clements is a formidable figure, wearing her authority as one born to uphold the law. Her voice, however, is mellifluous, and as she reads her judgement George is beguiled by the sound and finds it difficult to concentrate on the substance. Surely such a voice – cool and harmonious – can only speak of the beautiful and the good. How could such a voice pronounce a prison sentence?

She's a softie, his barrister had said with some scorn. *You'll get a suspended sentence for sure.*

'… So the defendant, George Johnson, acted in what he believed were the child's best interests.' Hearing his name, George pulls back his shoulders and listens more carefully. *I did. I did act in her best interests.* He glances around the courtroom, impressed with what he sees and hears. Justice will find a way. He's always believed that.

'However, though entering a formal guilty plea, at no time has Mr Johnson acknowledged an understanding of his wrongdoing. While taking account of his age and his previously unblemished record, I am cognisant of the fact that the law, and indeed the community, hold the abduction of a child to be a serious crime, warranting a stern penalty. I therefore sentence the defendant to five years' imprisonment with a minimum of two years to serve.'

George's dismay is manifested in that awful roiling of his guts. All he wants now is to get out of the courtroom, out of sight, in case he disgraces himself. He looks across at his little band of supporters, then bows his head as he is led from the dock.

*

Angie leaves the courtroom and, guided by her solicitor and her gran, pushes her way through the crowd. Gran seizes her arm with grim displeasure. 'I hope you're satisfied, young woman.'

'What?' Angie flops into a waiting taxi and looks belligerently out at the melee on the footpath. 'Why is everyone blaming me?'

*

The jail is low security, but at first they have to keep George away from the other prisoners. It seems that there are one or two who, believing him to be a paedophile, are out to teach him a lesson. He's scared, and lies in his single cell staring at the door, which is flimsier than he would like. He has been through the humiliating procedure meted out to an incoming prisoner and feels he has lost something important on the way.

So he lies in his cell and broods. At times, his bitterness is excoriating. *Angie*. Why couldn't she have left well enough alone? And how long would it be before she set off again in search of more 'fun'?

On his better days, he thinks, *At least they've given custody to Jeannie*. She's a woman to reckon with, is Jeannie, and he's confident that she'll never let Rory out of her sight. George takes some comfort in this thought and his anger cools. What's the point? What's happened has happened, and there's nothing he can do about it now.

In time, he is given a job in the prison library. He finds it congenial and the prisoners who borrow books seem to accept him. Some of them are professional people. With all those advantages, why would they knowingly break the law? He supposes they have their reasons, just like him. In here, he's lost the right to judge.

He has regular visits from all his friends, but not from Angie or Rory. He wonders if Angie feels any remorse for the part she played in his downfall. Jeannie thinks she might, but George is not so sure. As for Rory – he doesn't want her to see him locked up like a common felon.

When he can bear it, he looks into his conscience, trying to plumb the truth of his actions. There are times when all he can see is green, sludgy pond water, weedily opaque to his questing eye. But sometimes, when the water is clean and clear, he can explore the things that lie at the bottom. Love, for instance. Had his love for Rory been selfish? *Of course*, he admits as he stares into the bright waters. All love has an element of selfishness – that need the lover has for the presence, for the esteem, for the total commitment of the beloved. This isn't new to him. He'd loved Pen, couldn't imagine life without her, but in the end it took his best love to let her go.

*

So George does his two years minimum and is released into a largely indifferent community, returning to Mercy Street not quite the same man as the one who left. He goes for a drink with Redgum; has his morning tea with the Nguyens; both welcomes and resists visits from Shirl and Bree. It's all much as it was before, if only he can avert his gaze from the vast reality of absence.

Then, after a few weeks, Jeannie rings to arrange a visit with Rory. The solid, self-imposed order of his days is, after all, a chimera, easily vanquished by the magical uttering of her name. He prowls around the house, looking for things to do. Practical things that will keep him busy. He tidies her already tidy room, oils the swing, loads the fridge with Choc Wedges. Perhaps he should have bought chocolate teddies. He goes to the shops a second time and, along with the teddies, buys a cake for Jeannie's morning tea. He pauses at the bookshop. Rory would be too old for their favourite picture books now, and the saleswoman (a new one) recommends the latest fantasy novel. 'It's the first of a trilogy,' she tells him and he makes a mental note to look out for the sequels.

He returns home later than he meant to, and before he can regain his equilibrium, they arrive. Opening the door, he doesn't know what to do, what to say. Rory is taller (almost as tall as her grandmother) and it seems that she's grown up a lot in the nearly three years since he last saw her. She is almost, but not quite, a stranger. He scans her face for the sullen little waif she once was, and sees his own trepidation reflected in her eyes. It's comforting to know that she's feeling awkward, too.

'How's your mum?' he asks.

'Okay. Mum's okay.'

She's coming into focus. 'And Richie?'

'Good,' she says. 'We got him back – he's good.'

Jeannie rolls her eyes but says nothing.

Rory steps into the house and walks down the hallway, peering into her old room and then into the kitchen, before sitting on the sofa (bereft of protective covers).

'You went away,' she says, 'when I was in hospital. You promised you'd stay.'

Jeannie frowns. 'I told you. I told you he had to go.'

The young girl looks at him with a clear, green gaze. And offers her words like a gift. 'I've still got Slipper Dog.' The pause is minimal. 'Poppy George.'

Epilogue

Angie applies her lipstick, gives her hair an extra spray and peers more closely into the mirror. The lines are there, all right. And she doesn't want to know what colour (or lack of it) lurks beneath the black hair dye. She'll be forty next year. Never thought she'd end up working in a fruit shop – or looking after an old lady and a smelly old mutt. Given half a chance, she'd be on the road again, but with her gran nearly blind ...

She finds it hard to believe that Rory is twenty-four – that it's, what, nearly twenty years since she and George gave her that birthday party. She hugs the memory for a moment. Not many left from that day. Shirl carked it a few years back and she doesn't know what happened to the Nguyens. They'd have to be dead by now. And Redgum and Bree were killed in that car accident just after Rory started high school. She's glad she got back to talking to Bree again before she ... Anyway, that only leaves her and Rory and George.

George. She's avoided meeting him all these years. She's not sure why. Embarrassment, maybe. Then the longer you leave these things … *It's time*, she tells herself. And they could hardly not invite him to Rory's graduation, him helping out with uniforms and books and all.

She slips on her shoes. Killer heels for this special occasion. Who would ever have thought that her daughter would end up a lawyer? Well, beggars can't be choosers and lawyers are pretty good earners. All in all, she has to admit, the kid's done well for herself.

Angie is not reflective by nature. But she's been thinking a bit about George these last few days. They both did things they shouldn't have, but they were close for a while there in a funny sort of way. What she's come to think is that, by taking Rory away, George made sure she'd stick around to see her grow up. It wasn't his plan, but that's how it turned out.

Favour for favour, she thinks, they're even.

*

It's nearly five, and George is looking alternately at the clock and the door. A light knock. He touches his tie with a trembling hand. Wearing a tie is how he remembers that he's going out. He sits up straighter in his chair as one of a bewildering number of carers comes in and wheels him to the front room. 'Thank you, um … ?' It's on the tip of his tongue.

'Melanie,' she says in mock outrage. 'And I thought I was your girl!'

He's too polite to tell her that he only ever had two girls. There was a beautiful young woman with copper curls that spread across the pillow beside his. He spends much of his time now reliving their days together. She's elusive, though. In some way that he can't quite comprehend, she's out of reach.

Then there was the other one. A child with green eyes who called him Poppy George. When she appears in his reveries, he smiles. There was a dog and ice-creams on a stick (the names of both will come to him). There was a birthday party, too, and memories of a caravan holiday. The images of this little girl are sharp at first but suddenly lose shape. He reaches out and cups his hands to capture them, but they fall through his fingers like water.

Who is this smart young woman in a fancy skirt and jacket who kisses him on the cheek? Chatting brightly, waving to the other young woman whose name he has already forgotten, she wheels him out the door.

Strapped into a car, George feels the need for polite conversation. 'It's very kind of you to take me out,' he says. 'You have green eyes just like my little girl's.'

The young woman looks across at him. Her voice is soft and her eyes sad. 'A little girl? With eyes like mine?'

'A daughter. Granddaughter really, I suppose. But yes. I had a child. Just for a little while, mind – but I gave her my best love. And you know …' He struggles for a name. 'You know, young lady, I'm old and a bit forgetful, but I can guarantee you one thing – I may not have had her for long, but for me, a little while was good enough.'

Acknowledgements

The birth of a book requires many midwives. My grateful thanks must go to my agent Gaby Naher for her professionalism and understanding, and my editing team from Harper Collins, Catherine Milne, Jude McGee and Alex Nahlous. Their sensitive but rigorous editing enabled *Mercy Street* to become the novel I wanted it to be. I am also indebted to Darren Holt for the stunning cover design.

Thanks, as always, to my first reader, Carolyn Evans and my children, grandchildren, friends and family, who encouraged me along the way.

Finally, I want to thank most sincerely the readers of my other novels, whose letters and emails sustain me in my efforts. I hope you enjoy reading *Mercy Street* as much as I enjoyed writing it.

Reading Group Notes

The inspiration for *Mercy Street*

I began writing after a 23-year career in the TAFE system, the majority of which was working with long-term job seekers, many of whom were the victims of social deprivation or recession. This cohort included early school leavers, women returning to the workforce, indigenous trainees, those with psychiatric and psychological disability, labourers, tradespersons and professionals from age sixteen to sixty-four. What I came to understand in those years was that everyone has a story and that each story matters. So when I'm asked where my ideas come from, I believe that, at bedrock, it was this long immersion in the lives of other people.

Specific stories come from a trigger that makes me start to think – or 'wonder' might be a better word. *I wonder what … ? or I wonder how … ?*

The initial trigger for my first novel, *Book of Lost Threads*, was an article I read about the issue of identifying sperm donors. *The Memory Tree,* my second novel, came from the death of an acquaintance at the hands of her mentally ill partner. A story grows from the questions surrounding these triggers. For instance – I wondered what would happen if the adult child of an anonymous sperm donor knocked at his door. Or, how could the family of a mentally ill killer cope with the consequences of his action?

Three elements came together in the genesis of *Mercy Street.*

I tend to eavesdrop on the train – a favourite occupation, sadly less frequent now with everyone playing on their iPhones. One day, I overheard two women loudly discussing the problems they were having with their school-aged children. The problems were typical of normal parents with normal children and the women were just having a normal parental whinge. As they left the carriage, I caught the eye of an elderly man sitting opposite. He shook his head. 'They don't know how lucky they are,' he said wistfully. Had he lost a child? Was he childless? That made me start to think of men I know for whom children are a joy. And so George was born.

The character of Angie had been waiting in the wings for years. Years ago, my husband and I acted as respite foster carers for young children. During the training, we were told to accept that while some homes might not meet our standards, we must accept that 'good enough' is good enough. This stuck with me and I have always wondered where the line might be between good enough and not good enough. Is it rigid and unchanging or something fluid and situational? Angie tests these questions.

George and Angie came together when she saves him from an assault. This reminded me of my father, who told me that if you save someone's life, you owe them. I found this theory counter-intuitive as a child, and examined its veracity as the story evolved.

Of course more questions arise as a story unfolds and it is in the exploration of these questions that the narrative progresses and our understanding of the characters is enriched.

Questions

1. George thinks: 'She (Angie) isn't what you would call a good mother in the general way of things, but she's good enough and deserves a break.' Do you think Angie is a 'good enough' mother?
2. Was George a 'good enough' carer? Had Rory stayed with him, could he have continued to be 'good enough'?
3. How did George's life with Penny inform his thinking with regard to Rory?
4. Were any of the online groups that formed before George's trial justified? Which one, if any, would you join? If you wanted to get signatures for a group like change.org, before the trial, what would your petition be?
5. George committed a crime. Should he have been jailed? Is this a case of the end justifying the means?

6. 'And he hasn't seen her for well over a year. People mature in that time. He's an old man, yet since Rory, he has changed. So how much more might a young person be able to grow in understanding? And change as a result of that growth?' Did George change during the course of the novel? If so, how?

7. Did Angie grow or change?

8. How would you describe George's attitude to Angie? Does it change? Could it ever be called a 'relationship'?

9. Who had the greatest influence on George's life: Pen, Shirl, Redgum or Rory?

10. Should George have fought to keep Rory? Why did he seem to let her go so easily in the end?

11. Who was your favourite minor character? Why? What does he or she add to the novel?

12. 'All love has an element of selfishness.' Do you agree?

13. It seems that a number of characters give their 'best love' when called upon. Discuss how love, in the broad sense, is demonstrated by action throughout the novel.

14. Shakespeare tells us that mercy 'blesses him who gives and him who takes'. Discuss in the context of the novel.

15. Angie sums up her relationship with George in the following way. 'Favour for favour [we're] even.' Do you agree?